"You saw Jake this morning?" Leah asked.

"Sure. It's Saturday," Abby chirped.

"And that means . . . ?" Leah's eyebrows climbed her forehead a fraction or so.

"It doesn't mean anything," I said quickly.

Abby began to dance around us, pausing occasionally to admire herself in the full-length mirrors on the closet doors. "Saturday morning means . . ." Pose. Pause. Twirl again. ". . . that Uncle Jake stops by . . ." Pose. Pause. Twirl. ". . with a yummy muffin for me and a big tall coffee for Mommy." Pose. Pause. No twirl, just a little bow.

Now the corners of Leah's lips threatened to climb up with her eyebrows, "Uncle Jake stops by every Saturday morning with coffee and baked goods? How nice of Uncle Jake! What does Uncle Jake get in return?"

Abby cocked her head to one side while she thought. Her brows drew down in concentration. "Get? He gets to spend time with us, I guess." She pirouetted away, bored with us.

"It's not like it sounds," I said. "He's just looking for a little . . ."

"Companionship?" Leah suggested.

"Maybe."

"Just remember, dear," she said. "There comes a time in a relationship when a man wants more than just *companionship*."

Do Me, Do My Roots

Eileen Rendahl

doWn tOwn press

New York   London   Toronto   Sydney

An *Original* Publication of Pocket Books

DOWNTOWN PRESS published by Pocket Books
1230 Avenue of the Americas, New York, NY 10020

ISBN: 0-7434-7114-8

First Downtown Press trade paperback edition April 2004

10 9 8 7 6 5 4 3 2 1

DOWNTOWN PRESS and colophon are
trademarks of Simon & Schuster, Inc.

Manufactured in the United States of America

Designed by Jaime Putorti

For information regarding special discounts for bulk purchases,
please contact Simon & Schuster Special Sales at 1-800-456-6798
or business@simonandschuster.com

To all my intrepid sisters who have loved, lost, loved again, lost again, maybe even loved and lost a third time around and have still just kept going for it.

Acknowledgments

There are so many people to thank. I have to start first with my sisters, Marian and Diane, for allowing me to take our relationship apart, examine it, and put it back together for everyone to look at. I also want to thank my niece, Sophie, for giving me a glimpse of what it might be like to be the big sister. Special thanks to my many non-biological sisters for help, support, insight, and letting me use bits and pieces of their lives. A complete list of you would take forever, but here is a partial: Maureen, Celine, Sara, Rayenna, Ellen, Donna, Colleen, and Barbara. I could not have written this without my many writing sisters. Thank you Sacramento Valley Rose RWA Chapter. Thank you also to my unique critique group: Jean, Barbara, Christina, and Teresa. Thank you to Pat and Karen for pie and margaritas (although not at the same time) and to Antoinette for all the coffee. Thanks to Tina for the Hair Diary. Thank you to my father, Frank, the best daddy a girl could have, duct tape and all. Thank you to my mother, Debbie. Every strong woman I write has a kernel of you at her core. Thank you to my children for their patience and for putting up with my writing books whose titles they can't say at school. Thank you to Andy, my own personal Jake, for inspiration, laughter, love, and rare (if frightening) glimpses into how men think. Very, very special thanks to Pamela Ahearn for seeing the potential in this book, and to Micki Nuding for helping me turn it into what it is today.

Do Me,
Do My Roots

Prologue

There's a home movie I just love of my two sisters and me with our dad. I'm maybe three or so. There I am, Baby Emily, with that ridiculous pixie cut that my mother was so fond of. I have on a little checked pinafore with little matching bloomers. Honestly, I look precious, although it was my mother's insistence that I wear this kind of outfit that would mark me as a complete loser by the fourth grade.

Anyway, if I was three, Claudia would have been about five. Her hair is pulled back in glossy black pigtails so tight that she almost looks Asian. Leah would have been close to seven. Her hair is in one long reddish-brown braid straight down her back. The braid is so thick it must have weighed a ton. It's nearly as thick as her skinny little arms that stick out of her starched white blouse, the one with the little blue-and-pink flowers embroidered on the collar.

Many of my memories seem tied inextricably to the length of our hair and hemlines. A particular hairstyle or a particular blouse can slam me back in time like a door banging open in my head. Some people say that the sense of smell is the most evocative. For me, it's the length of my bangs and the height of my heels.

All three of us are a little obsessed with our hair. At least it's something we can all agree on.

I actually have a vague memory of the day the movie was taken. Maybe it's the pixie cut, but more likely those damn bloomers. They had elastic at the legs so tight it threatened to cut off my circulation. I'd still have red rings around my thighs the day after I wore them. It was one of those rare sunny, warm summer days that nobody thinks Seattle ever has. We were all so happy that my parents had taken out the movie camera, even though it wasn't anyone's birthday.

In the movie, we're all hopping around Daddy. He looks so young and strong. His hair is still dark and he still has most of it, too. He's wearing a plain white T-shirt and khaki pants. The belt has already started its upward creep, but you wouldn't even notice it if you didn't know how high it would go in later years. One at a time, he's picking us up and swinging us through the air.

I remember the sensation of flying. I remember the thrill of leaving the ground in the completely safe haven of my father's arms. I remember the pure joy of being loved.

I remember how hard it was to wait my turn, to let Leah and Claudia have chances to soar. I remember begging to be lifted.

In the film you can see our mouths moving, but home movies back then didn't have any sound. I know what we were saying, though. We were each begging for our turn.

We were chanting over and over again:

Do me! Do me next, Daddy! Daddy, Daddy, do me!

*   *   *

Now that we're adults, my sister Claudia has developed a way of describing even things that aren't funny that makes you laugh. If you could hear her tell about trying to get to the hospital in time to have her second child while her husband was going through heroin withdrawal, you'd understand what I'm talking about. I've heard that story at least a dozen times over the years, but it still makes me laugh so hard that I'm practically screaming.

Sometimes I try to get her to tell me about my own life, so I can laugh about it instead of crying.

It took me close to a year to figure out exactly how heartbroken I actually was. Until then, I'd reasoned that I'd done most of my mourning before my husband died. Watching him lose his hair, the ability to drive, to read, to speak, and eventually to even move, was a series of little deaths on the way to the Big Kahuna, and I mourned each loss as it happened. So I thought that was why I felt as little as I did. I'd cried so much before that, there weren't really any tears left.

I was wrong.

People talk about denial like it's such a bad thing. You hear it all the time, "Oh, he's just in denial." They all nod their heads wisely with knowing looks on their faces. I personally like denial a lot. It can get you through a lot of pretty bad days.

Unfortunately, like any good thing, denial has to come to an end. That happened on the first anniversary of my husband's death, which—far from coincidentally—would also have been our ninth wedding anniversary.

So after two years of keeping a stiff upper lip (I held up really well during the year he was sick, you can ask anyone.

That little episode in the Walgreens pharmacy could have happened to anyone), I pretty much fell apart. Without my sisters, I'm not sure my daughter and I would have come through the other side. They made food and made me eat it, too, drove car pool in my place, forced me to get out of bed and take showers, vacuumed my house. They stood watch and held me when I cried, and eventually Abby and I did make it through. Not unscathed, mind you. Even the highest-quality sister love can't do that, but we're here and we're functioning. So are my sisters.

We're still all over one another. Claudia says that we're overly enmeshed, but we like it like that. Rarely a day goes by that one of us doesn't end up at another one's house, but we religiously do one another's hair at least once a month. We can't go much longer than that because then my sisters' gray hairs start to show. We gather in Leah's kitchen while Claudia's boys watch Abby for me, and my two sisters do each other's roots.

CHAPTER ONE

There Are Some Events to Which You Don't Want to Be Invited

Leah

One part Apricot Glaze (#38), one part Titian Red (#74), one part developer. Forty minutes. Some people are born to be redheads even though they're not born redheads.

Claudia

Two parts Medium Ash Brown (#28), one part developer. Twenty minutes. Roots a little light, but acceptable. Is acceptable good enough? We say no: we will not bow down to hair color mediocrity.

My alarm clock read 2:47 A.M. when the phone jarred me awake. After I'd hit the snooze button several times in a futile attempt to get the noise to stop and finally answered the phone, my mother's voice chirped unnaturally brightly into my ear. "Hello, dear. Did I wake you?"

"Well, yeah, it's almost three o'clock in the morning." In these situations, it's my usual practice to lie. Oh, no, I'll say.

Of course I wasn't sleeping at 6:00 A.M. on a Saturday morning on one of those rarest of days that my daughter might actually sleep in. Why, I've already dusted and vacuumed the house and was getting ready to do push-ups.

Why do I do this? I have no idea.

Is there any shame to sleeping? There are news reports all the time about how sleep deprived we are, and how dangerous it is with drivers falling asleep at the wheel and machine operators pushing the wrong buttons. I'm actually performing a public service by sleeping. Maybe I'm worried that they'll think I'm lazy. At three o'clock in the morning, however, I figured subterfuge was pointless.

"I'm sorry, dear. It's just that . . ." Here she paused and tittered. No one can titter quite like my mother when under stress. Many have tried and failed. I myself usually let out horrible wheezy laughs or occasionally an hysterical squeal, but I can't titter worth a damn. "Well, your father has had an event."

An event? What, did he suddenly get up at two in the morning and decide to have a bar mitzvah, and they were calling to invite me?

"Mama," I said. "What are you talking about?"

"Oh, dear, well, it's just . . ." Her tone brightened more; soon she'd be chittering like a demented squirrel. "Your sister's here. I'll let her explain."

I listened to the phone being passed, hugging my knees under the blanket. My sister Leah's terse voice came over the line. "Daddy's had a heart attack. Find some place to park Abby and get your ass to the hospital."

*   *   *

I found them behind curtain number seven in the ER. Trust me, if Monty Hall had ever offered this as an option, *Let's Make a Deal* would have been a much tenser show. Choose Curtain Number One and you win an all-expense-paid vacation to beautiful Hawaii. Choose Curtain Number Two and you get a lifetime supply of Rice-A-Roni, the San Francisco Treat. Choose Curtain Number Three and we'll ram a really big needle into your wrist and shove a tube up . . . well, you get the point.

Tonight behind Curtain Number Seven, my sisters and mother sat watching my father's heartbeat on a monitor screen with more interest than they'd jointly showed in anything since the moon walk.

I kissed my father's forehead. It felt clammy against my lips. He looked kind of yellow and a lot smaller than he had the day before. "How ya doin', Daddy?"

He shrugged. "I've been better."

Under the circumstances, it seemed as good an answer as any.

Claudia jumped up and gave me a quick hug. She looked like she'd been dressed for hours. She had on a pair of khaki flat-front pants and a really cute sweater. Her makeup looked perfect and her hair didn't even look like she'd slept on it.

I had pulled on a pair of jeans under the oversize thermal shirt I'd worn to bed and thought I'd done the world a favor by brushing my teeth. Over that, I had on a hooded zip-front sweatshirt and one of Vince's old baseball jackets. I'd pulled my barely brushed hair back into a ponytail and pulled a baseball cap on over that. Mascara hadn't crossed my mind, much less my lashes.

"Where's Abby?" Claudia wanted to know.

"I wrapped her up in a blanket and took her to Kim's. She never even woke all the way up. I hope she doesn't wake up there and freak out."

Claudia gave me a sympathetic grimace. Her boys are old enough to stay alone.

"Come on into the hallway. I'll fill you in."

We stepped out from behind the curtain and walked a few steps on the yellowed linoleum. The glare and hum from the fluorescent lights were already starting to get to me. "Exactly how much time did Mama spend with the admitting clerk?" I asked.

"I'm not sure. Why?"

"Because when I stopped to ask how to find you guys, she said, 'You must be Emily.' Then she hugged me and offered me condolences on my loss."

"She advised me to sue Mark for more child support." Claudia popped her gum. There's something about the way she chews gum that always fascinates me. Maybe it's because her mouth is such a perfect little cupid's bow and her lips are so raspberry red. Abby had tried to lick them once when she was a baby, as if they were some kind of lollipop. I find myself mesmerized by Claudia's mouth when she pops her gum like that. I stared at it now, barely registering the words she spoke while I watched her lips move. It's like when you're driving and you find yourself more caught up in the rhythm of the broken yellow line in the middle of the road than in what's actually on the road in front of you.

The unending buzz from the light was like a siren call to the headache that was starting in my right temple. "Spread," it whispered. "Encircle her whole head." My eyes felt gritty.

"So what's the deal with Daddy?"

"Oh, yeah." Claudia jumped as if the question came out of nowhere. "They think he's had a small heart attack. It doesn't look like there's any permanent heart damage, but it is a warning."

"A warning of what?"

"I don't know, Emily. They have to do more tests."

"What kind of tests?" I started to feel a little frantic; I didn't like the sound of any of this. Heart attacks? Damage to heart muscles? Tests? The thought of sitting in waiting rooms again, hoping a doctor would come with a little good news, had my skin prickling. My lungs tightened at the memory of the hours I'd spent in this hospital and how little they were able to do in the end.

"Emily, I don't know! He's only been here an hour and I only got here about fifteen minutes ahead of you. Now chill out. I know it's hard for you to be here, but you're going to have to ride this out with the rest of us. Try just to deal with what's in front of you."

I felt tears start to slip out underneath my lids. I hadn't even felt them start. No chance to fight them at all. "Sorry," I mumbled.

She hugged me again. Have I mentioned that my sister Claudia gives the best hugs ever? "It's all right. Let's go sit with the others."

When we got back, a doctor who didn't look old enough to drive was checking out all the readouts from the various parts of my father's body that were hooked up to machines. I gathered from the way his hands trembled that he'd either had way too much coffee or Leah had already been working him over.

Even at four o'clock in the morning with her hair in a jumble, she can be pretty formidable.

Claudia said hello and the doctor turned to smile at us. It was a mistake. I understand the need for orthodontia, but this poor guy's braces made even Doogie Howser jokes something beyond a cheap shot.

"Dr. Hill is an M.D., Ph.D. from Northwestern," my mother informed us with a proprietary note in her voice. She has been wearing her dark, remarkably more-pepper-than-salt hair in the same no-nonsense way since I was in diapers. It's a sensible cut. Short, but not too short. Takes advantage of her natural wave, but not too curly. My mother doesn't like a lot of curls. Or a lot of frills. She likes things simple and straightforward. She likes things that make sense. She likes for men and women in their thirties to be married to people of approximately the same age, socioeconomic background, religion, and color as themselves.

She was clearly revving up to fix one of my sisters up with Dr. Metal Mouth, even though he looked young enough to be jailbait. I was grateful that she generally left me alone these days, though she'd started making noises about Derek Zaretsky, a boy that I'd hated since we used to carpool with his family to third-grade Sunday School, and saw no reason to like any better now that he and his wife had just divorced. He was, however, a stockbroker, which made him third only to a doctor or a lawyer as a son-in-law candidate. She seemed to have missed the fact that Derek had stopped growing in fifth grade or so and I now towered over him by about five inches, or that he was still struggling with that whole adolescent skin thing. She claimed that oily skin would help him age well by delaying wrinkles.

Claudia jumped in to save the day before Mama got going with introducing Braces Boy to her single daughters.

Claudia is an emergency room nurse and she knows all the right questions to ask. Suddenly things moved smoothly. Nurses filled out forms and made phone calls. Orderlies showed up and pushed beds. My father checked into a room. We trooped wearily down the halls, carrying the plastic bag that held his clothes and shoes.

His belongings seemed pathetic enclosed in that bag. The shoes, pants, and shirts looked forlorn and abandoned somehow. As if Daddy hadn't changed clothes but had shed them instead; left them behind him the way a butterfly leaves a cocoon or a snake leaves an outgrown skin.

The few windows we passed reflected our sad little parade back at us against the complete blackness outside. It was still the middle of the night. Inside, everything was overly lit, like it always is in hospitals. Mama's sensible shoes—I think she and her friends could single-handedly keep Rockport in business— made little squeaking noises on the linoleum floor. Somehow this all made me amazingly weary. The lights, the squeaking shoes, the *beep beep* of machines as we walked passed the semi-open doors of patients sleeping that in-between sleep that people sleep in hospitals . . . I wanted to lie down on the floor and doze off myself. We kept walking.

Daddy looked so tiny in the hospital bed. I remember when I thought he was the biggest, strongest man on earth, when he'd lift me up in the air and I'd feel like I was flying. Part of me still wanted to think that, still wanted him to lift me over his head while I squealed and giggled. He can't even do that to Abby anymore. Sometimes reality just sucks.

We lined up in age order to kiss him good night, just like we had when we were little girls. Leah first, then Claudia, then me. I kissed his forehead and whispered, "Good night, Daddy." I didn't trust my voice not to waver if I said it any louder.

He grabbed my hand and pressed it against his cheek. The light gray stubble scratched my hand. "Don't work yourself up. This will be all right."

I blinked and tried not to let my chin quiver. "Sure it will. I'm just tired." I tried to smile.

He tried to smile back.

Neither of us achieved much success.

We split up in the parking lot. Leah followed my mother home, to make sure she got there all right. Knowing Leah, she probably went in and made her a cup of tea, too, yet would still be at her desk by 8:30 A.M. I retrieved Abby from my friend Kim's house and tucked her back into bed. She never stopped snoring. I doubted if she'd remember any of it the next day. I wished I wouldn't. I crawled back into my own bed, pulled the blankets up to my neck, and started to shake.

CHAPTER TWO

Hook Up the DieHard and Let 'Er Rip

Leah

One part Apricot Glaze (#38), one part Titian Red (#74), one part developer. Forty minutes. Excellent coverage. Good, subtle color. So what else is new?

Claudia

Two parts Dark Ash Brown (#24), one part developer. Forty minutes. Oh, my God. What were we thinking? Way, way too dark. Shampoo! Shampoo immediately! *Arrgghhh!* Shampoo again!

My father's heart attack, or his "event" as my mother keeps insisting on calling it, turned out to be a nonevent. Even Derek Zaretsky's bar mitzvah changed our lives more. After Derek's bar mitzvah, I had to change the route I used to walk home so I could avoid him following after me and telling me how he was now a man. Yes, it was as creepy as it sounds.

In comparison, after a cardiac catheterization showed no blockages in Daddy's arteries, the hospital sent him home with a raft of follow-up appointments with cardiologists and rehab specialists. We didn't even change our toenail polish, much less anything significant.

Things had returned to some semblance of normal while we waited to hear what changes he would be expected to make. So, of course, we were all at Leah's. It was hair dye night. In all honesty, we would probably have been there making sure no one had gray roots even if my father had been in the ICU with all his breathing being done by machine.

Claudia actually has a living will stipulating that if she's ever in a coma, we must come in regularly to do her hair, pluck any stray chin hairs, and keep her toenails painted. To anyone who thinks that's shallow, she says that everyone has their own priorities.

Make no mistake about these evenings. This is a serious ritual, despite any resemblance to a mere beauty regime or a paean to vanity. We have meaningful food, which means that I make snacks that center around a theme. There's always alcohol, even though none of us can hold our liquor worth a damn. And we wear sacred vestments. All right, so they're just ratty clothes we don't mind getting splattered with dye—we each have a designated shirt for root night that never varies. We can identify different time periods based on the different colored stains. I'd say that makes them sacred. Before each coloring, someone has to make the pilgrimage to the beauty supply store where our oracle, Catherine, reigns supreme over choices of brand and color. The entire evening is one of worship to the goddesses of hair and tint.

As youngest (and don't think I don't lord that over Leah and Claudia as often as possible) and inheritor of our mother's excellent hair genes, I don't have to do my roots since I haven't started going gray yet. I'm in charge of refreshments and marking down what we used on their hair, and for how long and how well we liked it. It's the only time I cook anymore, so I tend to go all out. I had decided on a Mexican theme for the evening.

Technically I'm not necessary at these evenings, but they were the first social outings my sisters could talk me into after my little breakdown, and they've gotten to be a habit. A significantly better habit than refusing to get out of bed and not brushing my teeth for days on end, in my opinion.

I held Claudia's margarita up for her so she could reach the straw. She took a long sip and sighed. "Excellent. Just what I needed."

"Tough week at work?" Leah stretched her pipestem legs out in front of her, clad in her usual pair of fashionably distressed jeans with slightly ragged, slightly belled hems. Her feet were bare. Her toenails were red. Since she was the one being "done" at that moment, I didn't need to hold up her drink for her. I offered her the tray of taquitos. She held up her hand to say no.

"Just the usual sort of week." Claudia sighed. She shifted back and forth on her feet, which were encased in incredibly ugly blue plastic clogs that she claims are the only thing standing between her and having to quit her job. Being an ER nurse is tough (especially on your feet), but Claudia thrives on it. Usually. It takes a certain personality—one that's addicted to crisis and adrenaline—to do what Claudia does, but every once in a while things get to her, too.

"Not just the usual if you're sighing like that," I observed. I started to wash off the baking sheets I'd used to warm up the appetizers. As I put them in the sink, one of them slid out of my hands and clattered against the porcelain. Claudia and Leah both jumped. "Sorry."

"I suppose not entirely the usual. There was a couple who came in last night that reminded me a little too much of Mama and Daddy."

"What was wrong with them?" Leah wanted to know from underneath the shock-straight cascade of hair pushed forward over her face.

Claudia rubbed at an itch on her cheek with her shoulder while her hands stayed busy with Leah's hair, soon to be uniformly reddish blonde. "She was senile."

I snorted. "Mama may be a handful sometimes, but she's far from senile."

"I know. That wasn't it. Maybe it was their ages, or how they looked."

"People don't go to the emergency room for senility," Leah observed. "It doesn't happen just like that." She snapped her fingers.

"Right. Senility was just the starting point. She got confused in the middle of the night and wandered out of their apartment. She fell down the stairs and broke her hip."

"So, this couple reminded you of Mama and Daddy how?" I asked.

Our mother has done many things to horrify and embarrass us over the years. For instance, I'll never forget the moment at the rehearsal dinner for my wedding, when she opted to recount in great detail the time I had dental work done when I was nine and had been convinced my nose had grown and had refused to come out of my room until the novocaine wore off. Everybody had a good laugh at that one while I tried to sink under the table.

Or the time she came to Claudia's second-grade classroom to discuss Claudia's long absence due to strep throat, and announced in her loudest stage whisper to the teacher that Claudia's temperature had reached at least 102 degrees when taken "rectally."

And let's not forget the magical moment right before Leah's junior prom, when Leah floated down the stairs in her beautiful dress with her hair up like a princess, just to have our dear mother point to Leah's feet and warn Leah's date to watch out for those "Suitcase Simpsons" when they were dancing.

She has, however, never, to my knowledge, traipsed out of the house in her jammies and fallen.

Claudia sighed again. "Oh, just the way he looked at her. The way he made sure she was comfortable and we were treating her right."

"Mama and Daddy never do stuff like that. Especially when they're stressed. They bicker to show their love," I pointed out.

Leah, who doesn't have a whole lot of patience for beating around the bush, said, "Come on, Claudia, spit it out. What's bugging you?"

Claudia paused in her patient parting and painting of hair. "Look, I know I'm better off without Mark. I know Todd and Randy are better off without him, too. It's just that when I see a couple like that, people who've been together for fifty or sixty years and are completely devoted to each other, I wonder what's going to happen to me when I'm eighty and senile and start traipsing around the city in my nightgown and curlers. Who's going to care enough to keep me safe?"

Leah and I exchanged meaningful looks. "We are," we said in unison.

At this point in our lives, and we are as surprised about this as anybody else, all three of us are single. Leah's never gotten married. For a long time, we all thought she was too focused on her career to bother with relationships. Then we thought that men were frightened of her success. Then we realized that the majority of them were frightened of her. After all, she scares the bejeesus out of us half the time, why shouldn't men be nervous, too? She's a powerful personality.

This isn't to say that she never dates or has relationships. There was even a live-in boyfriend for about two years that Mama was convinced was going to pop the question. Unfortunately, the only question he ended up popping was who got the cookware they'd purchased together at Williams-Sonoma when he moved out.

Claudia divorced her husband, Mark, about four years ago. I think I mentioned that pesky heroin addiction thing. He's maintaining on methadone right now, so at least he's providing child support, but beyond that and being the sperm donor that helped her conceive Todd and Randy, he's pretty much good for nothing.

"You two will be as old and decrepit as I am!" Claudia wailed.

"I'll be two years less decrepit than you," I pointed out helpfully while offering to refill Leah's margarita glass.

"No thanks. I still have to do Claudia." Leah turned in the

chair to look up at Claudia. "I have no intention of being decrepit at all, so I'll still be able to take care of you like I always have."

Claudia gave Leah's shoulder a squeeze. "That's sweet. Bossy, but sweet. It doesn't make me feel all that much better, though." She gave Leah a nudge. "Turn around and let me finish."

I took Leah's glass and headed to the sink to rinse it out. Halfway there it shot out of my hand. I mean, it just literally flew out of my hand like it had suddenly developed jet rockets. It hit the floor and shattered. Glass everywhere. Everyone shrieked.

"What is with you tonight?" Leah burst out as I ran for the broom.

"I'm sorry," I wailed while I swept. "It just slipped."

"It's the second glass you've broken tonight." Leah lifted her feet as I swept under them.

"Don't forget the pan she dropped, and the way she tripped over the doorway when she and Abby came in," Claudia chimed in.

I threw out the broken glass and slumped down at the counter. I knew what was wrong. I just couldn't get myself to talk to anyone about it.

"Do you think you're coming down with something?" Leah asked. "Did you get a flu shot this year?"

"Maybe it's PMS. Where are you in your cycle?" Claudia asked.

If possible, I try to blame all things on my menstrual cycle. My sisters know that and sweetly do their best to aid and abet it.

The problem wasn't my cycle, though. Hormones, yes. Cycle, no. I could take it no longer. I had to tell someone. These were my sisters, the two people on earth to whom I could confess anything and be certain they would still love me. I finally blurted, "I am so horny I think I am going to die," and then collapsed in a heap on Leah's kitchen island.

After they finally stopped laughing, they started arguing.

"Maybe she should try one of those computer dating services," Claudia mused. "I know a whole bunch of women at work who've used one of them and they've met some great guys. I'm thinking of trying it myself."

"A dating service?" Leah chortled. "Let's face it. Dating is simply not all it's cracked up to be."

"Easy to say when you actually get to go on a few." Claudia sighed.

I know I mentioned earlier that Leah can be intimidating. She's also really pretty. I'm the tallest of the three of us, but she's still five foot, seven inches or so. She runs a lot so she's thin, but in a strong-looking way, not an anorexic way. She has red hair and these very intense green eyes that get absolutely laser beam-like when she gets angry. She's the only one of us who dates anymore. The problem is, by the third or fourth date, the guy gets overwhelmed and runs.

"Well, the last thing Emily needs is a man," Leah pronounced.

Claudia arched a brow at me over Leah's head. "Are you suggesting she swing the other way? It's fine by me. I just want to be there when she tells Mama."

"I am not suggesting she swing the other way, for God's sake." Leah snorted in disgust.

"So, if she doesn't need a man and she doesn't need a woman, what does that leave? Transsexuals?"

"Be serious, Claudia." I'm continually amazed that Leah can talk about anything—and I do mean anything—and make it into a serious discussion. "It leaves machines."

"Machines?" Claudia's voice rose so high on the last syllable that it squeaked.

Leah twisted around in her chair. "Are you going to do my roots, or are you just going to repeat every other word I say?"

"Sorry." Claudia obediently returned to painting the dye on Leah's scalp.

Leah settled back in her chair. "Yes. Machines. Like a vibrator."

"A vibrator?" Soon only dogs would be able to hear my sister speak. Then they both looked over at me. "Maybe if it was hooked to a DieHard," Claudia said.

When they both stopped laughing again, they started arguing again.

"You're missing the point, Leah." Claudia was almost finished with Leah's roots. She had worked her way almost completely over to Leah's right ear. "She doesn't need an orgasm. She needs intimacy, contact, companionship."

"Intimacy? What on earth does she need intimacy for?" Leah stood up and went to check herself in the hand mirror and set the timer. "She has a job to go to, a daughter to raise, and aging parents to care for. The last thing she needs is another person to place demands on her."

"Maybe a partner would help her shoulder those burdens and meet some of her own needs, as well."

Leah snorted. "We are talking about a man, not a myth."

Claudia shook the comb at her. "I refuse to become one of those man-hating, male-bashing women who sit around and—"

"What you refuse to do is to see reality." Leah took the comb and gestured for Claudia to sit. "Don't you think you're projecting a little?"

"Don't you think *you* are?" Claudia shot back.

"Do I get a say in this?" I asked.

They both sighed just the same way I sigh when Abby interrupts me when I'm on the phone. I put my head back down on the counter.

I know this all sounds terribly trivial, but between the year my husband was sick and then the year and a half since he died, it had been a really long time for me, and I'm still young enough to have certain needs. Needs that hadn't been met in a long, long time.

Granted, for quite a bit of that time I didn't actually notice. When you're too depressed to get out of bed and brush your teeth, having sex isn't high on your priority list. I suppose I should have taken it as a sign of how mentally healthy I was becoming, but it was beginning to drive me crazy.

"Emily? Are you listening?" Leah's voice broke through my haze.

"No. Not really. I figured you'd let me know when you needed my input."

She rolled her eyes. "Really, Emily. You put the problem before us. You could at least listen to our suggestions."

"I'm sorry. Am I supposed to order it from a catalog or from the Internet?"

"Order what?" Leah looked at me with a blank expression on her face.

"You know, the vibrator."

Claudia started stamping her feet and snorting. Abby came in to see what was so funny and ask if she could have some chips. Todd and Randy came in and inhaled the entire tray of taquitos. Then both Claudia and Leah had to shampoo. By the time we got back on track, the discussion had thankfully moved on to our father's non-heart attack and our mother's reaction to it.

"I think she's doing it just to torment him, personally," Leah said. She had pushed away her margarita and had started filing her nails. It's one of her weight-control methods. She figures if both hands are busy doing a manicure, she can't be shoving food in her face.

"Doing what?" I asked, relieved that my hormones had left the limelight.

"You know, all that heart-healthy stuff." She pulled another tool from her little case and started pushing back her cuticles.

"How is that tormenting him?" My hands always look like they belong to a carpenter. A big, healthy male carpenter. Remember that *Seinfeld* episode about the girl with man hands? That's me. I stopped doing manicures because I thought they made me look like a transvestite. I'm still fascinated with watching Leah do hers, though.

"Well, his arteries weren't blocked, so why is she making him eat all that low-fat, low-sodium stuff?"

"Because it's good for him?" I ventured. "And she loves him and wants to keep him healthy?"

Leah slapped the cuticle shover down. I was a little worried she'd pick up the nasty little scissor thing and come after me, but she didn't. She glared at me instead.

"Or she's just using that as an excuse to make him crazy. Like the pulse thing. Why is she taking his pulse every ten seconds?"

"It's not every ten seconds, and I think it's because their doctor told them to keep a log. He thinks Daddy might have had some kind of arrhythmia. He said it would be good information to have." I looked to Claudia for support. She was rooting through the crumbs of chips left in the basket, searching for a tortilla of sufficient size to hold a little salsa. Her weight-loss program is to have two adolescent boys around who inhale everything in sight before she can get her hands on it.

Leah shook her head. "At this rate, she's going to annoy him to death long before he has another heart attack. What kind of doctor would want that?"

Claudia snorted and finally spoke up. "Mama picks doctors like I pick husbands. She looks for someone who's just slightly sadistic."

The shriek followed hard on the heels of the pop.

"Mommy, stop it," Abby squealed.

"It's not like I'm doing it on purpose," I answered.

Abby had decided to be a bunch of grapes for Halloween. Okay. Maybe I talked her into it. If I had, I was regretting it now.

My fabulous costume idea required me to pin about twenty purple balloons to Abby's purple leotard.

While she was wearing it.

Every time she wiggled or jiggled while I pinned, I'd miss and stick a pin into a balloon. Or my finger.

She's seven. She wiggles a lot.

If she didn't stop, she'd end up covered with deflated balloons, and look like I'd dressed her up as some sick condom ad.

Abby wore green tights and a green stem-shaped hat that I'd made out of crepe paper and pipe cleaners. It seemed like such a great idea at the time (and how many times have you said that after a complete disaster). Simple. Cheap. Cute. All I needed were purple balloons and crepe paper. We had everything else.

I hadn't reckoned with trying to pin balloons on an excited wiggly seven-year-old, or that the wiggler in question might be invited to an outdoor Halloween carnival, requiring her to ride in a car. With a seat belt. Across a lot of balloons. Or that it could easily drop to below fifty degrees at night at this time of year in Seattle, and that Abby would refuse to wear thermal underwear under her tights because you could see the bumps under the tights and she didn't want people to think she had bumpy skin.

"Who . . . *who* would think you had bumpy thermal skin?" I asked, head already bowed in defeat. I wouldn't win because I didn't really want to win this one. I remembered all too well my mother making me wear green sweatpants under my Girl Scout uniform on cold days. Just thinking about it brought back horrible memories of classroom coat closets with their musty sheepy smell of wet wool mittens, and little kids pointing at me and laughing. I focused on the balloons before my skin started to itch.

"No one," she said, her eyes narrowed. "But one of those icky, stinky boys would *pretend* he did and make fun of me all night."

"Icky, stinky boys?" My old friend, Jake, clicked a picture of Abby with her lip out in full pout. "Are we all icky and stinky?"

"Nearly." She tried to cross her skinny stick arms across her chest, but couldn't, due to the balloons.

"Me, too?" He pretended to be hurt, sticking his lip out in a pout just like Abby's. It didn't have quite the same effect with a goatee.

Abby relented. "Not you, Uncle Jake." She gave him as close to a hug as she could without popping her costume, and sniffed him. "You smell kind of like soap and peppermint."

Jake was the best man at my wedding. He and Vince had been best friends since Jake had blacked Vince's eye in third grade, in a dispute over whether a pitch had been a strike or a ball.

"So I'm not stinky." Jake smoothed his beard as if he were thinking deeply. "I'm only icky."

Abby giggled. "No, you're not icky, either. Silly, but not icky. Besides, you're not a boy."

His eyes went wide. "I'm not?"

"Trust me," I interrupted. "Jake was as icky and stinky a boy as there ever was. He's just one of the exceptions that grew out of icky stinkiness."

Now Abby's eyes were big blue marbles. "He was icky and stinky?" She whipped around to look at me, balloons riffling in the breeze she'd created.

I backed off a little. "Well, maybe not the ickiest or the stinkiest." Jake had always had a sweet streak. Even when he was in third grade and I was a shy little first-grader, too afraid to cross the street by myself. "But icky and stinky enough."

Jake crouched down next to Abby and whispered in her ear loud enough for me to hear. "Don't listen to her. She's just trying to distract me from remembering what a bad case of cooties she had."

"She did not!" Abby said hotly, with great indignation.

I had to admit I was pleased to see her defend me so quickly. I stuck my tongue out at Jake.

He stuck his out back at me after giving Abby a little squeeze. "Okay. You're right. It was only a mild case of cooties."

Jake straightened up and Abby skipped off to check herself in the full-length mirror in my room.

"Thanks," I said.

He grinned. "For admitting that your cooties weren't that bad?"

"No, Icky, Stinky Boy. For stopping by. She doesn't fuss as much when you're here. I don't think I ever would have gotten all those balloons pinned on if she hadn't been posing for pictures for you. My fingers look like pincushions as it is."

"No problem." He took my hand and examined my fingers, peering over the top of his glasses. He winced and then let my hand go. "I was in the neighborhood."

I wasn't sure how that could be. I lived in Lynnwood. Jake and Sandy's house was in Edmonds and he worked in downtown Seattle. That would put him "in the neighborhood" only if the neighborhood was some giant complicated figure eight cutting through most of the Seattle metropolitan area. Maybe he'd had to do something for his mother. She still lived about a half mile from my folks, which was less than a ten-minute drive to my place.

I shrugged. "I'm glad you were."

He checked his watch. "I've gotta go in a few minutes, though." He sighed a little.

"Us, too." I sighed also. I wasn't sure I felt completely up to this carnival, but I didn't have much choice. Crowds with noise and confusion still made me want to hyperventilate, although I no longer had to carry a paper bag in my purse all the time, just in case. Times of forced gaiety still weighed pretty heavily on me, but Abby was excited and she deserved a little normal fun.

Abby skipped out and finally decided her costume met her expectations. I won't detail the argument over pinning balloons to her bottom. We'll just say that she was pro and I was con. I put a denim jacket on over my turtleneck and wool sweater, and tucked my feet into boots with a good thick rubber sole. At least one of us would stay warm. Jake helped me tuck Abby into the car and thread the seat belt through the balloons.

It was drizzling (surprise, surprise). No chance the carnival would be canceled, though. Pacific Northwesterners treat drizzle like the rest of the world treats sunshine: we think it's good weather.

I could feel my hair starting to frizz around my forehead. I slipped into my slightly beat-up Jeep Cherokee (parking is simply not my forte) and belted myself in to get out of the rain. My hair was a lost cause already, but I didn't have to get drenched all the way through before we even got there.

Jake kissed Abby's forehead. "I want some candy, you know."

Abby's eyes narrowed. "What kind?" I didn't raise any fools; we protect our chocolates at all cost.

"What don't you like?"

"Licorice and caramel."

"I'll choose from those."

She nodded. He shut the door and we drove off. When I turned the corner, I could see him still standing in the road looking after us. The rain beaded in his black hair, making it glisten a little in the streetlight. For a minute, it almost looked like he had a halo.

CHAPTER THREE

He Played My Body Like an Instrument. Unfortunately, It Happened to Be the Bongos

Leah

One part Apricot Glaze (#38), one part Titian Red (#74), one part developer. Forty minutes. Same as always. Yada yada yada.

Claudia

One part Light Ash Brown (#32), one part Dark Ash Brown (#24), one part developer. Forty-five minutes. A little better, but last month's blunder lives on in infamy. Who talked us into that anyway? Was it Catherine? Catherine must die!

He wanted to what?" My voice squeaked.

"He wanted to spank me." Claudia's face turned a mottled red, which was particularly charming with the ratty old pink towel wrapped around her shoulders and the combination of Dark and Light Ash Brown on her scalp. "Ow!"

Leah had slipped when she parted Claudia's hair and stuck the tip of the comb in her ear.

"And you let him?" Leah was as incredulous as I was.

"He was so cute! You don't know how cute he was!" Claudia begged for understanding while rubbing at her ear and glaring at Leah.

"I know how completely insane you are." Leah continued to methodically part Claudia's hair with a rattail comb and then meticulously brush dye onto her roots. "I mean, we can start with going home with a total stranger from a computer dating service on the first date, and progress pretty rapidly from there. Actually, you're lucky to be alive. He could have been an ax murderer."

"I think Claudia's being very brave to start dating again," I said.

"Brave?" Leah snorted. "More like crazy. More like lunatic. More like desperate."

"Did it hurt?" I asked. It wasn't precisely that I was ignoring Leah, but she didn't really expect anyone to comment on the lunatic hack anyway.

Claudia shook her head. Leah slapped her shoulder. Leah's used to us ignoring her sometimes, but it doesn't mean she likes it. "Don't move around so much."

"He didn't hit me that hard." Claudia looked up accusingly at Leah. "And he's not an ax murderer. He's an accountant and a spanker, but that doesn't mean he kills people."

I couldn't help it; I had to know. "Was it fun?"

"Emily!" Leah pretended to be shocked, but I could tell she was glad I'd asked. She wanted to know as badly as I did. She just couldn't bring herself to ask.

Claudia shrugged, careful not to move her head this time. "It felt goofy. He wanted me to stand there in front of his desk and then he told me what a bad girl I'd been."

"And then?" I asked, nearly breathless.

Claudia blushed. "Then he spanked me, and then we had some of the most fantastic sex I've had in my entire life right there on top of his desk on the leather blotter."

There was a moment of silent reverence. It had been a long time since any of us had had any kind of sex, much less the fantastic variety or the on-top-of-the-desk variety.

Leah broke the silence. "So, are you going to see him again?"

"I don't know. He's really cute. He's really smart. He's got a great job. He owns his own condo. He's got a nice car. But . . ."

"But what?" I asked.

"This came today." She nudged a bag out from underneath her chair with her toe.

I picked up the bag. Inside was a box from the Bon Marché. I arched a brow at her.

"Open it," she said. "Go ahead."

Inside was a white blouse with a Peter Pan collar, a navy blue cardigan with gold buttons, a very short plaid skirt complete with one of those giant safety pins, and a lacy white push-up bra with a matching lacy white garter belt and white stockings.

"No panties?" I asked.

She shook her head. "No panties."

We all stared at the ensemble for a few minutes, then I carefully packed it back in its tissue paper and put it away.

"At least it's from a nice store," Leah said thoughtfully.

"And he understands the importance of having the right outfit," I chimed in.

Claudia shot me a look as she changed places with Leah. "Pour me another martini, Emily, and get me another mushroom."

We were having vodka martinis with crab-stuffed mushrooms and scallops wrapped in bacon. I wasn't sure entirely what the theme was. Maybe some kind of fifties thing. Anyway, no one was complaining.

"Did Todd and Randy meet him?" Leah asked.

"No." Claudia shook her head. "They were out for dinner with Mark when he picked me up."

"Probably best that way," Leah said. "How is SOS these days?"

Claudia's ex is not exactly our favorite person on the planet. Quite a few years ago, we had started referring to him as SOS in front of the kids. It stands for Sack of . . ." Well, I'm sure you get the point. The kids have been hearing it for so long, they've never even asked what it stands for.

"Oh, him. I'm so mad at him, I could just spit," Claudia fumed.

Leah's eyes went round with surprise. It takes a lot to get Claudia mad and she'd just gone from zero to furious in about two seconds.

"Why?" I asked.

"Just for being Mark," she said succinctly.

"Okay," I said. "Being Mark is certainly worth being angry about. Are we angry about some particular aspect of being Mark, or just the general state of Mark-ness?"

Mark has definitely put Claudia and her boys through their paces over the years. He follows the standard drug-addict pattern of everything being secondary to his need to fix. The difference with Mark is that he's generally always held down a responsible job while maintaining his addiction. I've never been sure how he pulled it off, but he did and continues to do so, though I think methadone has a lot to do with it.

"He's stealing Randy's medications," Claudia spit out.

My jaw dropped. There's low and then there's really, really low. I personally think stealing your kid's ADD medications counts as the latter.

"I'm not surprised," Leah said airily.

"You're not?" I sure was.

Leah shook her head. "For all intents and purposes, he stole money from those children every time he bought drugs. Every time he shot up, he was taking food from their mouths, clothes from their backs, and opportunities that never come back." Leah shrugged. "Why should we be surprised that he would steal a few pills?"

Sometimes when Leah gets up on a soapbox, it's best to ignore her. Especially if she's right.

"Why would he steal them anyway, Claudia?" I asked.

Claudia sighed. "They took Randy off Ritalin. He was growing so fast, they were having to up the dosage all the time, so they wanted to try something else. They use Dexedrine sometimes, so they tried that. It didn't work so well, so we switched back to the Ritalin, and I had a leftover bottle of Dexedrine with the other medications in that cabinet over the kitchen sink."

"Dexedrine?" I asked. "As in Bennies and Dexies?"

She nodded. "The very same stuff. It makes most people hyper and jittery, but it has a calming effect on kids with ADD. That's why they call them paradoxical reactors. They react in the opposite way that most people do."

"What an incredible jerk," I said.

Leah nodded her head in agreement.

"And stupid, too," Claudia added. "I mean, how was he to know that the pills in that bottle were really what they were labeled to be? I could have filled that bottle with any little white pills."

"Yeah, but why would someone do that?" Leah asked.

"Oh, you know how you sometimes buy a big bottle of painkillers, and then use little bottles to carry them around in your purse or whatever." Claudia took another sip of her martini. "Let's face it, though. If you're willing to buy a pile of powder from a total stranger on the street and then put it in a syringe and shoot it into your veins, you're willing to take a chance on what your ex-wife might put in a pill bottle over the kitchen sink."

"Good point," Leah agreed. "What are you going to do about it?"

"I'm not sure. Probably just toss the pills. I just wish there was some way to get back at him without confronting him and having a huge scene."

"It's not worth it. Just throw them out."

"I know. I'm just so sick of him getting away with everything," Claudia huffed.

We all pondered the many, many things Mark had gotten away with over the years.

For instance, there was the night before our grandfather's

funeral, when Mark went out at ten o'clock to buy Claudia a box of tampons and didn't show up until six o'clock the next morning, leaving her grief-stricken, worried, and cramming toilet paper in her underwear. He'd said he had a hard time finding a store that was open. Or the time that he'd actually fallen asleep behind the wheel at a four-way stop, with both kids in the car. Or, my personal favorite, vomiting on Claudia's head while she was asleep when he was in withdrawal and couldn't remember even which side of the bed he was on. The list is really too long.

"Let's talk about something else," Claudia said. "Didn't you have a date with that cute service rep this weekend?"

Leah nodded. "Had one set up, but didn't actually have one."

"What happened?"

She shrugged. "I got to the bar we were supposed to meet at and my cell phone rang. He'd gotten hung up with a client and was bushed, and wanted to reschedule."

"Did you?"

She shook her head. "That's the second time he's done something like that to me. I don't feel like playing that game."

That's my big sister: two strikes and you're out. Why wait around for the third one?

"Poor you." Claudia leaned down and gave her a quick squeeze. "What did you do?"

"It turned out okay. I had a drink, listened to the music for a while. I was fine."

"You should have called one of us."

"You were at work, and what would Emily do? Tart up Abby and meet me downtown? I don't think so."

"I could have left her with Mama and Daddy," I protested.

"It's not your scene." Leah turned her attention to me. "So, what are you and Abby up to this weekend?"

"Not too much," I said. "Abby has a soccer game late on Saturday. Jake said he'd come to watch her, and then maybe we'd have a picnic together afterward."

Claudia arched a brow at Leah.

Leah nodded and smiled her special little lips-pressed-together smile that means she thinks she knows something you don't, which she usually does, which can be a little annoying.

"What?" I asked.

Claudia looked at me and then at Leah. "Do you really think she doesn't know?"

"I thinks she's clueless," Leah answered.

I stamped my foot. "What are you talking about?"

"Jake," they said in unison.

"What about him?"

They both cracked up. Wiping her eyes, Leah put her hand on my arm and said, "We think Jake might be the solution to your, uh, 'little problem.' "

"My little what?" Here's the bad part of being youngest. As much as I enjoy being the last to go gray, and probably the last to have things start to sag and the last to have hot flashes, I am also always the last to know. From the moment of my birth, my two sisters have always been a little more knowledgeable, a little more experienced, a little more clued in than I am. I thought it had mostly evened out as we hit our early thirties, but apparently not. They still treated me like their slightly imbecilic little sister.

I occasionally still *am* their slightly imbecilic little sister.

"You know." Claudia winked at me. "Your little problem that we were discussing last time?"

It finally dawned on me what they were talking about. "Jake and I are not romantically involved."

"Yet," Leah threw in.

"Ever," I threw back.

"Well, sweetie," Claudia said, "you might not be romantically involved with him, but I think he might be with you."

"Aren't you forgetting one little detail?" I said in a voice that I hoped was dripping with sarcasm, and not just shrill and defensive. "Like the fact that he has a live-in girlfriend?"

"Exactly how long has Jake been living with Sandy?" Leah asked with feigned casualness.

I thought for a moment. I remembered being at the moving party when the two of them moved into their house together. It was after Abby was born, because I remembered her playing in their yard, but it had to be before Vince got sick, because I remembered him helping carry some monstrosity of a couch up the stairs.

I know it's a strange way to keep track of when things happen, but since the two most significant events of my adult life have been becoming a mother and becoming a widow, everything else sort of exists in relation to those two happenings. It could be worse. I have an aunt who factors everything off of how old my second cousin Robbie was at her wedding.

"They've been living together for at least three or four years, I think," I finally said.

"And there's no wedding date, no engagement ring, no nothing?" Leah asked.

"No, but so what?" I countered. "Lots of people live together happily for years without getting married. Maybe they just don't see the need for a piece of paper from the government saying that they're a couple."

"Maybe they're just not meant to be together," Claudia chimed in.

I shook my head. "Sandy aside, Jake is not interested in me that way."

Leah smiled. "He sure spends a lot of time with you and Abby for a guy who's not interested."

I knew that was true. I was also pretty sure I knew why. Jake had spent a lot of time with Vince in those last few months when it was clear that he wasn't going to make it, but wasn't quite gone yet.

"I think he made a promise to Vince," I said softly. "I think Vince asked him to look after us."

Claudia and Leah exchanged another long look, but it didn't even bother me this time. Then Claudia hugged me. I'm pretty sure I told you already what good hugs she gives. "That may be so, sweetie, but there's looking after and then there's looking after, if you know what I mean."

"We need to talk about Thanksgiving."

I wondered when my mother had stopped saying hello when she called. I'd pick up the phone and say hello, and she'd just start talking. It was the telephone equivalent of flinging the door open, marching into the house, and taking over, which she is also perfectly capable of, so I don't know why the whole lack of telephone etiquette thing surprised me. I guess "surprise" isn't the right word. It's more that I wasn't sure when it had started. Had she been doing this for months? Years, even? Had I just not noticed? Or was this new?

Since my father's non-heart attack, she's been a little tense. Well, maybe not tense, but at least a little pinched. And definitely a little harsh. Especially with Daddy.

I didn't ask her about any of that, though. I figured I'd run it by my sisters first. Instead, I cradled the phone on my shoulder and turned back to my computer monitor, to continue re-formatting the proposal I was laying out.

"Why do we have to talk about Thanksgiving, Mama? Did they move it? Have we decided not to celebrate it for religious or political reasons? Are we not feeling thankful this year?"

She sighed. "You know, at least when you were depressed you didn't wisecrack all the time."

I smiled. It was safe; she couldn't see. No one could see. My desk resided in one of the most far-off, isolated little cubicles available at Reed, Myers & Anderson Architectural. "Sorry."

"If you were sorry, you wouldn't be smiling like that."

I cringed. How did she always do that? It makes me almost as crazy now, as it did when I was nine. I wiped the smile off my face.

"That's better."

I imported the style sheets from the last proposal that I'd worked on, for a small office building in an industrial park. It was my turn to sigh now. "What did you want to tell me about Thanksgiving?"

"We need to discuss the menu."

Our Thanksgiving menu has essentially been unchanged forever. We roast a turkey. Sometimes someone is feeling wild and crazy and changes the ratio of sage to rosemary or thyme in the herbs they rub on it, but it remains a roasted turkey. No fancy stuffings; just plain, ordinary, normal stuffing. The sweet potatoes have glaze and little marshmallows across the top. The green beans have the little french-fried onion thingies on top of them. We have one canned cranberry sauce and one from fresh cranberries. The fresh one has a lot of cinnamon in it. The mashed potatoes have nearly lethal amounts of butter in them and are whipped until they're fluffy, and then rebaked to brown the top. And gravy. Lots and lots and lots of gravy. I love gravy.

"Why?" I asked. "Why do we need to discuss the menu? It's Thanksgiving. Isn't that all we need to know?"

"Not in light of your father's condition," Mama said with great finality.

"But Mama, it's a holiday," I whined. I stopped trying to paginate the proposal; this required my full attention. I knew where she was going: she wanted a low-fat Thanksgiving. I'm no expert, but I'm pretty sure gravy and butter are not on the approved cardiac diet eating plan, and I had a bad feeling that if Daddy wasn't going to get butter and gravy, that I wasn't going to get it, either. "It'd be mean not to let him splurge."

"You think it would be nicer to kill him with unhealthy food? Is that how you would show your love, Emily? By killing him slowly with fat and salt? If we make an exception for the holiday, then we'll make a few exceptions on the weekend. And after that, we'll be making exceptions because it's Wednesday or it's raining or because we just plain feel like it. Before you know it, they're cracking your father's chest open to Roto-Rooter out his arteries. Is that what you want, Emily?"

"No, Mama. Of course it's not what I want. I just meant that—"

"I know what you meant, Emily, but sometimes true kindness seems cruel on the surface. It's still kindness underneath."

Round One to Mama! I take that back. Round, schmound; it was a TKO, and I'd barely set foot in the ring. I don't know why I even bothered. "What would you like me to make, Mama?"

"I think you should do dessert. You're always so creative when it comes to sweets. Remember that Hannah Kauffman will be there, too, so make at least one choice that a diabetic could eat. Oh, and Milton Feinstein will be there, as well, so one thing with no wheat products."

"Okay."

"And, Emily?"

"Yes, Mama?"

"What do you know about Tofurky?"

Greeeeeaaaaaaat.

Abby streaked down the field, dodged between two defenders by deftly kicking the ball to the left while she dodged right, and then quickly cut back to the left again. She booted the ball and it sailed waist high past the goalie through the posts.

"Holy shit," Jake said.

I elbowed him sharply in the ribs.

"Sorry," he mumbled. "I meant, Holy cow."

We were already getting a lot of sidelong glances from the other parents on the sidelines without him swearing like a sailor. They all knew I was single, or at least had guessed it, and everyone clearly wanted some explanation for Jake's presence. His looks probably were making them a bit nervous, as well. In our suburb of Seattle, there weren't a lot of men with wild, black curly hair past their shoulders and goatee beards.

Don't get me wrong; Jake's not unkempt. And he certainly has the hair for it. I personally would kill to have my hair naturally curl like that.

He doesn't look like a bum. He does, however, look a little like Satan's messenger boy in black jeans, a leather jacket, and boots.

It works for him, but it also clearly made the Soccer Moms and Dads a little nervous. They're more a polo-shirt-and-khakis kind of crowd on their most ribald days.

I decided to ignore the curious looks and focus on Abby running up the field, blonde braid streaming behind her and fists pumping in the air.

"You didn't tell me she was that good," Jake said, his eyes following Abby as she ran.

"Because she isn't," I said. "She's a reasonably solid little player, but she's never done anything like that before. I think she's trying to impress you."

He arched one wicked brow at me. "Really?"

I shrugged. "It's all I can come up with to explain the sudden flash of brilliance."

"That's gratifying. I don't usually have that effect on women." Jake smiled.

"Don't get cocky. She's only seven."

Abby continued to play better than she ever had. Wherever the ball was, Abby was there, too. She was a one-girl offensive and defensive dynamo. When the game was over, she raced across the field to jump into Jake's arms, screaming, "Uncle Jake! Uncle Jake! Did you see me?"

Jake twirled her around and assured her that we had seen every fabulous move that she'd made, that he hadn't taken his eyes off her for a second, that he'd been riveted the whole time. All of which was true.

I could see the faces of the other parents change as Abby called Jake her uncle. I don't think they would have minded if they knew he wasn't really a relative; they just wanted an explanation for his presence and were too polite to ask.

Jake and I look enough alike to be siblings anyway. Jake's hair and skin are a shade or two darker than mine are. My eyes are blue while his are sort of hazel, but we have the same long, straight nose, the same cheekbones and slightly slanted eyes. We're even pretty close to the same size. Jake skims in just under six foot and I'm a little over five foot nine.

In fact, we look so much alike that I used to tease Vince that he'd only fallen in love with me because it wasn't socially acceptable to marry Jake. At least not at the high school we attended.

They were that close—Vince and Jake. I think that's why Jake watches Abby so hungrily. I find myself doing it, too, sometimes. She looks so much like Vince. Same blonde hair. Same ski jump of a nose. Same blue eyes. Same stubborn little chin. She has so many of his gestures and expressions, too, that it's like catching glimpses of him again.

There are times I wish his face wasn't so clearly in front of me every day. The constant reminder can be hard when you occasionally want to shut down, but mainly it's comforting. I don't know how Abby feels about it, exactly. She plays her cards pretty close to her chest, especially when it comes to how she feels about her dad. I can see it being difficult as she grows older and hears over and over again how much she looks like a father that she may barely remember.

She was only five when he died, and the last few months of his life he didn't look or act a whole lot like most of the pictures of him that decorate our little house.

We spread our picnic out under a tree near the playground. It was a little chilly for eating al fresco, but not bone chillingly damp, so we took advantage of what passes for good weather up here. Abby bolted her sandwich and, after giving us both peanut buttery kisses, ran off to play with her friends. I sighed as I watched her strip off her cleats, long socks, and shin guards and abandon them in the wood chips that covered the ground around the play structures. I retrieved them and came back, picking bark off the socks.

I sat down next to Jake with a thump and said, "This is how I get wood chips in my underpants."

He stopped chewing and looked at me, brows creased with concern. "You've been dropping your underpants on the playground and running off to play on the swings?"

"No!" I punched his shoulder. "Abby leaves her socks in the wood chips, and then when I do laundry they all seem to collect in my panties. The wood chips, I mean."

He grabbed a bunch of grapes and laid back on the blanket. "That may have been more than I needed to know. Besides, I think I liked the concept of you playing on the swings with no underpants better."

I blushed. "It's better than the words, I suppose."

"Words?" Jake looked up at me, his head cocked a little to one side. "There are words in your underpants?"

I nodded.

"What precisely are your underpants telling you, and can anyone else hear them?" He looked like he couldn't decide whether to laugh or be worried.

"It's not just my underpants, but it does seem to surprise me most when they drop out of my drawers."

Jake waited a few beats before saying, "Emily, you're scaring me. Back up and explain."

"Abby had one of those magnetic poetry sets. We had it by the washing machine. I don't know why she liked it better there than on the refrigerator. I think nobody else was willing to sit on the floor in the laundry room to play with them, and that way nobody changed her words around. By the way, I think the washing machine is leaking a little."

"I'll take a look at it when we get back to your place."

"Anyway, the little container still had a whole bunch of words in it, and it was sitting next to the washer, which I had left open, and Shadow must have knocked it into the machine."

"The cat. You're blaming it on the cat." He put his hands over his eyes.

"I tried to get all the little words out, but they're stuck to the drum and they're hard to see—it's dark in there, you know—so now, every once in a while when I'm folding laundry or we're getting dressed, words just fall out."

"For example . . ." He let the words trail off.

I shrugged, not sure I was ready to share this or not. Something possessed me and I decided to plunge ahead. "For example, 'butterfly,' 'joy,' and 'dance' fell out of my underpants this morning."

"'Butterfly. Joy. Dance.'" He said the words very slowly, letting each one hang in the air between us. "In your underpants."

I nodded and gulped a little. I couldn't believe I was saying any of this out loud. I especially had trouble believing I was saying it out loud to Jake. "I thought it seemed particularly ironic, since there hasn't been any butterfly joy dancing in my underpants in quite some time."

One of those wicked eyebrows arched up again. "Do you want there to be butterfly joy dancing in your underpants again?"

I sighed and hugged my knees to my chest. The sky had clouded over and it had started to get chilly, but my face felt hot. Wasn't I too old to blush? "I suppose so. I'm just a little leery of everything you have to do to get the butterfly joy dancing in your underpants."

Jake laughed. "You're a woman. As I recall the dating scene, all you have to do is show up and say yes."

"I don't think so," I said, shaking my head. "You should see what Claudia's going through."

"Claudia's dating?"

"Mmm-hmmm. And speaking of more than you need to know . . ." I proceeded to fill him in on her latest adventures, including the package from the Bon Marché which is, of course, what had brought the whole thing to mind.

"*Ewww.* You guys tell each other everything!" He crinkled up his nose.

I giggled, spraying a fine dust of cookie crumbs on his

shoulder. I swiped at them, hoping he wouldn't notice. No such luck. He shook his head at me and wiped them away himself.

"Yeah. Don't guys? I thought that was what the whole locker room—talk thing was all about."

Jake shook his head. "Not at that level of detail."

"So what level of detail do you get to?"

He shrugged. "One guy might say to another one, 'So, didja do her?' and then the other guy would say, 'Yeah,' and the first one would say, 'Cool.' That's about it."

"Oooh. Very deep." I punched his shoulder again.

He popped a grape in his mouth and chewed. "You didn't ask for deep. You asked what we said."

By the time we'd convinced Abby to come in off the playground and head home, it was almost dinnertime. I couldn't blame her for wanting to stay. It was a gorgeous afternoon. The sun even attempted to make an appearance. It felt like one of those little warmer lights they used to have over buffets. You could almost notice the heat from it if it was just a little closer.

We headed back to my little house, where Abby was immediately dispatched to the bath. Though she was covered with grass stains, wood chips, and sweat, she protested that she wasn't dirty and that she'd had a bath just yesterday. I made her go anyway.

Jake twisted some hose thing around in the back of the washer and pronounced it fixed.

"Thanks for coming this afternoon. Abby doesn't say much about it, but I know she notices the other girls' dads always being around. It's nice for her to have a man besides her grandpa come to one of her games."

Jake went very still. "You know, it isn't a chore for me. It helps me to be around you two." He walked back to the kitchen with me following. He suddenly became very busy with making sure the Saran Wrap was pulled very tightly across the empty paper plate of cookie crumbs.

I put my hand on his shoulder. Grief is a very selfish emotion. Sometimes I forget that there are people besides Abby and me who still miss Vince. "He'd like that we're all helping each other out."

"I know." Jake reached around and put his hand over mine, but he didn't turn to look at me.

There's a danger when someone dies, especially if they die young, of turning them into a saint or a hero. I try to keep my memories and Abby's memories of Vince honest and true, but it isn't always easy.

He really was a terrific guy. Smart, funny, kind, good-looking. It was easy to put him up on a pedestal when he was alive. It would be easy now to turn him into some kind of folk hero: Vince Bunyan and his Blue Ox, Emily. Vince's not being around to screw things up by not mowing the lawn or forgetting Valentine's Day or not taking out the trash makes it even easier.

I wasn't sure how honest or true I was being when I told Jake that Vince would have been glad that we had banded together. I do think he would have been glad that we were helping each other. I just also know how much he must hate not being there in the middle of it. He was that kind of guy.

Jake drew a deep, raggedy breath and finally turned back to face me. He gave me a lopsided grin that looked pretty weak, then looked at his watch. "Guess I better be going. Sandy will be wondering where I am pretty soon."

"You know, she's welcome to come along on these things, too. I don't mean to exclude her." I wasn't sure I really meant that even as I said it. Sandy is a fairly high-powered salesperson for a computer software company. She's smart, gorgeous, driven, and very good at what she does.

Vince disliked her.

Not because she's an ambitious woman or because she's hard; at least, I'm pretty sure those things hadn't bothered him. He adored Leah, after all. I think it's just that she's Jake's opposite—all restless energy where Jake is mellow, judgmental where Jake is tolerant, all sharp edges where Jake is soft. Vince couldn't see why or how they got along, and I guess if you pick a mellow, tolerant, easy-going guy as your best friend, it might just indicate that you're not interested in hanging out with restless, judgmental, sharp-edged people.

On the other hand, maybe he just didn't like her.

I always reminded him about that whole opposites attract thing, but he didn't buy it then. I'm not sure I buy it now.

Jake shrugged. "Maybe if we plan some kind of grown-up night out. Kids are not Sandy's thing."

My head shot up. Jake had always doted on Abby, had always been in the center of whatever gang of kids happened to be around at any given moment. I'd just assumed that he wanted kids of his own.

"Is that a problem for you? I mean, you've always seemed to love kids."

He grimaced. "I don't know. It's something we're talking about."

"That sounds a little grim."

"It's not that bad. I never thought that procreating was the only path to happiness. On the other hand, I like being around kids, but if you hang around the local playground too much without one of your own, eventually the police stop by to question you."

My jaw dropped. "No. They didn't."

"God, you're gullible, Emily." He snorted. "Of course the police haven't stopped by and I'm not loitering around playgrounds, either. Except when I'm with you and Abby." Then he gave me a hug—a really nice, warm one—and made me promise to call if I needed anything, and left.

I spent the rest of the evening wondering why those butterflies had taken up residence in my stomach, if they were supposed to be joy dancing in my underpants.

CHAPTER FOUR

Tattoo My Ass

Leah

One part Apricot Glaze (#38), one part Titian Red (#74), one part developer. Forty minutes. In light of recent behavior, perhaps something scarlet would be more appropriate?

Claudia

One part Light Ash Brown (#32), one part Apricot Glaze (#38), one part developer. Thirty minutes. Hmmm. Kind of a banded effect we hadn't counted on. Too bad nurses don't wear those little caps anymore.

We have to take care of this before we turn fifty. Before we're too old to do it, we must get something really funny or sexy or interesting tattooed on our asses. That way, when we're in a nursing home, everyone will want to come and wipe our asses for us just so they can see our tattoos." Claudia announced this as if she were starting us on a new multivitamin regimen: it was to be undertaken for our own good.

"What brought that on?" Leah peered around Claudia to try to get a glimpse of her face, and nearly lost her balance.

I'd opted for a French theme for our refreshments. I'd made a baked Brie, a quiche, and a lovely tossed salad, and chilled a bottle of champagne. The champagne might have been a mistake. There's just something about those bubbles that go straight to a girl's head.

"Dating, I bet," I mumbled around a mouthful of cracker crumbs and cheese.

"I'm giving up on it," Claudia said.

"I thought you had a great time with that guy you went out with last weekend." Leah parted Claudia's hair, but it came out more like an MTV-generation zigzag thing than her usual precise straight line. She slapped the dye on anyway. "Saturday morning you said he was charming."

"Yeah." Claudia sighed. "Charming, attentive, constantly giving compliments."

"Sounds like an absolute nightmare," I agreed. "I hate it when men are charming, attentive, and full of compliments. What are they thinking?"

"It was just a facade." Claudia picked at the towel on her lap. "Only a facade. They're all just big, dumb facades."

I looked at Leah, who was a teensy bit out of focus. "Do you have a feeling there's something we don't know about?"

"Yeah, but does it matter? They're just facades." She looked like she was going to cry.

I sat down on the floor in front of Claudia so I could see her face better. "What happened?"

"We went out on Friday night after work. Met for a drink.

He was wonderful. Kept telling me how beautiful I was, how smart I was. We ended up having dinner. I could barely eat. He was just so . . . I don't know, exciting to be with." She covered her face with her hands.

I patted her knee. "I'm so sorry. Too much excitement."

She leaned down to get her face close to mine. "I was good, though," she said earnestly. "Even though I had a lot of wine and not very much food and he was really cute, I was good. I didn't go to bed with him that night."

"Good for you," I half mumbled back. We can't drink champagne. We love it, but we can't handle it.

"We made out a whole bunch and I really wanted to, but I didn't do it. It was like a movie. You know, where you're pressed up against a wall and he's kissing you and nibbling on your neck and sliding his hand up your shirt, and your knees feel all wobbly and he smells really good, and he's all pressed against you and you can feel . . . well, you know." She sat back and shook her head. "But I didn't do it. Nope. Didn't do the deed."

I raised my glass to her. "To no deeds! Didn't do! Did the room suddenly get a lot hotter? I feel warm."

"L'chaim," Leah added. She slipped down onto the floor next to me. "To the deed!"

"No, Leah," I said. It suddenly seemed very important to me that she get it right. "To *no* deed."

"The next day he sent me flowers." Claudia moaned.

"Oh, no. Not flowers." I shook my head, then stopped because the room went off-kilter. I shut my eyes and opened them again and this time the room stayed still. Maybe it was my contacts.

"Yes. Flowers. And he called. He wanted to go out again that night."

"Two nights in a row?"

"He said he couldn't stand to wait to see me."

"Who could?" I asked. "I can barely wait to see you most days, and I don't stick my hand up your shirt."

"Know what you mean," Leah agreed. She nodded her head, looking for all the world like one of those little doggies people put in their cars' back windows. "Love to see my little sisters." It actually came out more like "Love to shee my liddle shishters."

"Oh, Leah." Suddenly I felt all mushy inside. What could be better than having sisters who love you, even if they call you their "shishter"? "I love to shee you, too." We embraced right there by Claudia's knees.

"Will you two morons stop slobbering on each other and let me finish my story!"

We looked up, surprised.

"I'm not done yet!" she said.

"Flowers, compliments, hand up your shirt? There's more?" Leah looked dumbfounded. It's not easy to make Leah look dumbfounded. For that matter, it's not easy to make her look dumb anything. Darn that champagne!

I wrapped my arms around my knees. "Let's hear it." Sitting on the floor, looking up at Claudia, I felt like I used to at story time at the library when I was a little girl. I liked it.

"We went out again Saturday night," she began, her voice hushed.

"Did he stick his hand up your shirt again?" Hearing about some great-looking guy putting his hand up my sister's shirt wasn't as good as having a great-looking guy put his hand up my shirt, but at least I could live it vicariously.

"Don't rush me."

"Who's rushin'?" Leah slurred.

"Boris Yeltsin!" I yelled.

Leah and I collapsed in hysterical yowls of laughter.

"Have I mentioned that the two of you truly are morons?" Claudia yelled.

We laughed harder.

It took a while for us to calm down; champagne giggles are like that.

"So you slept with him, didn't you?" Leah asked Claudia when she could finally talk again.

Claudia nodded miserably.

"And . . ." I urged.

"And what?" she asked.

"And was it good? Was it great? Did the earth move and the stars explode?" Leah prompted.

Claudia blushed. "Not really."

"So, it was just okay? Not great and not bad?" I suggested.

Claudia blushed harder. "Let's just say that he, uh, left me to, um, dial O on the little pink telephone all by myself."

"You're kidding." I was a little disappointed. After all the buildup, I expected the guy to have a Ph.D. from Kama Sutra U. Apparently, Claudia had, too.

She shook her head. "Then he left."

"Right away?" Leah asked.

Claudia nodded. "Pretty much. I'd dozed off, and woke up just as he was walking out of my bedroom door at two A.M."

"Maybe he didn't want to run into Todd and Randy in the morning," I suggested.

"Maybe he felt awkward," Leah offered.

"Maybe he's blowing me off," Claudia said.

We waited.

"He didn't call the next day, but I didn't know what his plans were and figured he was busy."

"Reasonable." I laid my chin on Claudia's knee. My head was getting heavy. "Besides, maybe he was waiting for the flowers to be delivered." It felt funny when my jaw moved against her knee. I giggled.

Claudia smacked me on the head. "No flowers. No call. No nothing. I figured he'd call the next day. On Monday."

"Did he?" Leah asked.

I didn't even have to look up. Through her knee, I could feel Claudia shake her head. Maybe the true seat of our soul is in our knees. I giggled again. I liked that thought about seats and knees; I just wasn't sure why.

"So I called him."

"What happened?" I asked her knee.

"Nothing. His secretary said he was out and took a message. He didn't call back."

"Maybe he had a lot of meetings," Leah suggested.

"All week?" Claudia asked.

"He never called?" I asked.

"Never."

"Did you call him again?" It was Leah's turn.

"Three times. Once more at the office and twice at his house."

"No flowers?" I started to feel sad. If you get to vicariously have a great-looking guy put his hand up your shirt, then I suppose you had to vicariously share in getting blown off.

"Nope. No flowers. A big, fat nothing. I slept with him and he disappeared."

"Nothing?" I asked again. I felt a little desperate. What had we done wrong? What had we said? How could he have dumped us like that?

"Hmmmm," was all Leah said. I thought she had a funny look on her face, as if she had bitten into a lemon, or some of our late grandmother's homemade gefilte fish.

"Hmmmm what?" I asked her across our sister's lap.

You could have knocked me over with a feather when Leah burst into tears. Considering the amount of champagne I'd drunk, you could have probably knocked me over with a feather anyway, but Leah bursting unexpectedly into tears really added to my sense of imbalance.

"I'm just a facade," she wailed.

"What?" Claudia and I said in unison.

She grabbed the edge of the towel draped across Claudia's lap and blew her nose into it. "I'm just a facade, and now someone else will have to get their ass tattooed because of me."

My mouth had dropped so far open that I had to wipe the drool off my chest.

"Remember when I told you about the guy who sort of stood me up?" Leah asked.

I nodded. I think Claudia probably did, too, but I couldn't take my eyes off Leah to check.

"And how he called me on my cell phone at the bar to tell me he wasn't showing up?"

I nodded again, I hoped in an encouraging fashion.

"So I figured I'd finish my drink before I left. I mean, it was a perfectly good drink. It would have been wasteful to leave it on the bar. Right?" She looked from my face up to Claudia's, as if this point needed corroboration. "Right?" she repeated.

"Absolutely," I said. "It would be a shame to waste it. Might as well flush your money down the toilet." Sometimes it helps to have Depression-era parents.

"Completely," Claudia chimed in.

"So I'm sitting there drinking the perfectly good drink that shouldn't be wasted because some idiot of a customer service rep would rather take clients out to dinner than meet me like we planned—"

Claudia hissed. "What kind of jerk would do that? Worse yet, what kind of jerk would be jerky enough to tell you he was doing it?"

"Claudia, hush," I said. I wanted to know what the point really was. "Go on, Leah. What happened next?"

She took a deep breath. "This guy walks up to the bar and orders a club soda. I turn to look, and it's like all the air goes out of my lungs."

"It does?" I asked.

"Why?" Claudia asked.

Leah went on as if we hadn't said anything. "This guy is so cute and young and so unbearably sexy. He has on jeans and a leather jacket. His hair is a little too long in the back and he has one of those scruffy little beards that look so stupid on most guys. But on him it looks great."

"How young?" I said.

"How sexy?" Claudia asked.

Leah squinched up her eyes. "I think he's about thirty."

I considered for a moment. "That's young, but not gross young. At least he could have ordered a drink if he'd wanted to."

"How sexy?" Claudia asked again.

Leah looked up at her from the floor. "So sexy I had to cross my legs."

"Wow," Claudia and I breathed in unison.

"He turned to me and said hi." She paused. "And he smiled."

I sighed.

"We started talking. It turns out he was in the band that was playing there. That's why he wasn't drinking. He doesn't like to drink until after his shows. Sometimes not even then. He's very serious about his music."

"Leah," Claudia said quietly. "Do you know his name?"

She nodded. "His name is Chase."

I thumped my hand to my heart. "Wow! What a name!"

"Leah, what happened?" Somewhere, at some point that I wasn't completely aware of, Claudia had stopped sounding drunk. She sounded sober. And serious.

"I waited around and watched him play. I mean, it's not like I had anywhere else I needed to be, and I can't quite explain how I felt when he smiled at me. I don't think someone's taken my breath away like that since Trevor Kraft in eleventh grade."

I had only been in seventh grade when Leah dated Trevor, but even I remembered the three weeks she spent crying her eyes out when he dumped her for the dishwater blonde that worked at the KFC with him. Mama even let her take her dinner on a tray in her bedroom for three nights in a row.

"Wow," I said again.

Claudia kicked me. "Stop saying wow."

"Ow," I said. "What happened next?"

Leah looked from Claudia to me. "I watched him play. I kept watching his hands on his guitar. How sensitive they were. How strong they looked. The way they cradled the neck of his guitar and strummed the strings. I started imagining his hands on me—how it would feel to have those fingers on my body. Every now and then he'd look over at me and smile again and I felt like I was melting, like he'd lit a flame inside of me that I could feel everywhere from my face to my, well, you know . . ."

I sighed, careful not to say wow. I didn't want bruises.

"You took him home, didn't you?" Claudia's voice had an accusatory note in it.

I craned my neck to look up at her. I hadn't thought it was possible to press Claudia's lips together tight enough to make them disappear, but she was doing a pretty good job.

Leah nodded. "He was amazing. The first time we did it, I figured it was that good because it had been so long for me. But then it was just as good the second time, and the third, and the fourth . . ." Her voice trailed off.

"Four times?" I felt my eyes go wide.

Leah shrugged. "He's only thirty."

Claudia stood up to check the timer, dislodging Leah and me from her knees. I leaned my face against the wooden chair. It felt cool. The champagne had started to wear off, but my face was still flushed and warm. From my vantage point, I watched Claudia's knees pace back and forth across the kitchen.

"And you think I'm nuts for going home with an accountant?" Claudia demanded.

"Not just an accountant. An accountant and a spanker," I pointed out.

"Be quiet, Emily. You're drunk," Claudia snapped.

"So are you!" I looked up at Claudia, but she didn't seem drunk at all anymore. Not even post-champagne sleepy. "Well, you were. At least, I think you were."

"Exactly what do you think you're getting yourself into, Leah?" Claudia asked, her voice sharp.

"I'm not getting myself into anything," Leah wailed. "That's the problem."

I put my head back down on the chair. It was nice and solid. It wasn't exciting, but at least I knew what to expect from it. "I don't get it."

"He keeps calling. And sending notes."

"Do you want him to stop? Have you asked him to stop?" Claudia asked.

"I haven't talked to him. I'm screening my calls and not taking his. Not returning his messages. You know, what you just described, Claudia. I just realized how despicable I'm being. I just realized that I'm putting someone else in the position where they're going to have to have their ass tattooed."

Claudia tossed some dirty silverware into the sink. "You have to see him and break it off."

"I'm worried that if I see him, I won't be able to break it off. You don't know what it was like. The second our eyes met in that bar, I was on fire. I don't think Daddy standing in the door with a shotgun would have stopped us. I'm not sure nuclear war would have stopped us."

Claudia tossed the pan in along with the silverware. "Then you have to do it over the phone."

"That seems so cold," I said. "The phone thing."

"I know," Leah agreed. "I can't stand to do it over the phone."

"Are you sure you want to break it off?" I asked. Feeling like a towering inferno just from a glance and a smile didn't seem all bad to me. This guy Chase was only six years younger than Leah was. If it were the opposite way around, no one would be batting an eye. And as to his profession, well, it wasn't like Leah needed a man to support her. So, if what she *did* need a man for was the whole hot-and-sweaty thing, it sounded like Chase fit the bill.

Leah handed me a crumpled piece of paper that she'd dug out of her pocket. "This was under the windshield wiper of my car when I came out of work this afternoon."

It was a poem. Or a sort of ode. Whatever it was, it was for Leah and it was so hot it practically singed my fingers.

"Wow," I breathed, and handed it to Claudia before I'd thought better of it. She didn't hit me, though, for which I was grateful. I figured the champagne would give me enough of a headache without her adding to it.

"Under your windshield wiper," Claudia repeated, voice shrill. "That sounds like he's stalking you. Leah, you don't know anything about this man. He could be dangerous. If he's following you around, leaving filthy notes on your car, maybe you should make a police report."

"It's not filthy, Claudia. I think it's sexy. I think they might be song lyrics. I think he might be writing a song about me."

"Then it's a filthy song. And your windshield wiper isn't the place for it, especially if your car is parked in the lot by your office. And whether you call the police or not, I think you better talk to him and break this thing off before it goes any further."

"Why?" I asked. "Why does she have to break it off? I don't see why she can't date him!"

Leah sighed. "We spent practically the whole weekend together and then when I got to work Monday morning, it suddenly occurred to me what it would be like to show up with Chase at the company Christmas party."

I still wasn't following. "It's not even Thanksgiving yet. Why do you have to worry about Christmas? Besides, we're Jewish. We don't even celebrate Christmas."

"Emily, it's not about the holiday. It's about how things look. It's about being with someone appropriate. It's not appropriate for a woman executive in her late thirties to be hanging out with a barely thirty-year-old musician."

Leah sounded convincing, but there was something in her eyes that made her look like the people in the Calypso scene in *Beetlejuice*. You know, their mouths are singing the song and their bodies are dancing the dance, but their eyes look desperate to stop. She had that same look. Like her mouth was saying words she had no desire to say.

"Who cares about your office Christmas party? That's one night a year. There are three hundred and sixty-four others to get through, and I don't think his age or his profession should stop you if you like him. He's thirty. He's a musician. It's not like he's eighteen and asking if you want fries with your order at Burger King," I said.

"And if he was, would that finally make you understand what inappropriate means, Emily?" Claudia snapped.

"Not if he made Leah happy!" I snapped back.

Leah mumbled something about brushing her hair out and stumbled from the room.

"So what's the deal, Claudia?" I couldn't believe she could stand there and stack dirty dishes as if nothing had happened, after she'd decimated Leah like that. "If you can't be happy, nobody's allowed to be happy? Is that it, Claudia?"

She threw the spatula in the sink and wheeled on me. "What the hell is that supposed to mean, Emily?"

I didn't feel like backing down, for once. "I think I made myself pretty clear."

Claudia stared at me until my eyeballs felt hot, but I didn't blink.

"I'm just trying to protect her," she finally said.

"From what? An unpleasant dose of happiness and fun?" I shot back. "Lord knows we can't have any of that! Between your divorce and Vince dying, we've probably gotten to the point where we can't even digest happiness! We don't have the right enzymes anymore. Even a little glee might make us sick or something."

"Don't be so naïve, Emily," she snapped. "Do you have any idea what the whole music scene culture is like?"

"No. And neither do you."

She closed her eyes and breathed deeply in and out twice before she answered. "I have enough of an idea to know that it's rampant with drugs and alcohol abuse. And what about the hours they keep? They're in and out at all times of day and night. A family needs a schedule."

I put my head down on the counter. "Is that what this is really all about?"

"Of course."

"Not of course, Claudia. Just because the guy can play a guitar doesn't mean he shoots heroin. After all, Mark can't even pick out 'Mary Had a Little Lamb' on the piano and look at him. And speaking of irregular schedules, did you ever really know where he was?"

"And just because he's cute and good in bed doesn't mean he should be anywhere near our sister."

"It's not just that he's cute and good in bed, Claudia. Did you see Leah's face? Did you see the glow on her? He made her feel good. He made her happy. Isn't that worth something? Isn't it wonderful to see her like that?"

"You know it is. But I don't think it's worth the risk of having her end up like me, picking up the pieces of a life that's half ruined by drugs."

"Well, I think it's worth taking a risk so she doesn't end up like me, alone and lonely and feeling like half a person."

We were still staring at each other and breathing fast through our noses when Leah walked back into the room.

"Did I miss something?"

I waited, holding my breath, to see what Claudia would say. She dried her hands on a dish towel and gave Leah a brittle smile. "Nope. Nothing worth repeating."

My parents live in a fabulous split-level home in Edmonds that they could never afford if they had to buy it now. We moved into it when I was four. It's been paid off for five years, and it's worth easily ten times what they paid for it. When they still had mortgage payments, they were less than what Vince and I paid for monthly rent on the one-bedroom apartment we lived in when we first got married.

When we all lived there—Leah, Claudia, me, and my parents—it was all families like us. Parents with decent jobs and a few kids. Now, with the exception of a few old-timers like my folks, it's all highly paid, upwardly mobile professionals.

After I picked Abby up from the bus stop, we had had to run some errands that took us pretty close to their place, so we decided to drop by. I rang the bell and waited for my mother to answer the door. My father never answers the door. He sits in his favorite chair in the living room, reads the paper, and if the bell rings, roars out, "Jessica, doorbell" as if she would be too deaf to hear the bell, but not too deaf to hear him yell. I have a key, but don't like to let myself in when they're there.

I could feel my mother look through the peephole at us. I don't know how; it's not like I could hear her footsteps or anything. I just always know when she's looking at me. I get a prickly feeling on the back of my neck. Especially if she's looking me right in the eyes.

The door opened. "Gordon, Abby and Emily are here," she yelled.

Abby skipped through the door, pausing to give my mother a brief hug around the legs before plopping down in the living room that opened to the left off the central hallway, and pulling out the basket of Barbies that lived under the coffee table. There has been a basket of Barbies under the coffee table ever since we moved in. Leah put it there the day we arrived and no one has ever dared get rid of it. When Todd and Randy were little, the basket accumulated some superheroes and a few trucks. It was still the same basket, though.

I followed more slowly. I felt it was undignified to skip, although there's something about walking into my parents' house that makes me feel like I'm the right age to do it. "Hi, Mama." She might have wanted to do away with salutations altogether, but I wasn't ready for that radical of a move.

"So, what are you doing here?"

"Terrific to see you, too," I replied with a big, bright smile.

She shot me a look and then gave me a really weird, brittle smile. "It's lovely to see you, too, Emily. Just unexpected."

In the dining room opposite the living room, my father sat at the heavy mahogany table on one of the gold cushioned chairs. Mounds and mounds of colored paper and binders and old photograph albums and banker's boxes, so old their corners had turned to dust, covered the entire surface. I looked back at my mother, who had followed me in. She shrugged and smiled that weird, brittle smile.

"What are you doing, Daddy?"

"I'm scrapbooking!" he said with an enthusiasm that I hadn't heard in his voice since the last time my mother made triple-chocolate cheesecake. Which in a way was good, because I didn't think Daddy was going to score any triple-chocolate cheesecake for a long time, so he might as well be enthusiastic over something else.

"You're what?"

"Scrapbooking." Mama rolled her eyes. "Last week, Charlotte Harris invited me to come to a scrapbooking party. They're like Tupperware parties, but instead they sell you all this junk to make these scrapbooks."

"Not junk," Daddy growled. "These papers are archival. Acid-free, so they won't yellow your photos or get brittle and fall apart."

"For what they cost, you'd think he was preserving the *Mona Lisa* with them," Mama grumbled.

I saw Daddy look at me from under his half-closed eyelids. He never lifted his head, and if someone hadn't really been looking, they would have thought he'd never looked up from the photos he was rifling through. You always had to watch him. I can't tell you the number of times I'd gotten busted as a kid sneaking Hershey's Kisses from the candy dish in the living room by his favorite chair when I thought he was asleep, but he was really watching everything through the teensiest little crack of open eye. "Preserving the story of my life apparently isn't worth a few extra pennies to your mother."

"That's not what I said, Gordon. I thought it was a lot of money to spend on a hobby that you weren't sure you were even interested in yet."

"Wait a minute," I interrupted. "Charlotte invited Daddy to the scrapbooking party?"

Mama sighed. "No. Your father drove me there. He was going to have a coffee in the kitchen with Jack while I went to the party, but before I knew it, there he was like a great big bull in a china shop, pawing through all the stickers and papers and borders."

"It was interesting." He shrugged. "It looked like fun. Why should the women get all the fun?"

Mama puffed up like one of those prairie chickens you see on nature shows that try to make themselves look too big for the snakes to eat. "All the fun? All the fun? How about all the cooking and the laundry and the cleaning? We shouldn't have a few minutes to ourselves to remember the few good times you've allowed us, without you horning in on it?"

"Horning in on it?" Daddy yelled back. "You didn't even want to go! You almost called and pretended you were sick, so you wouldn't have to go. You didn't have the slightest interest in this!"

"And you made sure I never would, didn't you?" Mama shot back. "You had to go out of your way to make it so I wouldn't have some hobby, or something to think about or do, that didn't center around you."

Daddy stared at her for a second. "You're welcome to participate if you want. We could do it together. It's mostly about you, anyway." He looked back at me. "Come. Sit here next to me. I'll show you." He patted the chair next to him.

I slid in. He'd assembled a photo of himself in his army uniform with his arm slung around my mother's shoulders, a yellowed napkin embossed with "Clarice and Elmer," and some stickers of wedding bells and doves. In the photo, my mom was wearing a floral-print dress with a lace collar. Her waist looked so small you were almost afraid the belt around it would snap her in two.

"Mama, you look gorgeous. Who are Clarice and Elmer?"

Mama had sat down on the other side of me. She ran a finger slowly down the scalloped edge of the photo. "Clarice was a second cousin on my mother's side. They moved away a long time ago. I don't think you ever met them. Your father was my date to her wedding to Elmer."

"And you kept a napkin from their wedding all these years?" I couldn't imagine it. To keep an embossed napkin from the wedding of a second cousin who you never saw for all those years.

Mama smiled. "Your father proposed to me that night."

I felt all gushy inside. I loved all the old stories about my parents' courtship. It was all so romantic. They were young and in love. Mama got to wear fabulous suits that actually worked with our tall, somewhat too curvy figures. "Oh, Daddy, that's so sweet that you're making a special page for that day."

"Yeah, it's like writing a memoir, but more fun."

"What other days are you making pages for?" I asked.

He snorted. "I think today will be a big one."

The comment froze me. Had Daddy decided to do his memoirs so we wouldn't forget him after he died? Was that why all the stickers and colored papers and cutouts and photographs were strewn across the table?

My little out-of-the-blue visit was actually planned to coincide with their return home from my father's cardiologist appointment, because I was worried. Maybe even a touch anxious. Maybe even a little scared. For more than thirty years, my parents had represented everything stable and secure in my life. Their getting older and possibly ill would change it much more than I was ready to allow.

The cardiologist, Dr. Shakira, was the biggest cheese of all the doctors who were poking and prodding my father after his nonheart attack. He was the one who would make the final decisions about my father's treatment. I prayed he hadn't been offended by my father's lame jokes about "too many chiefs and not enough Indians," or if he was, that he hadn't take it out on Daddy with some horrible and bizarre treatment option.

Mama got up from the table and left the room.

"Really? What about today makes it a big one?" I asked with feigned casualness.

"Well, your mother's feeling much better."

I stared at him for a second. "I thought Dr. Shakira was your doctor. I thought this appointment was for you."

"It was." Daddy looked suspiciously like he was about to laugh.

"Want to explain?"

My mother bustled into the room and handed each of us a glass of iced tea. "Let's go into the living room to talk."

My father sat down in his favorite chair by the big reading lamp, snapped the newspaper open, and hid behind it. It seemed to me it trembled a little.

"He doesn't want to explain. He's having a little chuckle at my expense," Mama said.

I looked back at Daddy, who was definitely fighting back a laugh now. "What happened?"

"Something that could have happened to anyone," Mama said sharply. "I don't see why he's making such a big deal about it."

The paper snapped down. "Because you didn't see yourself! Jumping around, smacking yourself on the head and yelling! You looked like a crazy person!" My father grabbed his sides and doubled over as the laughter bubbled out of him.

I stared, openmouthed. "Mama, why were you jumping around and hitting yourself on the head?"

"A bug," she said, her lips pressed primly together.

"A bug?" I repeated.

Apparently, as they'd walked into the medical building, some gnat or little bug had flown into my mother's ear.

At first she'd shaken her head a little and kept feeling around with her pinky finger, which apparently just pushed the little bug in farther. By the time they got to the doctor's office, she was pulling frantically at her ear and shaking her head violently.

When Dr. Shakira came out, she was jumping up and down, slapping herself on the side of the head and yelling, "It's walking! It's walking! It's walking and buzzing!"

"They tried to give her lithium," my father gasped out between guffaws. "They thought she was nuts! They thought she was having a psychotic episode right there in their waiting room!"

My mother still wasn't laughing. "Thank goodness, I got them to check my ear first. Dr. Shakira's nurse ran down the hall to some pediatrician's office and borrowed one of those otoscope thingies, looked in my ear, and then plucked the bug out with a pair of long tweezers."

"Its legs were still wriggling." Daddy grinned.

Mama shivered with disgust.

"But then they knew you weren't crazy? Right?" I asked. "They stopped trying to shoot you up with psychotropic drugs and restrain you?"

"Of course. But it wasn't funny, Gordon. They thought I was crazy. They wanted to send me off to a loony bin, and you did nothing to help. I hope you never get a beetle in your ear and need help getting it out." Mama sniffed, clearly hurt.

He laughed harder. "It wasn't a beetle. It was a little gnat. Besides, I thought you were crazy, too. I was going to help them put you in restraints."

"It was twice the size of a gnat. It was a beetle." She leaned forward in her chair and shook her finger at him. "Someday when you're in need, I'll laugh at you and you'll see how it feels."

"It was barely the size of the tip of my fingernail, and I've been in need plenty of times and not had any help," he roared, not laughing anymore.

My parents are like that. In high school, my friends liked to come over for dinner because it was like visiting a sitcom. One second they're laughing, the next they're fighting, then they're laughing again.

My mother stood and put her hands on her hips. "It was too a beetle, and when have you ever been in need and not had me drop everything to help? When?"

"Gnat. And what about the time I cut my hand fixing the washing machine? What about that time?" He was on his feet now, too, feet spread, shoulders squared.

"Beetle. And I helped. I drove you to the hospital to get stitches." My mother sat back down and primly crossed her legs at the ankle. "Right after I finished the dishes."

"Gnat. I almost bled to death, waiting for you and your lasagna pan."

"*Ach,* you did not. The bleeding had practically stopped, and at least I didn't take a picture."

"You took a picture?" Normally I stay quiet while my parents work these things out; the question burst out of me on its own.

"A picture, and he made the nurse write a little note." The note of hurt in Mama's voice couldn't have been missed by a deaf man.

"And I have the gnat!" Daddy said triumphantly. He zipped into the dining room and came back with a tiny Ziploc bag, the kind I use to put carrots in Abby's lunch.

I peered into it. As usual, they were both right and wrong. Definitely bigger than a gnat, but not quite as big as a beetle.

"It's gonna make a heck of a page in the ol' scrapbook," my father chortled. "I can't decide whether to use that paper that has the little ant border, or the stickers with the stethoscopes."

Abby looked up from where Barbie was vanquishing a Teenage Mutant Ninja Turtle by running him over repeatedly with a truck. "Why don't you use both, Grandpa?"

He froze for a second, then clapped his hands. "By George, Abby, you're right! Why not use both?"

"Oh, maybe because you might want your wife to retain some shreds of her dignity and self-esteem," Mama suggested.

I could hear the heat starting to turn up again in the room, and Abby was starting to make strangled little whimpering sounds as she watched her beloved grandparents bicker. I knew how she felt. I'd spent a good seventy-five percent of my childhood making little whimpering sounds in the corner.

"Could someone tell me what Dr. Shakira said about Daddy's heart today?" I asked.

They looked at me as if they'd forgotten all about Daddy's heart. In fact, they probably had.

Dr. Shakira had decided that given the fact that my father was sixty-eight years old and had survived forty years of marriage to my mother, even if she hadn't been jumping around and smacking herself on the side of the head for the entire time, and had managed to raise three daughters without jumping around and smacking himself on the side of his head, his heart was in relatively good shape.

He'd probably had an atrial fibrillation. It's a flukey thing that happens sometimes. He should come back to the hospital if he had another one, because repeat episodes could mean something bad. But right now, this one meant nothing.

I hadn't realized quite how tense I was about it until Abby and I left, and I realized that my knees were shaking.

"You made it," I said to Jake as he slipped into the chair I'd been saving for him next to mine.

"Sorry I'm late. Traffic was a bitch," he said.

I kicked him and he winced a little as he turned to wave at my father and mother, Claudia, Leah, Todd, and Randy. We were crammed together on folding chairs in the multipurpose room of Abby's school. The primary grades were giving a performance. Abby might not have a dad there to watch her play, but we were going to try to make up for it with sheer numbers. Quantity if not quality.

"Sandy couldn't make it?" I asked, trying not to sound snide.

"This isn't exactly her idea of a night out at the theater," he answered.

"Too bad. She missed a lot already." I double-checked my program. "The kindergarteners did a square dance. That little boy over there in the red overalls swung his partner so hard I thought she was going to fly off the stage. Two of them tripped during a do-si-do and almost brought the whole group down like dominoes, and one little girl burst into tears and wouldn't dance anymore because her partner said she had cooties."

"Sounds memorable." Jake nodded.

"The first-graders just finished singing what I think might have been the Washington state song, but I'm not sure, and Abby's class is about to begin."

Jake frowned down at his program. "Shouldn't this be some kind of Thanksgiving pageant?"

I sighed. "The teachers decided the whole pilgrim-and-Indian thing was too political and potentially divisive, so they decided to go with something different."

"Yeah, but *The Little Red Hen?*"

"Maybe it's a statement about poultry liberation. How should I know?" I shrugged.

Jake considered it for a moment. "Freedom for Fowl. I could get behind that."

I thought of the Tofurky. "Be careful what you wish for."

The lights went down, and Clarissa from down the block came out in a red leotard, yellow tights, and red construction paper wings and started to recite her lines in a lisping monotone.

"Is she talking?" my mother stage-whispered.

"Of course, she is. Can't you hear her?" my father stage-whispered back.

Other parents started to turn to look at them.

"Maybe that gnat damaged your eardrum," Daddy suggested.

"Well, wouldn't that give you the last laugh," Mama huffed.

"*Sssshh,*" I hissed at them.

Jake elbowed me. "I thought you said Abby had the starring role."

"She does."

Jake looked down at the program and then back at the stage. "The play is *The Little Red Hen*. I'm pretty sure that's the little red hen up there talking, and I'm equally sure that it's not Abby. I think that's Clarissa from down the block."

"It is Clarissa. Just because the little red hen is the title role doesn't mean it's the starring role," I whispered back.

Leah leaned forward. "Last week, a soccer ball bounced off the back of Abby's head when she wasn't paying attention, and one of her teammates kicked it in for a goal. Emily claimed it as an assist for Abby."

My father poked me in the side with a rolled-up program. "Be quiet. You children are disturbing the people who are trying to pay attention."

I rolled my eyes, slumped back in my folding chair, and waited for Abby's big entrance.

When she came on, it was like the beginning of a great fireworks display. The whole audience let out a collective *aaahhhh*. She had on a brown leotard and black tights. I'd sewn fake fur on the arms of the leotard and made a little matching fake-fur miniskirt, too. She had little fox ears and a little fox tail and a painted-on fox nose and whiskers, and was basically the cutest little fox ever to enter a henhouse.

Then she started her little fox song-and-dance routine, about how good the bread smelled and how she was going to trick the little red hen out of it without doing any work. Her voice piped high and sweet and clear through the auditorium. She stumbled a little bit in the dance, but it made her only more darling.

I thought my heart was going to break.

The show ended and everyone leaped to their feet when Abby came onstage for her bow. I could barely breathe.

Jake took my arm. His hand felt warm and strong and I leaned into him. Having him next to me helped. It didn't quite make it all right, but it definitely helped.

"You okay?" he asked.

I shook my head, not quite trusting my voice yet.

"What is it? Abby was great. You should be proud."

"I know. I think that's the problem." Abby skipped through the crowd, threading her way toward us. Sheer delight shined from her face as every adult she passed told her what a great job she'd done, how cute she was, how well she sang and danced. "Look at her."

"I am," Jake said. "Hardly anybody here can take their eyes off her. She glows."

I turned to face him. "He should be here to feel like that, too."

Jake shut his eyes slowly. "I know. I thought of that, too."

"It's totally unfair," I said, trying to talk quickly so I could be done before Abby got over to us. "Vince should be here. He should be here to see her sing and dance and be cute. He

should be here to hug her and tell her she's special. I don't
know who got the rawer deal, Vince or Abby, but they both
got robbed."

"And you," he said quietly. "You got a raw deal, too."

I turned to face him and saw the pain naked on his face in
a way that I'm not sure I'd ever seen before. "And you," I said.
"You, too."

Abby and I had joined a bereavement support group for families who had lost a loved one, not too long after Vince died.
On the second Wednesday of every month, we all meet for
pizza in a church basement and then break up into small
groups. Abby fits into the group for the littlest kids. The kids'
therapists use a lot of art therapy and role-playing. The grown-
ups sit around and talk about our feelings.

Abby always called it the Bereavement Party. It makes
some sense if you think like a little kid. First, everyone gets
together and eats, then the kids go off to play games. How
different is matching colors to emotions from pin the tail on
the donkey, anyway? Then at the end, there's candle lighting
and singing. Ta da! A bereavement party. Happy Depression,
everybody!

Abby also has a bad habit of referring to the urn in
which Vince's ashes reside as "Daddy's can." She was only
five when he died. She fit what was happening to her into
the only framework that she knew. Sometimes, when your
grief partner is a small child, it's hard to take sorrow seriously.

Anyway, at first the support group seemed hokey. Then it
seemed like I didn't have anything in common with those

other sad people. We sat and stared at each other while the facilitator, a woman named Joanie who was sweet but had a penchant for the worst shade of coral lipstick I've ever seen on anyone, talked about finding something positive that came out of each of our personal tragedies.

I could not possibly imagine anything positive that came out of watching Vince die, or trying to keep my life together without him. The idea that anything positive could ever come of that seemed outrageous and even insulting to Vince.

Then one night this woman named Lisa started talking about the last days of her husband's life. I don't know what sparked it, but the words tumbled out of her like she couldn't stop them. She talked about those horrible hours caught between praying for him to die, so all the suffering and horror would be over, and panicking every time she thought he was going, because she didn't know how she'd go on without him.

I felt like she was describing my life. By the end of the night, we were all group hugging and crying. More sisters and a few brothers.

"It looks like my dad is going to be okay," I announced to the group on this particular Wednesday night.

"That's wonderful, Emily," Christine said. Christine's husband died of leukemia. It took twelve years. She has one of the darkest and raunchiest senses of humor I've ever encountered in another woman. "You must be relieved."

"Yeah, and vaguely guilty," I admitted.

"Guilty over what?" Joanie asked.

"Guilty over how relieved I am that I don't have to start taking care of him." It's amazing how liberating it is to say some of these words out loud. Sometimes I just love my support group.

"Why would it have to be you to take care of him? You have sisters. Your mother's in good health," Joanie said.

I shook my head. "It wouldn't be just me; we all would do it. But I didn't even want to do my little part."

"You can say no, you know," Christine said. Like she ever said no. Like she didn't dedicate her whole life to taking care of her husband.

"No. I couldn't. He's my dad. Although he probably wouldn't want me to; I'm such a lousy nurse." I cannot begin to recount the ways I got things wrong trying to take care of Vince. Claudia started referring to me as the Keystone Caregiver at one point.

"Emily, please don't start that again." Joanie leaned back in her chair and sighed. "I thought we'd gotten past that."

"How can you get past it?" I turned to Christine. "Don't you wonder about it sometimes?"

"No," she said flatly. "I do not. I do not walk those paths."

I didn't believe her. One of the worst things about Vince's being sick in the way he was sick was that I had to start making all the decisions about his treatment for him. He was in no shape to read research reports and decide which kind of chemo or what kind of surgery he thought he should have. On the face of things, when I force myself to be relentlessly logical, I know it probably didn't matter.

The kind of brain tumor he had was so fast growing and so invasive that most people don't last more than six months. But there are a few flukey cases where people do survive. In the back of my head, I always wondered. Maybe if I'd insisted that he have the gamma knife treatment before his first rounds of chemo? Or maybe if we'd inserted Gliadel wafers at his first surgery. Or what if we'd flown off to Mexico to have him treated with Laetrile and concoctions made of his own urine? I'll never know. I'll never stop wondering, either.

"But it doesn't matter, does it?" Joanie said reasonably. "Your dad's fine. It's a moot point."

"Yeah. I'm so relieved." I smiled around at everyone.

"So, how are you doing, Emily?" Joanie asked.

"Me? I just told you."

"No. You didn't. We've heard about your dad, your mom, your sisters, Abby, a few cousins, but we haven't really heard how *you* are."

"I'm fine."

Everybody groaned.

"Really. I'm okay." I looked around the table. They were all rolling their eyes. "What?"

"Are you fine?" Lisa asked. "Or just functional?"

I thought for a minute. What was I anymore? I got out of bed every day. I brushed my teeth, showered, got Abby to school, got myself to work. Definitely a huge improvement over the weeks where I refused to wash my hair or do much of anything besides watch cobwebs forming in the corners of my bedroom. At least on the surface of things.

But how was I really? I spent a lot of energy making sure I didn't have to *know* how I was really. I figured I couldn't do much about a lot of it, or at least about the worst of it. Which was the loneliness. The incredible resounding emptiness in my heart, in my arms, in my bed.

Tears started to well up in the corners of my eyes. "I'm fine. Just fine."

"Yeah. You look fine," Christine said, sarcasm dripping off her words.

Sometimes I hate my support group.

CHAPTER FIVE

By the Sweat of Our Brows

Leah

One part Apricot Glaze (#38), one part Golden Copper (#40), one part developer. Forty-five minutes. Very glamorous. Maybe we'll find out if blondes do have more fun.

Claudia

One part Light Ash Brown (#32), one part Apricot Glaze (#38), one part developer. Thirty minutes. Sassy! Now, if we could just find eyebrow pencils to match.

I burst into Leah's condo running so fast that Abby trailed behind me like a balloon tied to my wrist. Her feet barely touched the ground.

"Where are you?" I gasped. "What's the emergency?"

Leah had called thirty minutes earlier with a terse command to get to her condo as fast as I could. She can do this thing with her voice that makes you feel like you're in trouble, even if you didn't have anything to do with it. It doesn't even matter what "it" is. Leah can make you feel responsible and vaguely guilty just with her tone of voice.

I think she learned it from our mother.

"Over here," a small voice said from the living room.

Claudia sat with her head bowed down on Leah's Pottery Barn couch with the taupe slipcovers. She wore a black baseball cap that said *Lou's Sports Bar & Grill* on it in white and yellow. She had it pulled down very low over her forehead. Claudia never wears baseball caps. I occasionally wear them when I can't be bothered with blow-drying my hair, which happens more often than I'd care to admit. Leah wears them when she runs, with her long, red ponytail flying out the back, but hats squish Claudia's curls and give her horrible hat hair, so she never ever wears them. This one didn't even go with the pink sweater she was wearing.

A beauty emergency dire enough to get Claudia into a baseball cap must be a real doozy. I sat down next to her and put a hand on her arm. "Let's see."

She shook her head. "It's too humiliating. I'm not sure I can." Her big brown eyes filled with tears.

"I can't help you fix it if you won't show me." I kept my voice soft and gentle, like Robert Redford in that movie about the horses. Claudia had that look. Like some poor creature that had been traumatized by a barn fire or terrible flood and hadn't realized yet that it had been adopted by some impossibly pretty girl who would heal her own wounds by making it well. "Come on. How bad can it be?"

She bit her lip. "Let's put it this way. I'm not sure if it could be worse."

"Don't say that," I said quickly. Maybe a little too quickly. That phrase had become poison to us when Vince was sick. Any time we said it, things did seem to get worse, as if fate wanted to prove to us that it had the upper hand.

I think the worst time was the day that we were so caught up in taking care of Vince, who was having a particularly rough day, that no one noticed Abby hadn't eaten anything but chocolate-covered doughnut holes all day. A big storm rolled in at about four o'clock that afternoon. It was garbage day and we had too much garbage to fit in our cans, which meant that I'd have to run up and down the block in the rain after all the neighbors put their cans out, and see if there was room for our extra garbage. Then Abby projectile vomited chocolate-covered doughnut holes all over the wall. I burst into tears. In an effort to comfort me, Leah had said that things couldn't get much worse. That's when the power went out.

"Take the hat off, Claudia," I commanded.

Slowly, with shaking hands, she removed the cap. I felt my head tilt to the side. Abby did the same thing. Most of the right side of Claudia's right eyebrow was gone, leaving her with a sort of apostrophe or maybe an accent mark over her right eye. That would have been bad enough, but her left eyebrow was even more spectacular. The whole center of the eyebrow was gone, so it looked like a double dash.

I would have laughed, but it would have been cruel. I also didn't quite know what to say to a woman with eyebrows like that. I went with, "The accent mark over your right eye has a certain élan."

From the way Claudia's face crumpled, that hadn't been the right choice. "Where's Leah?" I asked, deciding that changing the topic might be a good idea before the waterworks got going.

"At the drugstore, buying a hair waxing kit and some eyebrow pencils. We figure the only thing to do is to take the rest of them off and then draw them on until they grow back."

It was a desperate plan, but you know what they say about desperate times.

"Just think, you'll look like Shirley MacLaine." By the tears that had started to drip down her face, apparently that had not been the right choice of things to say, either. I decided to stop trying to make her think it wasn't so bad.

"How did it happen?" I wasn't sure I wanted to know, but figured it would be good to avoid whatever Claudia had done so I didn't end up with random punctuation marks on my forehead one day.

Claudia grabbed a tissue from the box on the coffee table and blew her nose. "I went to get my eyebrows waxed."

"By whom? A blind beautician? Are those like some kind of Braille message?"

She hit me. "No. By Mandy. At my usual place. Over by the mall."

"No wonder those places go out of business so fast." I shook my head. She hit me again.

"Will you listen for a second?" She put her face in her hands. "Why won't anyone in this family ever listen to anything I have to say? Why are you always interrupting?"

I shrugged, but remained silent. At least I know when I'm in the wrong.

"I decided to get my eyebrows waxed as a reward for not calling that guy again and not acting desperate. I'm sitting there chatting away at Mandy, who's supposed to be waxing my eyebrows, about how this is my reward for not trying to call this scumbag, and I notice that her hands are shaking."

"You should have left then," I observed.

"Do you think I don't know that?" Claudia wailed. She grabbed more tissues and blew her nose harder.

"I'm sorry. Go on."

"Anyway, the shaking hands made me a little nervous. I mean, she's about to put hot wax on my face and rip my hair out by the roots. I want her to feel confident about it. So I asked if she was okay or if something was wrong."

"Very nice of you," I said. "Most people would have suddenly realized they'd forgotten an extremely important meeting across town. What did she say?"

"She didn't say anything. She started painting on the wax and then she burst into tears."

"So she's crying and waxing at the same time?"

Claudia nodded.

"You didn't stop her?"

"Emily, what was I supposed to do? I'm lying on my back. She's holding hot wax and sharp objects and hovering over my face. I was just relieved when she blew her nose and the snot didn't get mixed in with the wax."

"Did she say why she was crying?"

Claudia nodded again. "She's been dating this guy, Darryl, since she was seventeen. They were seniors in high school. Now they're twenty-four. He's got a great job. He's taken her on some fabulous vacations when he's had to go to Europe on business. Everything's wonderful."

"This doesn't sound like a reason to cry to me."

"It would if you'd stop interrupting and *listen* for a minute."

I mimed locking my lips and throwing out the key.

Claudia continued, "Darryl comes back from a week in Zürich. Goes straight to her place. Hugs her. Kisses her. Tells her how much he missed her. She's catching him up on all the family news, and tells him that her sister is pregnant with her second baby and how happy her whole family is."

A million questions popped into my head. Is the sister younger or older than she is? Does the sister have a job? Is it a better job than hers? What does the sister's husband do? Is he as good-looking as the boyfriend? Do they own their own home? I figured if I asked any of them Claudia would hurt me, so I kept my mouth shut.

"Darryl says something about how Mandy's sister is the obedient little robot, getting married and reproducing like the family expects her to. So Mandy says that her family is starting to wonder when she and Darryl are going to get married."

I couldn't help it. "She asked that? She said that out loud? I haven't been on a date for more than a decade, and even I know that that question is poisonous!"

Claudia just sighed. "So he says he doesn't know if they are going to get married. He doesn't know if Mandy is who he wants to spend the rest of his life with. So Mandy says that if he doesn't know after being with her for seven years, then maybe they shouldn't be seeing each other at all. She waits for him to protest, to tell her he loves her, to say he didn't mean it. Instead, he says, 'Okay.' And walks out."

"She told you all this while she was waxing your eyebrows?"

Claudia nodded. "She kept putting on the wax and then yanking it off while she was talking. Then she'd pluck and pluck and pluck. . . ."

"How'd you find out what you looked like?"

"I sat up just as the receptionist poked her head in to tell Mandy that her next customer was ready. The receptionist screamed. I looked in the mirror and screamed, and then Mandy screamed, and then I ran straight here."

"Did she say anything? Apologize or something?"

Claudia smiled ruefully. "She wants to come help us with our roots when we get together next, and I say the only solution is still to tattoo our asses."

"We are not tattooing our asses, Claudia." Leah came in through the front door of her condo with a bulging bag from Fred Meyer. "At least not with the type of thing you're suggesting."

I hissed at them both and looked pointedly at Abby, who had switched on the TV and found Nickelodeon. A little girl with braces and glasses was talking to a polar bear. Apparently she had to save it from some hunters who had mixed up the nice polar bear with a mean polar bear, without letting anyone know that she could actually talk to animals. A pretty problem, if you ask me. If I could talk to animals, I'd tell everybody about it. Then again, if we weren't embroiled in a beauty crisis, I'd probably be watching the show. I'm not always the most mature one in the room, even when I'm just with Abby. But that didn't mean that I wanted her to start talking about tattooing her ass at school.

I took the bag from Leah and started sorting through the variety of hair removal kits she'd chosen. There was a waxing kit, a sugaring kit, two different kinds of depilatory creams, three tweezers, a cream bleach, and four different shades of brown eyebrow pencils. "Nice selection."

"I thought I'd let Claudia choose." Leah plopped down on

the other side of Claudia and eyed the mountain of boxes thoughtfully. "They all seemed to have pluses and minuses. Waxing and sugaring seemed like they'd hurt. You know, that whole ripping-hair-out-by-the-root thing."

I winced, thinking about it. "Plus, it's what got her into trouble in the first place."

Leah nodded. "On the other hand, I can barely stand the smell of those hair removal creams when they're on my legs, and I thought they might sting her eyes."

"We could cover her eyes up with a washcloth," I suggested.

"Good idea," Leah conceded.

"What about this?" I asked, holding up the little jar of cream bleach.

"Well, the bleach wouldn't take the hair off, but you wouldn't notice it so much and you could work around it. Anyway, the kid behind the counter said we could return anything we didn't use, as long as the box wasn't opened."

We both looked at Claudia. "So, what's it going to be?" I asked.

With a shaking finger, she pointed to the bottle of depilatory cream that had baby oil added to it.

I read the back of the bottle. "It says we should test it on a section of your skin to make sure you don't have a reaction. Wanna take some hair off your arms?"

She shook her head no.

"You just wanna go for it?" I asked.

She nodded.

"Let's go, then."

I made sure that Abby was comfortable, and then Leah and

I each took one of Claudia's arms and marched her into the bathroom.

Once she was lying down on the bathroom floor with a towel under her neck, Claudia seemed to relax a little.

"We could keep the cream bleach," she said as I draped a damp washcloth over her eyes. "Randy has been wanting to bleach the ends of his hair. We could do it next time we do our roots."

I giggled. "I'm sure it'll only require a few years on the couch to overcome being part of his aunties' root-dying ritual."

"It'll be a blip compared to the years required to overcome his relationship with his father." Claudia lifted one corner of the washcloth to peer up at us. "Besides, all the kids are doing it."

In unison, Leah and I chanted, "If all the kids were jumping off a cliff, would you want to do it, too?" A mantra our parents recited at us endlessly over everything from mascara to crop tops to coed camping trips.

"Probably." Claudia giggled.

Leah took Claudia's hand away from the washcloth. "Leave this on; we don't want to drip anything into your eyes." With a Q-tip, Leah painted the depilatory on what was left of Claudia's eyebrows. "Set the timer for seven minutes, Emily."

"Why don't we make it five?" I suggested. "Claudia's skin is so sensitive." If Claudia looks at poison ivy, she has to be on Benadryl for a month. If someone washes her clothes with detergent that isn't dye- and perfume-free, she'll be slathering herself with hydrocortisone creams for days.

Leah frowned at the bottle. "The bottle says seven to nine. We're already picking the low end of the time limit, and it says here that you can't repeat it for forty-eight hours. If we take it off too soon and it doesn't remove the hair, she's stuck with those weird tufts for two more days."

"I think they look a little like punctuation marks," I said.

Leah cocked her head to one side and then the other. "I see what you mean. That one looks a little like a semicolon."

"I suppose if you look at it from that direction, but I thought it looked more like one of those double dashes," I said. "See, sit over here by me."

"Has anyone set the timer for any amount of time at all?" Claudia asked, sounding a little tense. "Or are we all too busy using my eyebrows as some strange grammar Rorschach test?"

"Oh, yeah." I grabbed the timer and set it for seven minutes.

Leah and I leaned back against the bathroom cabinets. We sat for a while in silence, listening to the ticking of the timer.

"Are you guys still there?" Claudia asked, her voice a little tremulous.

"Of course, you ninny. Did you think we'd leave you lying there with Nair on your face?" Leah snorted.

There was another moment of silence. "Maybe," Claudia said in a really tiny voice.

I kicked her.

"Ouch!"

"Don't be an idiot," I told her.

"Well, talk then, so I know you're there. It's weird not being able to see."

"What do you want to talk about?" Leah asked.

"I don't know." Claudia shrugged and then folded her arms over her tummy. "Anything."

"Hey, Leah," I asked. "Whatever happened with that guitar guy?"

"Guitar guy?"

"Yeah, you know. The hot guy with the cool name."

"Oh, Chase." Leah's voice sounded a little hollow.

"Yeah, Chase." I probably should have noticed how Claudia's legs stiffened at that point.

"Did you break it off, Leah?" Claudia asked.

"Sort of."

I have never seen Leah look like that. She was all shifty and nervous and trying to avoid Claudia's eyes. This wasn't so hard to do, considering that they were covered up by a washcloth.

"How can you sort of break something off?" Claudia asked.

"Let's just say it didn't go exactly how I'd planned it." She snapped the Q-tip she'd used to put the lotion on Claudia's forehead in two. Then she twisted it around itself.

Leah was actually wringing her hands. I'd never seen Leah wring her hands. Of course, since I'd also never seen her try to avoid the eyes of a blindfolded sister, seeing her do things for the first time was rapidly losing its shock value.

"How did you plan it?" I asked. It was possible that some day I might need to dump a guy who left me incredibly sexy love poems under my windshield wiper. It could be good information to have. Perhaps not as crucial as knowing how to avoid letting some beauty technician turn your forehead into a grammar lesson for the blind, but still important. This whole night was turning into an awesome research project. It's very good to have older sisters. Also, I figured it would help to establish a baseline. At least we'd know one thing that hadn't happened.

"I planned to meet him for coffee or something in a public place, and tell him it couldn't work out. That it wasn't him, it was me. That I was sure he'd find someone much more appropriate for him. That he had to stop calling and sending me notes." Leah took the instruction sheet from the Nair box and started folding it over and over into a little fan.

"That sounds like a good plan," I said.

Claudia made a grumbling sound from underneath the washcloth. "Emily, she didn't stick to her plan. Remember? She said it didn't go the way she'd planned."

I gave her another little kick. "I know. I was being encouraging."

"Stop kicking me," she whined. "It's bad enough that I'm lying here on the floor blind, with depilatory cream on what's left of my eyebrows, without you physically abusing me."

I stuck my tongue out at her. Leah kicked me. I said, "Ow!"

Claudia sighed. "Leah, how did it end up going?"

"Well." Leah sighed, too. "He couldn't meet me for coffee because he was teaching back-to-back guitar lessons all afternoon. Then he had to pick up some equipment from a friend for a gig he was playing the next day, and he didn't know how long it would take. So he suggested that he could stop by here after he'd picked up the equipment, and we could leave for coffee from here."

"Sounds reasonable," I said.

"Yeah, it did to me, too." She looked like she was going to cry. She unfolded the little fan and began making folds that were perfectly perpendicular to the first ones. She seemed very engrossed in her little origami project.

"I take it that it wasn't reasonable in reality, though," I prompted.

"No." Leah shook her head. "No. It wasn't."

"Leah, what happened?" Claudia asked. "Did he hurt you?"

"No."

"Then what?" I grabbed the instructions from her and spread them flat.

Leah looked bereft. She gazed longingly at the instruction sheet in my hand. I gave her my best approximation of our mother's hairy-eyeball look. It's a squinty kind of thing that can look really mean when she does it. It makes Abby laugh when I do it.

"He came to the door. I opened it. Just being next to him made me feel like a volcano had erupted inside me. My face flushed. Everything got hot. I felt all liquid and melty inside."

"Maybe you're getting hot flashes," Claudia suggested. "I read an article the other day about perimenopause. You can start having symptoms years and years before you actually go through the change."

I kicked her again. "Leah is not going through the change."

Leah went on as if she hadn't even heard Claudia. "We took one look at each other and started kissing. Then it got really hot. We almost didn't get the door closed before we had our clothes off."

"Oh, Leah, you didn't," Claudia moaned.

"Oh, Leah, you did!" I exulted.

"You don't understand," Leah said desperately, looking from my face to Claudia's washcloth. "I thought I had it under control. I didn't. I can't, around him. I take one look at him and my body temperature goes up. The whole thing's a blur of hair and skin and teeth and lips. All I remember with any detail is heat."

"That's great," I said.

"No, it isn't," my sisters said in unison.

"I think you're both wrong. I think it's great that Leah's found somebody that she really likes," I argued.

"She doesn't like him, she lusts after him," Claudia snapped.

"What's wrong with that?" I demanded. "A little lust can carry you through a lot of bad days. It's almost as good as denial. It requires birth control and wearing nicer underwear, which are definite points against it, but it's a lot more fun than denial."

Leah put her head in her hands. "I don't feel in control of myself when he's there. I'm not used to that. I don't like it."

"You do, too," I said. "It's probably a nice change for you. Don't you ever get tired of being in charge of everything?"

Claudia snatched the washcloth off her eyes and sat up to start to yell at me. She argued that Chase was a subversive force in Leah's life. I argued that it sounded like Chase was a force of fun and enjoyment in Leah's life. Leah moaned that she didn't know what he was, but she didn't like it when she couldn't even control herself. It took us a few minutes to notice that the timer had gone off, because we were all talking at once.

Anyway, I'm sure Claudia's forehead will look just fine as soon as those red marks heal.

"Your father is sucking the life out of me."

Generally, conversations that start this way aren't going to go well. I doubted this one would be any exception to that rule, but couldn't figure out how to stop it. I also found it interesting that the conversation still didn't start with "hello," either.

"Hi, Mama. I'm fine. Thank you," I said.

"Seriously, Emily, I'm not joking around. He's driving me to distraction," my mother snapped.

I so wished she'd decided to call Leah with this instead. I wasn't sure why I was being graced with these confidences, but there wasn't much I could do about it.

"What precisely is he doing, Mama?"

"Hiking."

I hadn't had enough time to conjure up some way that my father was sucking the life out of my mother, but even if I had, hiking probably would never have come to mind. I would have gone with something more vampirelike, but then again, I watch too much TV.

"What happened to scrapbooking? I thought that was his new hobby."

"He said a man can't sit and cut out pictures all day long. He said a man needs to get fresh air every once in a while. He said a man needs to make new memories to put in the scrapbook of his life. He keeps talking about climbing Mount Rainier."

"Daddy's been talking about climbing Mount Rainier?" Terror struck my heart. I don't know what the rest of the country knows about Mount Rainier, but we're talking treacherous territory here. It's a fourteen-thousand-foot inactive volcano. Climbing Mount Rainier involves a more than nine-thousand-foot rise in elevation over about eight miles. It is not a climb for a sixty-eight-year-old man, with or without a heart condition. And it is no place for anyone in my family, with our co-ordination issues, to be traipsing around alone.

"Of course not," she hissed. "He's just talking about it. Incessantly."

Relief washed over me. "So, he's not actually doing anything. He's not actually hiking."

"No." Her voice wavered a bit, as if she were unwilling to concede the point. "But he is shopping and dressing for it. The clothes he's wearing! Velcro everywhere. Pockets all over. You could hang an entire kitchen off the man!"

"Why would you want to do that?"

"I don't, but your father's new clothing is not why I called."

"It isn't?" To my credit, it didn't occur to me until later to ask why she'd started the conversation that way, if it wasn't why she had called.

"I wanted to let you know that Hannah Kauffman's mother is coming for Thanksgiving, as well. You know, so you could factor it into your dessert plans."

Hannah Kauffman is older than my parents are. Her mother is older than Methuselah. In fact, Hannah Kauffman's mother might be older than Methuselah's mother. "I thought she'd had a stroke."

"She did, but she's feeling much better now."

"Great." I didn't know what else to say.

"Emily . . ." My mother hesitated.

"Yes," I prompted.

"I think you should warn Abby about old Mrs. Kauffman."

From visiting Vince in the hospital, Abby had seen a lot more neurologically compromised people than most seven-year-olds. I supposed it was fair to warn her, but I didn't think a sagging face or dragging leg or arm would even faze her after what she'd been exposed to while her father was dying. "What about her?"

"The stroke seems to have removed some of her, well, inhibitions about what might be considered appropriate conversation."

I didn't get it. "Huh?"

"That's all. Just, you know, maybe be ready to keep Abby out of earshot."

I wasn't sure quite how I was supposed to do that if we were all going to be sitting around the dining room table together, but I guessed that forewarned was forearmed, or some cliché or another like that. "Thanks, Mama. I'll keep it in mind."

"And by the way . . ."

"Yes, Mama?"

"What did you do to your sister Claudia? She looks like a burn victim."

"Nice job with the Alderwood proposal, Emily." Karen, my supervisor, dropped the sheaf of papers onto my desk. "It looks good. Really good."

"Thanks," I said. Then I waited. Karen always begins with a compliment. Then, as you're starting to feel pleased with yourself, she slips in her complaints in a sneak attack. I'm sure some management course she took or some business book she read recommended it as a way to make an employee feel appreciated and thus more open to constructive criticism. Unfortunately, since I resented the fact that I was her employee at all, it made me wary any time she said she was pleased with my work.

The fact that Karen is five years younger than me, has a penchant for filmy, pastel floral skirts in lime green and hot pink, paired with shoes that should only be worn by brides-maids, and has the job I'd thought I'd have before Vince got sick, probably contributes to my less-than-one-hundred-per-cent-stellar attitude. She looks like a particularly vapid Barbie doll wrapped in seventies-era wallpaper, and she's my boss.

"I've marked a few corrections."

Aha! See? I knew it! I gave Karen my best I'm-open-to-constructive-criticism smile and seethed inside.

"You put Dean Schonauer's photo by Dave Schneider's bio and vice versa."

My smile became a cringe.

"Hey, it's no big deal." She patted my shoulder, the conde-scending wench. "It could happen to anyone. Same initials. Similar names. Two middle-aged white guys in suits. Just switch 'em around and reprint it. I'll have Tony go over it this weekend, and we can probably shoot it out of here on Mon-day."

What she said was true. They did have the same initials, similar names, and they were both middle-aged white guys in suits, but they also had egos the size of major monuments to dead presidents. Having their photos by the wrong names would be a lot like giving Abby to the wrong mom after school and then shrugging it off because she was, after all, just an-other little white girl going home with another white mom.

Karen was also doing me a favor, and I knew it and I hated it. I didn't want to need any favors from Karen.

Tony is the VP of marketing. It's his say-so that gives you a raise, or doesn't give you a raise, or gives you a promotion or leaves you in your lonely little cubicle at the end of the hall-way, or keeps you on the list of necessary employees or lays you off when things get tight.

Karen has a great relationship with Tony. They chitchat by the copy machine and know what the other one likes in their coffee.

Tony has always made me a little uncomfortable. He has that slightly too-slick demeanor of the successful marketing guy. Whenever I talk to him, I don't know whether to emulate his attitude or respond the way I normally would. If I act like him, I end up feeling kind of slimy. When I let my normal re-actions show, I feel surly. I can't seem to find a happy middle ground.

Anyway, Karen's bringing me the proposal now and letting me fix it before Tony saw it meant that it was just one more of my incredibly stupid blunders that he wouldn't have to know about.

In a way, that was my problem with Karen.

It isn't really that she has a job that I feel I deserve. It's that we all know I don't deserve it anymore.

I'm lucky to have any job, really. I took a very extended leave of absence when Vince got sick. At first, we thought I'd be able to handle going to work around the schedule of his surgery and radiation treatments and first rounds of chemo. After all, there were hours and hours and hours in the day that I wasn't driving him to the hospital or taking care of him. The problem was, we never knew when something would come up. Every time things seemed to be settling down and I'd come back to work and start a project, something terrible would happen.

He'd have a seizure or suddenly lose a big chunk of peripheral vision. Then there were the biggies. When the tumor would recur, everything came apart at the seams. It finally seemed wiser to take a leave of absence until things were on an even keel. As it turned out, that didn't happen until after he died.

I probably came back to work too soon, but I was anxious to get out of the house. I felt suffocated there all day. My going to work seemed to make Abby feel that we were at least a little more normal again. And my boss, not Karen or Tony but the really big boss, had held my job as a graphic designer open for an awfully long time. I was really grateful. The best way I knew to show my gratitude was to get back to the office as soon as I could. Plus, I really thought I had it all together. I thought I was functioning fine.

I was wrong.

I designed a sign for the contributor's board at Lynnwood Memorial Hospital. Apparently, in my book, if you give a lot of money to a hospital, you can be an Angle of Mercy. I put the pages of a proposal in the wrong order. Then I sent the wrong photos out to the printers for a brochure, and nearly cost the firm $2,500 to print something that would have been worthless if Karen hadn't been there to catch it.

Yep. Sweet little Karen.

The low woman on the graphic design department totem pole had been there at the press check, caught my error, raced back to the office, found the correct photo transparencies, and got them back to the printers so we didn't even miss our press run, thus vaulting herself to the tippy top of our office totem pole.

Karen didn't even try to lord it over me. In fact, no one would have known about it except that she accidentally tripped the alarm when she came in to get the photos. She wasn't senior enough to have the code.

She was the heroine of the story. I was the bumbling idiot.

I hate her. I'm also indebted to her. This makes me hate her more.

I know it's not logical. Who said I had to be logical?

So Karen, who had been hired to fill in the gap when I took my leave of absence, now supervised me.

I wasn't on the ball anymore. I couldn't focus enough to do the work I was used to doing while paying hardly any attention to it. Worse yet, I didn't know that I couldn't focus. I thought I was fine.

Actually, looking back, I'm not sure what I thought. Everything is a little hazy. I suppose it's one of the kind things your mind does for you at those times, blurring the really painful things, softening the edges of the sharp things that can cut you and make your heart bleed.

I know it's true of the day that Vince died.

For instance, I remember calling my parents to tell them it was finally over. I remember my father answering the phone. I don't remember anything else of that conversation.

I know I called Leah and Claudia, but I don't even remember dialing the phone.

I remember showering and blow-drying my hair. I was standing in our bathroom, bent over to give my hair a little extra volume, when it hit me that nobody would even care what my hair looked like that day. I turned off the blow-dryer and went to where my husband's body lay in the rented hospital bed a few feet away, and held his hand. It was cold. His fingernails had turned blue.

I looked at his face. It was so clear that he wasn't there anymore. Whatever metaphysical or physical thing that made Vince the man I'd fallen in love with had gone. I knew standing there holding his hand would make no difference to him. He was beyond that. Beyond my reach.

Then it occurred to me that having my hair look lousy wouldn't really help anyone, either, so I went back to the bathroom and finished drying my hair.

For a long time, mundane tasks like drying my hair, brushing my teeth, sweeping the floor, all had that effect on me. I had to stop and consider each one. Did it help anything? Did it hurt anything? Eventually, I think the psychic burden of weighing each action like that became too much and I tuned out.

It's actually pretty common. The other people in my support group say they went through similar states of numbness.

Thus, at work, in a tuned-out state into which I hadn't realized I'd gone, I'd do my job in what I thought was the same way I always had. Then someone would send back a proposal where I'd mislabeled all the graphs and nearly gotten the firm into a situation where they could get their rear ends sued off.

"Emily, seriously, it's not that big a deal. That was the only slipup in the whole proposal." Karen was still talking about the photos being switched. I'd been so deep in my humiliation and self-hatred that I'd missed what she had said.

"I appreciate your letting me fix it before Tony sees it." I owed her that acknowledgment. I actually owed her more than that, but I couldn't quite bring myself to get right down on my knees and stick my nose up her rear end. Worse yet, she didn't even seem to want that.

She shrugged. "If my people do good work, it makes me look good, Emily. We all work together, remember? Besides, this doesn't even set us back on our schedule at all. It's a win-win situation."

Oooh. That burned me. Hating her would be so much more satisfying if she was a bitch.

Kim picked up her glass of iced tea, took a long sip, and then set it back on my coffee table.

Everyone should have a friend like Kim. She's perfect. She has just enough problems to keep me from being jealous of her all the time, but not so many that she's in constant crisis and unavailable to worry about me. She's upbeat, smart, and always fun. If I could have another sister, it would be Kim.

She's the friend who talked me into going down the water slide when I thought I was too scared, and made me say hi to the boy who kept looking my way during the basketball game, and held my hand when I got my ears pierced.

She's divorced. No kids. Blocked fallopian tubes from an infection she never knew she had caused her to be another casualty on the highway we always thought led to happier-ever-after. Kim never complains. She's braver than me. Taller and skinnier, too, but I forgive her those sins.

I shook a T-shirt loose from the laundry basket to fold it. A tiny magnet fell to the floor. Kim scooped it up and set it next to the ones she already had. She had on flat-front khakis and a black sweater and somehow managed to look elegant draped on my sofa with mounds of laundry around her.

"Anything interesting?" I asked.

"Maybe." She cocked her head to one side and squinted her eyes at them. "So far we've got 'sad muffin.' What do you think?"

"I think I have two more loads to fold after this one."

"You make a lot of laundry for two people." She grabbed one of Abby's socks and put it on two of the fingers of her right hand. "Especially when one of you is so small."

"It's actually the small one who makes the most laundry. I think Abby changes outfits with every mood."

"So, listen," Kim said. "I met this great guy at work. He's new in the training division for the customer service reps."

Kim is forever meeting "great guys" at work. She works at this giant insurance company. She only dates outside of her division—she says it's like the difference between first and second cousins—and since there are about twenty-seven divisions, there are a lot of choices. Considering the turnover, as well, the possibilities for a vivacious, outgoing woman are nearly infinite. According to Kim, she gets more action in the company cafeteria than in any singles bar she's ever hit.

"That's nice." I folded three more T-shirts with no words coming out. I hit pay dirt on the fourth one. Three magnets fell out of that one. Kim grabbed them. "What's his name?"

"Gary. And he's a doll. Does his hair in kind of a fifties slicked-back thing, drives an old Corvette, and he's got a friend."

"That's nice," I said.

Kim pounced. "So you're interested?"

"Excuse me?" My mind drew a blank. I couldn't imagine what she wanted me to be interested in. "Interested in what?"

"His friend?"

"Whose friend?"

"Gary's friend."

"What about his friend?" I felt like I'd wandered into a conversation between Abbott and Costello.

Kim put her head down on the coffee table. "Emily," she said with exaggerated patience. "Would you like to go on a date with Gary's friend?"

I stared at her, almost unable to process the question, much less answer it. "I don't even know Gary. How would I know if I wanted to go out with his friend?"

Kim started to knock her head very gently against the table. "Because I want to go out with Gary and I asked him if he had a friend, because I thought I had a friend who was ready to start dating."

I slid a stack of T-shirts where she was bouncing her head to cushion the blows. "Dating?" I squeaked. "You mean me?"

Kim sighed. "No. I mean my imaginary friend Melissa. Of course, I mean you, Emily."

"I don't think I'm ready to start dating." I shook my head. For a second, the thought of how good Jake had felt when I leaned against him at Abby's play flashed through my mind. It would be nice to have that again. Someone next to me. Someone warm and strong.

"What happened to the woman who claimed she was so horny she thought she was going to die?" Kim demanded.

"She's more scared than she is horny," I answered, but even I could hear the doubt in my voice. "Did I tell you about Claudia's eyebrows?"

"Yes, but I don't think your sister's hair removal issues have anything to do with this."

"Lisa from my support group went away for the weekend with her new boyfriend, and when she came back, her kids had locked her out of the house and claimed they didn't have a mother."

"We're talking about an evening, not a weekend. Your parents will watch Abby. She probably won't even notice you're gone. Lisa's children are teenagers and would be torturing her about something else if they didn't have this excuse handy. Abby isn't old enough to lock you out of the house on purpose."

"How do you know?"

"I know." Kim shoved the last three magnets at me. Her eyes closed to a squint. "Read those."

They were "silly," "cocoon," and "girl."

"They're just magnets, Kim," I said.

She pursed her lips and shook her head. "It's a sign, Emily."

"A sign that you're a lunatic?"

"No. A sign of what we're supposed to do."

"About what?"

"Fear. What are we supposed to do with our fears, Emily?"

"Wrap them up in cozy blankets and give them hot chocolate?" I suggested.

"No," Kim shouted, banging her fist down on the coffee table. Magnets, T-shirts, socks, and panties all leaped. "We face them."

She rose to her feet. "We do not lie low and wait for fate to come to us. We are not namby-pamby women who sit around bemoaning the bad hands fate has dealt us in the past."

She grabbed my arm and dragged me to my feet. "We are wild women! Women who never get the blues. We will not bow down. We will take our destiny in our own hands."

By the time Abby came out to complain that we were too loud and had woken her up, we were marching around the living room with my best panties on our heads, singing, "We Will Go on a Date" to the tune of "We Shall Overcome."

And we hadn't even been drinking.

CHAPTER SIX

Chi, You Look Terrific!

Leah

One part Apricot Glaze (#38), one part Golden Copper (#40), one part developer. Forty-five minutes. Blondes apparently don't have more fun. Or if they do, they don't tell their sisters about it.

Claudia

One part Light Ash Brown (#32), one part Apricot Glaze (#38), one part developer. Thirty minutes. Finally, fabulous. Seriously. She should have gone redder a long time ago, although I suppose she had to wait until Leah went blonde. Everybody's soooo territorial.

I figured out what to do! I figured out what I'm doing wrong!" Claudia triumphantly dumped a stack of books on Leah's counter like a retriever dropping a dead bird on his master's boot. Her eyebrows had started to grow back. They were a little thin yet, but she'd finally managed to master drawing on fake ones that were roughly symmetrical. With a huge grin, she announced, "It's our houses. They're all wrong!"

Leah set down the bag that held the gloves, bowls, and spoons and picked up the top book. *"Feng Shui Falls in Love?"*

"Yep," Claudia said excitedly as she spread the rest of the books out for inspection.

"What's this about?" I looked over Leah's shoulder.

"It's not me," she crowed. "It's my house! It's your house, too, Emily. You wouldn't believe how blocked your chi is. It would be so simple to fix it, too!"

"Would it require ripping out the carpeting?" I asked. "I've been thinking about how easy Pergo would be."

"Aren't you worried it would end up looking like you'd floored your house in plastic?" Leah picked up a book called *101 Feng Shui Tips for a Better Love Life* and riffled the pages.

"Maybe, but at least it would be different. I'm bored. Maybe a change would help."

Leah looked up from the book. "Couldn't you change something less drastic than your flooring? I mean, think about how disruptive it would be. You'd have to move all the furniture out and leave it out for days."

She had a point. I picked up the hair color box that Leah had set down. "What about your house anyway, Claudia? What's wrong with it?"

"Everything's arranged wrong." Claudia looked around, shaking her head. "Your condo could use some work, too, Leah."

I actually liked Claudia's house. It seemed fine to me. Cozy. Comfy. A little cluttered, but you have to expect that with kids around. Hey. This box said that it would leave someone with my dark hair with auburn highlights. Auburn highlights sounded like a nice change.

"Everything's wrong?" Leah asked. "Are you sure?"

"Absolutely. I mean, my bedroom alone has probably been

blocking any possibility of good relationship chi coming my way."

"What do you think I'd look like with auburn highlights, and what the hell's chi?" I asked.

"Energy. You know, life force," Claudia said impatiently. "And why do you want auburn highlights? Your hair's fine the way it is."

"I don't know. Leah said to change something less drastic than my flooring. My hair seems like an option. C'mon. Do me tonight!" Just like that. Excitement. Spontaneity. Change.

"No," my sisters said in unison.

"How exactly is your bedroom blocking your chi?" Leah asked.

"Why not?" I demanded.

Claudia ignored me and pulled out a sheet of paper with a hand-drawn floor plan of her bedroom. "Look here and here." She pointed to a block labeled "dresser" and another one that said "armoire." "Do you see how the points of the furniture are angled toward my bed?"

We nodded. I wasn't sure there was any way to arrange the furniture without the corners pointing toward her bed. It wasn't that big a room, and there were doors and windows and closets to work around.

"Well, all those corners are sending poison arrow darts right at my bed." Claudia thumped the box marked "bed" with great vehemence. "And that poster over my bed?"

"The one with all the peonies?" Leah asked.

"Exactly! It says right here in *Shift Your Stuff and Change Your Life*—" she grabbed one of the books and opened it to a page she'd marked with a paper clip— "that peonies make men wander away. The guy who blew me off couldn't help it. I practically shoved him out of my life with my stupid bedroom furniture arrangement, the damn peonies, and all the other stuff!"

"Other stuff?" I echoed.

"Yes. Other stuff," Claudia said in a voice laden with disbelief at my ignorance. "According to *Ancient Chinese Astrology and Modern Love,* I should have no wood or metal in the southeast corner of my bedroom, and that's where I have my desk with the wood-and-metal mail rack. And the mirror over my dresser? Well, it's got to go. There's so much wrong with it, I can't even begin to list everything. You have to be very, very careful with mirror placement. They're quite powerful."

We all knew that. We'd had to cut a shopping trip short once when we'd looked into a magnifying mirror at Bed Bath & Beyond and discovered forests of previously unnoticed facial hairs. Claudia bought a pair of tweezers and we plucked each other in her station wagon right there in the parking lot.

"I won't even start to discuss my downstairs love corner," Claudia continued. She opened the dyes and began measuring them into a bowl.

Leah snorted. "Downstairs love corner? Sounds dirty to me."

"That's because you have a dirty mind." Claudia sniffed. She tested the consistency of the dye with the long-handled brush my sisters use to part their hair and put on the dye.

"So what are you going to do?" I asked.

Claudia whipped out another floor plan and slapped it down on the counter.

I rotated it around ninety degrees. Then I did it again. I

looked up at Leah. She was nibbling at her lower lip, which she always does when something perplexes her. "I don't get it," I finally said.

"What's to get?" Claudia asked. "I put the bed here under the window, then move the dresser here and the armoire over there." She tapped on the different labeled boxes as she spoke.

"I'm not sure, but doesn't that mean you'll have to climb over part of your dresser to get into the room?" I asked.

"Just the end of it."

I paused. It is not my role in the family to rain on other people's parades; that's Leah's job. Occasionally our mother pitches in, too. I didn't think a furniture arrangement that required you to climb over any portion of your dresser was functional, but everyone is entitled to an opinion.

"Claudia, that's absurd," Leah said.

"No, it's not." Claudia stuck her chin out.

"It is, too." Leah squared her shoulders.

"It's the only way to arrange everything so there are no poison arrow darts headed to my bed."

"No, it's not." Leah grabbed the floor plan from Claudia, scribbled a few notes on it, and shoved it back at her.

Claudia looked it over through squinched-up eyes. "Where's my desk?"

"Move it downstairs into that corner of the living room by the plants. Then you can keep your mail rack."

"What's that?" She pointed at an unlabeled square.

"It's your bedside table. You forgot to put it in your plan." Leah tapped it with the pencil eraser.

"Oh." Claudia shoved Leah's floor plan back inside one of her books without saying anything else.

Tension stood thick in the room. Leah can be a frustrating big sister to have sometimes. She simply does everything better than everyone else, and more effortlessly. It's handy, but occasionally hard on the ego.

I decided a change of subject might be a good thing. "I'm going on a date."

It was like throwing blood into a tank of sharks. They swarmed me.

I took a good hard look at my house when I got home that night. I hadn't rearranged things for quite a while. I hadn't even thought about it. The furniture had been sitting in the same spots since Vince got sick. At the very least, I reasoned, it would be bad for the carpet to leave it like that.

It wasn't like I hadn't changed anything in the house. Right after Vince died, I redid the bedroom in a sort of Caribbean theme. I cleared out his side of the closet, bought new sheets, new curtains, and a new comforter. I painted the walls lilac with tangerine trim. It had been too disorienting to wake up in our bedroom with only me in it. There was no mistaking it for our bedroom anymore; Vince would have screamed bloody murder at the color scheme alone. After that, however, I lost interest in home decor. Along with everything else.

At some point, Leah had decided the living room was too dark and dragged me out to buy new curtains and slipcovers. Somewhere in there, Claudia had also decided that the flower bed in front of my house needed updating, and had convinced me to replant it with herbs to use when I cooked. I didn't cook anymore, but I liked the herbs anyway. They make me feel very hip and organic.

Looking back, I realize those decorating and gardening efforts had been my sisters' attempts at therapy for me. It probably helped. At least a little bit. But when you're at the bottom of a very deep well, a few steps up the ladder still leaves you pretty deep in the dark.

The next morning was Saturday morning, so I called Jake and he agreed to come over and help. I should have sensed trouble when I asked if Sandy would mind and got a noncommittal grunt back in response.

"So, what prompted this sudden burst of interior design?" he asked from behind the other end of the sofa.

"Oh, Claudia got some new books out of the library about feng shui and I thought the place could use some updating." I felt a blush start to rise to my cheeks. With any luck he'd attribute it to the effort I was putting into shifting the couch, and not ask too many questions about Claudia's books. I didn't even want to admit to myself that I thought rearranging the furniture would help with what my sisters were still calling my "little problem." I couldn't imagine admitting it to anybody else. "Balancing energy and harmony and all that stuff."

He nodded as we dropped the sofa into its new spot. I tried to remember what Claudia's books had said about love corners and flowers. Maybe I should ditch the yellow slipcovers with the big blue and gray flowers and get something in a solid color. I didn't want to go with anything striped or geometric. The armchairs already had blue-and-white stripes, the kind you see in cottages that are supposed to look like mattress ticking.

"You know about it?"

He nodded. "Sandy went through a feng shui phase. That

was after her Martha Stewart phase, but before her HGTV phase. Actually, I didn't mind the feng shui phase too much. It might have been one of my favorites. Everything's simple and uncluttered and very functional."

"The other phases weren't?"

He shook his head. "The Martha Stewart phase was painful. Everything had to be just so and handmade and nothing was ever easy to live with. It all required so much effort. The HGTV phase at least had a lot of color, but it stressed her out too much. Too many ideas at once, I think."

"Did you have a phase?"

"Nope," he said, dusting off his hands. "I think rearranging furniture is one of those girl things. I'm just relieved you're not faux-finishing the entire place to look like it's covered with marble. Also, just so you know. If you tile something, it's permanent. It won't work to ask me to crack the tiles off later."

"Men don't rearrange? Or paint? Or tile?" I started to pick up the coffee table. It wasn't very heavy, but Jake took it from me anyway. I pointed to where I wanted it and he dropped it there. I put a red pillar candle that had been gathering dust in a cupboard onto the table, with some small stones that Abby had picked up on a trip to the fish ladder.

"Men don't paint unless the place actually needs to be painted, and we don't rearrange unless we've purchased new electronic equipment that requires it." He shifted the table with his toe to line it up with the couch. "I actually think it's a metaphor for the whole relationship thing."

"You do?" I dropped down on the sofa to see if I liked the distance between it and the coffee table. I pushed it back a little with my feet.

"Sure. I mean, why are you doing this? Why did Sandy re-arrange furniture every other week?" He dropped down next to me.

"Because a little change is nice sometimes?"

"Ah! That's exactly it." Jake jumped up and began to pace back and forth. "Women want change. When a man puts a chair in a certain spot, he puts it there because it's the best place to watch TV or read or eat, or whatever purpose that chair is supposed to serve."

He shifted one of my armchairs over and angled it toward the TV set as if to demonstrate. "A man won't move the chair again unless the chair's purpose changes or he gets a new TV. A woman will move it for no reason whatsoever. She'll move it just to move it. She'll slipcover it even if it doesn't have a stain. She'll give it new throw pillows and put the old ones in the closet for no reason whatsoever. If the chair is fine in that corner one week, a man won't see any reason to move it to an-other corner the next week unless something else in the room changes."

"Maybe the spot she put it in wasn't the best one and she needs to find out if it's better in the other corner, and there's no way to find out without trying it out." I got up and moved the other armchair so it was at the same angle as the one Jake had just placed.

"But it won't be better in the other corner. It'll just be the same chair in a different corner," he countered. "Maybe that chair was as good a chair as it could be. Putting it in a different corner won't make it a better chair or even a different chair. It will always be the chair that it is."

I thought for a moment, then straightened both chairs back

out into their original angle. "Then she can put it back." I sat down on the couch.

Jake shook his head slowly. "Sometimes the chair simply can't go back." He sat on the couch, too. "Sometimes a chair can only be moved so many times before it just gives up its stuffing."

Abby bounded in from her room with her Game Boy. "Mom, Mom, Mom. I finally defeated Growlithe!"

"You did? Sweetheart, that's wonderful! How did you do it?" I had no idea who Growlithe was. Well, I had a little idea. I knew Growlithe was a Pokemon. I didn't need to know anything else. Asking who Growlithe was would get a thirty-minute lecture on Growlithe's various forms, evolutions, strengths, and weaknesses. I didn't want to know.

"First I used a freeze attack on him and then I used confusion," Abby explained in way more detail than either of us could follow.

Jake grunted. "Sounds like you've been taking advice from Sandy."

My head shot up. "Trouble at home? I mean, besides rearranging furniture."

"I guess you might say that."

Abby bounded back out with her thumbs still frantically working the Game Boy.

I waited. One thing I learned from being married was that sometimes not asking questions got you more information than asking. Perverse, I know, but it worked more often than not on Vince, and I was rewarded once again this time.

"She's moving out this weekend," Jake finally said.

"Jake." I reached over and rested my hand on his forearm. "I'm sorry."

He shrugged. "Don't be. It's been coming for a long time. We just don't seem to want the same things."

"Like what things?"

Jake leaned back and shut his eyes. He gave my shoulder a squeeze. "Like each other, I guess," he said.

I had known, of course, that we hadn't been talking about chairs earlier, but I hadn't realized how irrevocably his chair had been moved into a different corner, or that he felt he had no more stuffing. I also hadn't known that hearing that he couldn't go back to his earlier corner would make my stomach churn and make my breath catch in my throat.

The other thing I didn't know was what to say. So I said the first thing that popped into my head. "Want to come to my mom's house for Thanksgiving?"

It was after ten o'clock on Sunday morning, the morning after my double date, and I was still in bed. Abby was watching cartoons in the living room.

"Well, that wasn't a complete disaster," Kim said as she plopped down on my bed. She slid her jacket off and toed off her boots before she lay down next to me. I could smell the brisk morning air on her along with a faint whiff of peppermint shampoo.

I pulled a pillow over my head. "What part wasn't a disaster?"

She pulled the pillow off. "You looked really cute. That was a great outfit."

"Kim, it was your outfit. I borrowed it. Remember?" I

grabbed the pillow back. I smiled a little, though. I *had* looked great. Brown suede miniskirt with a black sweater, black tights, and boots.

I hadn't been on a date, even a husband date, for more than two years. My closet now looked like a store in which I wouldn't have been caught dead shopping a few years earlier. One side had work clothes: sensible skirts, appropriate dresses, a few suits. The other side had Mommy clothes: jeans, sweat-shirts, a few sweaters. Nowhere was there anything cute, sassy, or sexy. I wondered about that. Just because there was no man in my life didn't mean I couldn't be cute, sassy, and sexy. I used to be at least cute and sassy nearly all the time. Or at least I think I had.

Regardless, I'm pretty sure I once owned cute, sassy, and sexy clothes. Otherwise, why would Kim have been over here borrowing stuff all the time? So, where did all those clothes go? I know I cleared out a lot of my own stuff when I cleared out Vince's closet, but had I also decided to completely remove my personality?

I honestly don't remember. That might say more about it than I could ever figure out.

Anyway, it had felt great to stroll through the restaurant and see a few heads turn as I went by.

"Yeah." She smiled. "I've got great taste, don't I?"

"And I need to go shopping, don't I?"

"You got that right." She handed me a tall paper cup from the corner coffee shop. "Sit up and drink this."

I could feel the warmth through the little cardboard cup-condom. I took a small sip. A mocha. It's good to have friends. "I'm really sorry," I said. "I know you really liked Gary."

She patted my thigh. "It's okay. It'll make a good story later when you're ready to laugh about it."

"I don't think I'll ever be ready to laugh about it."

"Oh, please, it was pretty funny. Besides, it was his own fault. Who wears white pants in January? It's just wrong."

"It's white shoes after Labor Day that's wrong. I think white woolen pants are still considered okay." Besides I thought those rules had all changed. To be honest, it seemed like all the rules about everything had changed since I had last dated.

"But white pants on a guy?"

"Well . . ."

"And who wears wool with no underpants? I mean, it's got to be itchy, not to mention the whole hygiene issue."

I started to laugh despite myself. I just couldn't help it. "I doubt he expected anyone to dump most of a pitcher of ice water in his lap."

"You can say that again! Did you see the look on his face?"

I blushed. "No. I was too busy looking at . . . well, where his . . . you know . . ."

Kim cackled. "You mean where his thingie should have been?"

I blushed harder. "You couldn't see it, either?"

"Even allowing for shrinkage from the ice water, that looked more like an extra pinky finger to me."

I put my face back down in the pillow.

You know what happens when white T-shirts get wet, right? Well, the same thing happens when white pants get wet. They're just lower.

"So, why'd you dump the ice water on him anyway?" Kim asked.

"I didn't mean to. It was one of those instinctive, automatic things, really." I groaned into the down. "He startled me, is all."

"Startled you? How?"

I didn't answer. She nudged with an elbow. "How? How did he startle you?"

"He touched me."

She gasped. "Where? Under the table?"

I shook my head. "No. My shoulder."

Kim didn't speak for a few seconds. From where I was buried in the pillow, I heard a few gasping sounds of the sort you associate with fish flopping around in the bottom of a boat or a bad asthma attack.

"You dumped an entire pitcher of ice water in a guy's lap because he touched you on the *shoulder?* Girl, they're gonna have to rewrite *The Rules* for you!"

"It wasn't a punishment! It was an accident! A reflex! He startled me! He should have warned me before he did that." I get defensive when I do stupid things.

"Before he touched your shoulder? He should have warned you? How? With a siren?"

"I wasn't expecting it. If I'd been expecting it, I wouldn't have jumped like that."

Kim sighed. "Girl, we have to get you out more."

"I don't think I can take it, Kim."

"Emily, it was just a pitcher of water."

"No, it wasn't. It was the whole scene. I don't think I can do this. Leaving my little girl so I could go out with some man I don't even know, and probably won't even like me. I can't do it." I pushed myself up on my elbows so I could shake my head. "No. I think I belong right here in my nice, warm bed in my flannel jammies."

"First of all, it's not like you abandoned Abby. Your parents took her out to a movie and for ice cream, and then tucked her into her own little bed and waited for you to come home." Kim wriggled around on the bed until she'd made a little nest for herself in the comforter and then propped the pillow up more to her liking.

I groaned again. "That's part of it. You have no idea what it's like to have your parents quiz you about your date when you're this old."

She giggled. "You're kidding. What did they ask?"

"I don't want to talk about it." I drank more of my mocha and then put my face back in the pillow.

"Come on, tell me." Kim scooched down next to me. "Knowing your folks, it had to be good."

Understand that my mother scoped out my husband's memorial service for good husband material for me. To see an unmarried person in my age range horrifies my mother. To see her own daughter, a nice Jewish girl in her thirties, unmarried through no fault of her own, was an abomination, anathema. She'd tried to act calm, but she was so thrilled that I was going out on a date that she didn't even care that he wasn't Jewish, or that Kim (who she hasn't trusted since that unfortunate experiment with sloe gin fizzes in eleventh grade) had fixed me up with him.

"Mama just wanted to know if I had a nice time." And if the young man had "prospects" and who his people were and a score of other questions I didn't want to go into right now.

"What did you tell her?"

"I said it was fine, but I didn't think I'd be going out with him again."

Kim snorted. "There's an understatement for you. He didn't even want to sit next to you anymore."

"Shut up." I lifted my head from the pillow long enough to hit her with it.

"Still, that doesn't sound so bad," she observed after whacking me back.

"That wasn't the bad part."

"So, are you gonna keep me waiting all day? Tell me the rest." She extracted a bag from her jacket pocket and waggled it in the air. "There might be a blueberry scone in here for someone who talks fast."

"Mama said I deserved a little companionship. I agreed." I'm a pushover for baked goods. I think they represent true happiness. I could never be a spy; I'd sell my soul for a good éclair. Certainly, I could let state secrets go for a muffin. "Then Daddy took me aside and informed me that sooner or later in a relationship, a man would want more than just companionship."

Kim's jaw dropped. "He gave you 'the talk'?"

I nodded. "Can you believe it?"

"You're thirty-two years old, a widow with a child of her own, and your father gave you the talk about what boys want from girls when they take them on dates?"

I nodded again.

"And he called it 'more than just companionship'?" Kim crowed.

I kept nodding.

"Sheesh. Where was he when you were sixteen and Vince

spent the entire summer trying to get you out of your panties?"

"Busy, I guess."

Kim snorted. "Yeah, so was Vince."

I smiled. "So was I."

"Well, girl, I think it's time we got you busy again."

CHAPTER SEVEN

We Gather Together to Ask for Some Semblance of Normality We Are Not Rewarded

Leah

One part Apricot Glaze (#38), one part Golden Copper (#40), one part developer. Forty-five minutes. Leah is thankful that her hair looks great and that she hasn't gained weight this year.

Claudia

One part Light Ash Brown (#32), one part Apricot Glaze (#38), one part developer. Thirty minutes. Claudia is thankful that her eyebrows have almost grown back in. We tossed a little Apricot Glaze (#38) on them, too, for a festive holiday look.

Emily

I'm thankful I don't have to dye my hair! Ouch! Leah threw a brush at me. I'm telling Mama.

Ten A.M., Thanksgiving day. I'd curled Abby's hair into long ringlets and tied it back with a big blue velvet ribbon that matched her blue velvet dress with the white lace yoke. She wore white tights and patent leather Mary Janes. It was like getting to dress up a pretty dolly. She rarely submitted to this kind of masterminding of her clothes, so I really relished it.

I took a shower, then blew my hair out as straight as I could get it. Claudia has actual curls; I got waves that never seem to be going the direction they should. I put on a great blouse I'd scored at a vintage store in Capitol City, even though I knew my father would make some crack about it looking like pajamas. He thinks anything made out of a satiny material is clearly a nightgown. The blouse was made from a slick lavender material that clung to me as it draped down in a V-neck and long belled sleeves. I finished up with a pair of low-slung, pencil-legged slacks with boots.

Then I put Abby's hair up again since it had already slipped out of its bow, and had her change into a fresh pair of white tights since she'd run outside to play on our swing set and gotten them muddy. Interestingly, "glow" and "fly" had fallen out of the laundry basket when I was digging for her clean tights. I couldn't decide if it was advice or a warning.

The Mary Janes were filthy, too, so I cleaned the mud off them, and before my little darling could do any more damage to herself or her outfit, I packed up the sugar-free almond pudding, the wheat-free chocolate hazelnut torte, the low-fat-but-sugary-and-wheaty pumpkin pie, crammed us into my Jeep, and headed down the road for an exciting afternoon of turkey basting with my family.

Right after graduating from college, one of my old friends got a job with the City News Agency in Chicago. Being twenty-two years old but looking twelve, and being the new guy and from out of town, he got stuck with the morgue beat. After he'd been working a few months, he told me about "barbecue-related homicides."

Basically, on Memorial Day or the Fourth of July, families would get together and have a few beers. Then the temperature would start to rise. And eventually the humidity level would go up. Maybe somebody would make a joke about something that someone else didn't think was funny, or make a pass at someone else's wife, or finally confront their father with the fact that he'd always liked their older brother/younger sister better. Suddenly people would have the most astounding urges to stick meat forks (or knives or bullets) into each other rather than into the meat they were supposed to be roasting. Hence, barbecue-related homicides.

To my knowledge, no one has ever stabbed or shot anyone at any of our family gatherings. My cousin Julia once threw a small plate of after-dinner mints with the bride's and groom's initials on them across the table at her brother Robbie in the middle of a wedding reception, but trust me, Robbie deserved it.

That doesn't mean, however, that tensions can't rise. I always try to approach family holiday gatherings with an open mind and an even temper. I also try to get my father to open the wine as soon as possible. Sometimes Leah's right: the best defense is a good offense.

By two o'clock, I was sitting at the kitchen island in my mother's nice warm kitchen, dangling my legs and letting my feet kick against the cabinets like I'd been doing since I was four and Mama bought the three bar stools that still sat lined up along the counter.

Everything smelled like sage and rising bread and cinnamon. I had a nice buzz going from drinking a glass and a half of white wine on an empty stomach, while I listened to Leah and my mother argue about when they'd last basted the turkey and who had forgotten to set the timer to remind them to do it again. I was grateful to Claudia for talking Mama out of the Tofurky. I mean, turkey is low-fat to start with. Forming it out of bean curd seems like an unnecessary waste of fat and taste reduction. On the other hand, I'm not sure you have to baste tofu, an improvement I hadn't previously considered.

"It was one-thirty. I'm sure of it." Mama made a threatening gesture with the baster and dodged to the left in an attempt to get around Leah.

Leah stood her ground in front of the oven, arms crossed over her startlingly white sweater. She didn't budge an inch, despite the threat of a greasy baster coming perilously close to her top, which she wore over a long, straight gray skirt and a dynamite pair of boots. I tilted my head slightly to the side to consider whether I liked them better than the ones I was wearing. "It was one-fifty, and if you keep opening this oven up, the turkey will never get done."

My father clomped in from the living room, wearing a maroon down jacket with a big stripe of duct tape over the right shoulder. "I'm going to pick up Ilse and Hannah."

No, I decided, Leah's boots came up too high; they were almost to her knee. I'd never be able to wear them with pants. If I wanted to wear them with a skirt, she'd probably let me borrow them. Her feet were only a little smaller than mine, so they probably wouldn't pinch too much. It'd be fine as long as I didn't have to walk too far.

"I thought dinner wasn't until four. I told Jake to get here at three-thirty." I checked my watch. Two o'clock, almost on the dot. Hannah and Ilse only lived about fifteen minutes away.

Leah looked over at us. "I told Joe three-thirty, too."

While Leah was distracted, my mother dodged back to the right and yanked the oven door open. Leah scowled at her, but allowed herself to be outflanked. This time.

"Dinner isn't until four," Daddy groused.

"Five, if Mama keeps leaving the oven door open," Leah interjected.

Daddy waved her comment away with a careless hand, and I grabbed the bottle of wine before it went over. He never even noticed. "It'll take me an hour to load the old lady in the car. I hope she keeps her hands to herself this time. Last time, she tried to pinch my butt when I bent over her to buckle her seat belt."

"Do you want some help?" Claudia offered from the counter where she was slicing up sweet potatoes. She looked so sweet in a rose-colored knit dress that matched the flush she now had in her cheeks from the warm kitchen. With the white apron on, she looked like some colorized fifties advertisement for housewives.

"You're busy," Daddy said. "Besides, I think she knows how to buckle the damn seat belt herself. I'm not helping her this time. Or Hannah can."

Claudia didn't let up. "I'm busy, but Emily's not. She made all her desserts yesterday, and she's just sitting there at the counter getting tipsy like she always does on Thanksgiving. She could act as a distraction for Ilse, and maybe this time

Emily won't end up embarrassing herself by sliding under the dining room table before dessert."

I felt that was unfair. True, but unfair. The sliding-under-the-table thing had happened when I was nineteen and it was Passover, not Thanksgiving. Four glasses of wine is a lot for anyone.

Besides, I'd never liked the holidays that much to start with. Something about all that forced frivolity and happiness. They give me the same vaguely manipulated and icky feeling that going to Disneyland evokes in me. It was even worse without Vince. He'd had a way of teasing me through the whole season that I couldn't quite resist, even if I occasionally resented it.

Halloween is actually the only holiday that I like, although after the balloon-grape costume fiasco I'm starting to have reservations about it, too. If swilling moderately priced, overly chilled white wine in my mother's kitchen got me through Thanksgiving, I didn't think my family should be callous enough to bring it up in front of me. They should do what they always do and wait until I'm out of the room to discuss me openly.

"I could be more than a distraction. I could be a real help. I know how to fasten a seat belt and I bet Ilse wouldn't pinch my ass," I said indignantly.

My mother tsked at my choice of language. I actually felt myself blush. Who says you can't go home? Not only can you go home, you can revert to your twelve-year-old self within thirty seconds. I'm apparently still trying to be one of the adults and still not quite pulling it off.

"Nah. The old lady doesn't want the competition around. She likes to be the center of attention. Besides, Emily is still in her pajamas. I'd have to wait for her to get dressed," he said, smirking. I knew he'd say something about my top.

"I don't want to go, anyway. I was only offering to be nice. Last time I saw Hannah Kauffman, she went on and on about how my life was ruined now that Vince was dead until I cried, and then she told me I had better keep a stiff upper lip if I ever wanted to get another man." I drummed my toes against the cabinet a few more times. "By the way, Daddy, did you know there's a big piece of duct tape down the back of your coat?"

He zipped his coat. "It's been there for four years. You're just noticing now?"

My mother turned away from the stove and looked at my father's coat as if she had never seen it before, either. "Four years that duct tape's been there?" she said in a wondering tone.

He shrugged. "Maybe five." He left the kitchen through the door to the garage.

Mama stared after him, muttering, "Four years? Four years, I've been telling him to get a new coat?"

"So, who's this Joe guy you're bringing?" I asked Leah. I was a little disappointed; I'd hoped she'd bring Chase. I guessed he was out of the picture now that Joe had arrived on the scene. Joe was a fix-up, a friend of a friend of a friend. They'd gone out a few times. He was highly appropriate, which meant that he'd probably score about a zero on the entertainment scale for me.

"He's a nice guy," Leah said with a shrug.

"Nice enough to take to the office Christmas party?" I knew I was being snide but couldn't help it. Was I the only one who noticed how Leah's voice had no inflection when she talked about him? How her skin didn't glow when his name was mentioned? I think I missed Chase more than she did, and I'd never met him.

She turned to face me. "Yes, Emily. Nice enough for the office Christmas party. He's my age and he has a respectable job in the financial department of a big aviation company. Happy?"

"Not really." I drummed my feet some more.

"Stop kicking, Emily," Mama said absently as she took the potatoes that had been boiling off the stove.

"What about you and Jake? Is he here as your date? Does this signal a change in your relationship?"

I told you that Leah has always been good at using a good offense as the best defense.

"No." I stood up with as much dignity as I could, considering that the wine, along with the heels on my boots, had made my balance a little precarious. I swayed a bit, but tried to make it look like it was part of straightening my top. "It signals that his parents went to San Diego to see his sister for Thanksgiving, and that Sandy wasn't likely to invite him over to her parents' place since they broke up."

"A pity invitation, then," Claudia said.

"No. Not that, either." Somehow I found that very offensive. I didn't pity Jake and I didn't want anybody else to, either. "Just a friend offering to spend a holiday with a friend, okay?"

"Okay. You don't have to get up on your high horse about it." I could see Leah fighting the laugh that was turning up the corners of her lips. "I thought that now that you'd started dating again, you might want to bring one of your new beaus."

There were no new beaus and she knew it. I'd gone out on two more double dates with Kim. Neither of them were as disastrous as that first one, but I wouldn't hail them as successes, either. I apparently elicited awed pity from men these days. The last guy had actually burst into tears when we said good night and had told me that he respected my bravery and that I reminded him of his mother. I certainly don't want to remind anyone of their mother and I didn't want my bravery respected. I'm not sure I wanted to be respected at all. I was pretty sure I didn't even care if he would respect me in the morning.

I stumbled into the living room to check on Abby and to put some distance between me and my wineglass. I hadn't realized what a lightweight I'd become over the past couple of years. I abuse caffeine much more often than alcohol, and I didn't need to give my family any more ammunition than they already had.

This time, Abby had the Teenage Mutant Ninja Turtle running Barbie over with the army Jeep.

"Ooh, poor Barbie, what'd she do to deserve that?" I asked my angelic-looking yet clearly slightly demonic seven-year-old.

Abby shrugged. "She didn't have any more fun clothes to put on so I thought I'd run her over."

I nodded. It seemed fair. I hoped the same standards weren't going to be applied to me anytime soon. My closet did look pathetic. The new blouse helped, but I still had a long way to go. I sat down and stretched my legs out. Abby used the triangle made by my legs, the chair, and the floor as a tunnel through which the turtle could drive the Jeep. I heard Barbie ask him if he was going her way as I drifted off to sleep.

The doorbell jarred me awake. I jumped, tripped as I tried to stand up when my heel caught in the throw rug, then choked on the drool that must have pooled in my mouth when I'd fallen into my semialcoholic stupor while my daughter played dead Barbie. Sigh. There goes that Mother of the Year Award again.

Speaking of which, I heard Abby say, "Hi, Uncle Jake. Mommy must be excited to see you. She did a special dance in her chair when she heard the doorbell ring."

I checked my chin for residual drool then attempted standing again—slowly this time—and was rewarded by my body staying vertical.

"Well, I'm glad that my arrival is such a cause for excitement," I heard him say.

"Hey, Jake," I said as he came around the entry way. He'd dressed up in charcoal gray slacks, a blue silk shirt, and he even had on dress shoes instead of his usual sneakers. He gave me the little boy grin that used to be able to entice me to skip school with him and Vince, and then his brows creased.

He was across the room in two steps, dropping the bottle of wine he'd brought on the sofa. He took me by the shoulder and then held my face with his other hand and then he . . .

. . . wiped a smudge of something off my cheek.

"Sorry," he said, his voice gruff. "I think your mascara ran."

I put my hand to my cheek. "Oh, it must have run when I was sleeping."

"Em, have you been, uh, drinking?" he asked, a grin twitching at the corners of his mouth.

I checked again for drool, trying to make it look like I was just brushing back my hair, and gave an elaborately nonchalant shrug. "A glass of wine while everyone was cooking maybe."

He shook his head in wonderment. "We have to get you out more."

"So everyone is telling me," I said.

"Mommy went on a date and then she had to stay in bed all the next morning," Abby said in that high, piping voice that carries for miles.

I rolled my eyes. "It's not like it sounds."

His eyebrows went up. "Maybe we need to keep you in more instead."

I barely had time to rescue the bottle of wine from the couch before the doorbell rang again. Joe had arrived. Fast on his heels, Milton Feinstein showed up. As I was getting him a glass of wine, Daddy trundled through the back door with Ilse and Hannah Kauffman.

"Milt!" Ilse called across the room, waving from her wheelchair as my mother tried to take her coat. Ilse seemed blissfully unaware that the arm she was waving was still in her coat and that she was waving it around like a tweed flag. My mother lunged forward and tried to grab it, just to have it whip off in another direction before she could trap it.

After a few attempts, she managed to get hold of a corner and hung on like a terrier with a bone. Ilse finally noticed the dragging feeling and whipped around to see what was restraining her, and began shaking it like a dog that had sunk its teeth into her arm. "Jessica," she barked. "Get this damned thing off me."

"I'm trying, Ilse," my mother said through tight lips. "Just hold still a minute."

"Hold still, you say? What else can I do? I'm stuck in this damn chair, you idiot! I'm not likely to be dancing away." She turned to smile at Milt. "I used to be a wonderful dancer."

Milt nodded and smiled. "I remember," he said.

"Mama, that's no way to talk to Jessica," Hannah broke in as she hobbled up behind them with her four-legged cane. "She's just trying to help you off with your coat."

You could almost see the rational world swim back into focus behind Ilse's thick-lensed glasses. "Oh, in that case, I'm sorry I called you an idiot. But would someone get this goddamn coat off my arm?" she demanded.

Mama managed to maneuver the coat off Ilse and hang it in the closet. I poured glasses of wine for both of them (I figured Mama needed one by now), and settled Ilse's wheelchair next to where Milt sat on the couch. Hannah followed my mother into the kitchen to offer unwanted cooking advice.

"How's the world been treating you, Milt?" Ilse asked.

"I won't complain." Milt smiled gently. He really is a sweetie. He's eighty-some-odd years old and he looks like a turtle. "I could, but I won't. And you, Ilse? How are you liking your new living arrangements?"

Hannah had recently sold the house she and her mother had been sharing for the past twenty years and moved into one of those senior living communities that accommodates several levels of needs.

Hannah had her own apartment with a kitchen and bathroom. Ilse had something a lot more like a hospital room, but with easy access to nursing care, cafeteria meals, really loud TVs, and endless games of bridge.

"It's not too bad," she said as if the thought had just occurred to her. "It's nice to have so many people around and so much to do."

"That's nice. I'm happy for you." Milt smiled again. "Something to be thankful for on this wonderful day."

"What I'd be thankful for is a couple of live-wire guys like you around, Milt." Ilse winked at him. "Or maybe more like this prime piece of beefcake." She twisted around in her chair and came nose to cheek with Joe's backside.

I don't blame her for being impressed with the view. Joe was broad-shouldered, slim-hipped, well-groomed, and basically cute as a button. Leah said he was a runner like her, and I bet he worked out every day. Ilse clearly appreciated the results. She slapped Joe's rear like a cattle driver sending the first-rate animals into the branding pen.

Joe lurched forward, more from shock than the force of the blow. We are, after all, talking about a little old lady in a wheelchair here. When Joe lurched, the glass of red wine he was holding also lurched. Since he had been leaning against the mantelpiece in a very *GQ* pose while murmuring softly to my sister in her snowy white sweater, that meant the snowy white sweater received most of the glass of red wine's lurching power.

There were several moments of horrified silence. I didn't know what to be more horrified about—Ilse Kauffman feeling up Leah's date, or what was probably the total ruination of a brand-new and expensive sweater that I would now never get to borrow.

Finally, Ilse giggled and said, "Oops!"

That broke the ice. I grabbed Leah, who was staring at the burst of red wine down her front like someone in a movie looking at the blood seeping from a bullet wound—you know that moment where they look down in disbelief and then up at whoever shot them, right before they collapse to the ground—and hustled her into the kitchen.

Claudia and my mother took one look at her and shifted into high gear. In a matter of seconds, it seemed, Leah had on one of my mother's old cashmere sweaters from the fifties that we all covet, so she can't give them to any one of us without pissing off the others. Claudia had Leah's new sweater and was pouring club soda on the wine stain over the kitchen sink. Hannah Kauffman leaned over her, yelling, "No, Claudia! Not club soda! I'm sure it's salt that gets out red wine!"

"What about hydrogen peroxide," I suggested. I crowded in for a look, too. It wasn't pretty.

"Salt is too slow." Claudia shook her head. "Hydrogen peroxide is for blood."

"That's red like blood," I pointed out.

"It's a protein thing, Emily. Not a color thing." Claudia poured more club soda on the sweater. You have to take a lot of chemistry to be a nurse. You don't have to take it to be a graphic designer. The stain turned pink, but it was a long way from being gone.

"You could soak the whole thing in red wine," I suggested to Leah. Drinking makes me ever so helpful. "Then you could pour club soda all over the whole thing and maybe it would all be one color."

Leah closed her eyes. "If I decide I want a pink sweater, I'll let you know and we can do it together. It'll be like an art project. Maybe Abby can help, too."

I knew I wasn't helping, so I backed away. Hannah followed as if attached to me like Velcro.

"So, how are you doing, dear?" Hannah peered at me through glasses nearly as thick as her mother's, with eyes that were nearly as demented. "We haven't had a chance to chat yet."

I froze. I hadn't thought through how to play this beforehand. The wheels in my brain were churning so fast, I was surprised smoke wasn't coming out of my ears.

I'm sure Hannah's question would seem innocuous to most people. Not to a young widow with a child to raise.

One of the most interesting phenomena I observed after Vince died was people's knee-jerk reaction to talk me out of whatever emotion I was experiencing at any given moment, all done in the name of being supportive.

If I said Abby and I were okay, they would immediately launch into a diatribe about how I would never find another man like Vince (as if I didn't know that) and that my loss was devastating (as if I hadn't noticed) and that Abby's life would forever have a hole in it where her father should be (as if she couldn't tell me that herself), and they didn't know how I could get out of bed in the morning or go through my day without crying constantly because my life was so irrevocably ruined and lonely. Usually, by the time they were done, I no longer was okay. They had supported me right into deep depression.

If I said I was having a difficult time and that I missed

Vince terribly, the self-same people would begin to lecture me on how I was young (as if I didn't have access to my own driver's license) and that I had my whole life ahead of me (assuming I didn't get a malignant brain tumor or get hit by a bus) and that I had a beautiful, healthy child to raise (as if she wasn't hanging on my leg at that precise moment because she gets clingy when I get depressed) and that I needed to pick myself up, brush myself off, get on with my life, and stop dwelling in the past.

So you can see why Hannah's question might throw me into a quandary. Did I want to be badgered into tears and just get them out of the way for the day? Or would I prefer a lecture on pulling myself up by my bootstraps, as she had done after her beloved Walter died and as her mother had done after her beloved Carl had passed on?

A bolt of brilliance hit me out of the blue. I couldn't believe I hadn't thought of it before.

"You know how it is, Hannah. Good days and bad," I said.

The timer buzzed. Mama checked the turkey and pronounced it ready to carve. While my father carved it, I escaped to check on everyone in the living room.

Jake sat on the coffee table, out of reach of Ilse's hands, nodding at her description of her neighbor's kidney infection. Joe had switched from wine to straight whiskey from my father's liquor cabinet. He hadn't even put in any ice.

"Joe doesn't look too good," I whispered in Jake's ear.

He grinned and whispered back, "Ilse told him that he ought to come home with her, because she'd taught Leah everything she knew."

At the table, I was careful to put Joe as far from Ilse as possible. Somehow Jake ended up next to her, but he was still smiling and nodding. Now she was telling about her other neighbor's angioplasty.

My mother came out of the kitchen with a platter of turkey. Her face glowed from the heat of the oven and she looked triumphant. Leah followed with mashed potatoes, also a bit rosy. Claudia had a casserole full of sweet potatoes. Her cheeks always look rosy anyway.

All three of them looked at me and gave simultaneous, identical little head jerks to indicate that there were more things to come out of the kitchen and I should start to help. I started to giggle. It looked like they were about to break into a bizarre dance routine. I wished they had on those little headsets like Janet Jackson wears when she performs.

My mother's eyes narrowed and I scampered into the kitchen. I really shouldn't drink at family gatherings.

My father hummed as he continued to slice turkey with an electric knife. He was down to just dark meat, not my favorite. But there were lots of little shreds of white meat lying on the big cutting board. Those are my absolute favorite. I like them so much better than those big slabs of turkey flesh. I scooped up a few of them and shoved them into my mouth. He stopped slicing and eyed me over the top of his glasses. "That's enough, young lady."

I rolled my eyes. "Daddy, what difference does it make? There's plenty of food. This was just a nibble."

"You eat at the table with a knife and a fork like a person," he said, brandishing the electric knife at me.

I sighed and grabbed both dishes of cranberry sauce. *Sit at the table. Clean your plate. Don't you like it? Why aren't you having seconds? Have you gained weight?* It's a wonder that all three of us don't either weigh several hundred pounds apiece or have horrendous eating disorders.

Serving turned out to be a bit more of a production than we'd anticipated.

Conversationally, we had to gently guide Ilse away from a description of the draining of her downstairs neighbor's abscesses. We also had to pass dishes for her, since the stroke that had weakened her right side, added to some osteoporosis, made it nearly impossible for her to lift the heavy dishes. Hannah sat on one side of her, so you'd think that would help, but she'd apparently forgotten how to pass food. Ilse would give her a dish and Hannah would set it down in front of her and smile, leaving the other side of the table to look and salivate, but not actually taste.

Not that the tasting ended up working out all that well, anyway.

I was still busy cutting Abby's meat for her when I noticed the strange silence. I looked up to see Milt put down his forkful of mashed potatoes with an odd look on his face.

Ilse simply spit hers out and looked accusingly at my mother. "The sour cream you used in these potatoes must have gone bad, Jessica."

"That can't be, Ilse," my mother said serenely.

"Sure tastes like it can be," Ilse countered. "They taste like crap."

"There isn't any sour cream in the potatoes. I used yogurt instead." My mother ladled some gravy over her potatoes and took a bite. I'm sure she thought none of us saw the face she made when the potatoes hit her tastebuds because she covered it up so fast, but I didn't miss it.

I looked down at the big pile of potatoes I'd already put on my plate and sighed. They looked beautiful. Fluffy, smooth, lightly browned on the top.

"Yogurt?" My father looked down at his plate with an expression that was probably pretty similar to mine.

"That's right." My mother smiled around the table at everyone. "Yogurt and no butter and no sour cream. Why, you could eat as much as you want of these and not worry for one second about the fat or the calories. I got the recipe from one of Gordon's heart-healthy handouts."

"But it's Thanksgiving, Jessica." My father looked like a little boy with coal in his stocking on Christmas.

"That's no reason to not eat healthfully," my mother said, sounding very reasonable.

"The way these potatoes taste is a reason to not eat at all," Ilse said. "How about the dressing? Did you make some edible dressing, at least?"

The dressing had been made with fat-free, low-sodium chicken broth instead of turkey drippings, and was barely edible if you added about a pint of salt. The gravy didn't help. It was low-fat, too, and came from a jar.

Abby saved the day by motoring through a surprisingly large amount of turkey for someone who generally lives on air, and then skipping down the table to give my mother a big hug and thank her for the wonderful dinner. She then left to continue the degradation of Barbie at the hands of the Ninja Turtles.

I vaguely heard Barbie call Michelangelo "big boy," and decided my mother was right about keeping Abby away from Ilse Kauffman. Otherwise, we'd see Skipper being sold into white slavery.

Claudia loaded the dinner dishes into the dishwasher while Leah scraped and rinsed. I was putting leftovers into Tupperware when Jake backed through the swinging door with his hands full of wineglasses.

"Oh, thanks. You didn't have to help clear the table, though," I told him.

He blushed. "Actually, I wanted an excuse to leave the room."

I arched a brow at him. He blushed harder. "Is Daddy trying to pick a fight with you about politics or music or something?" Daddy can be very argumentative when he's had a little wine. He says he's trying to have some meaningful debate, but really he just wants to show everybody how much more logical he can be than everybody else.

He shook his head. "No. Your dad's fine."

"Bored?"

"No. Not really."

"Then what?" I'd had enough cat and mouse. Why can't men ever just answer you when you ask them a direct question that doesn't have to do with how big your butt looks in a particular pair of pants?

"It's the little old lady in the wheelchair."

"Ilse?"

He nodded.

"She's a tiny little thing in a wheelchair, for God's sake, and if you stay sitting down, she can't slap your ass. How can you be scared of Mrs. Kauffman?"

If he blushed any harder, something in his neck was going to burst. "I'm not exactly scared, and you don't know what she said to me!"

"Did she embarrass you with too much detail about her last colonoscopy?"

He went scarlet from the roots of his hair to the collar of his shirt and beyond, for all I knew. "Let's just say that when I stood up next to her, she offered to perform certain, uh, services that she could perform in precisely that position, but would require her to remove her dentures. She said Leah's date looked good but was a cold fish, and she thought I might be more to her liking. I'm supposed to be out here getting her a glass to put her teeth in, and you can't make me go back out there."

My mother closed her eyes and sighed, and then let out a bellow. "Gordon!"

He came bursting into the kitchen. "What? What is it? Is there something on fire?"

"Gordon, put the desserts on the table."

"The girls haven't even finished clearing yet," he protested.

"I don't care. Put the desserts out, please."

"But the table's messy." He really was whining.

"Gordon," she snapped. "If you aren't willing to help, just say you won't help. If you are willing to help, put the goddamn desserts on the goddamn table."

Silence reigned again. Mama never talks like that. She certainly never talks like that to my father. They argue, they bicker. But she doesn't swear at him.

My father picked up the almond pudding and the torte and headed out of the kitchen. Claudia followed with the pumpkin pie and some forks, her eyes as big as saucers.

"I swear," my mother said as she measured decaf coffee into the coffeemaker. "That man will be the death of me. Why can't he even once just do as I ask? Why do I always have to *explain* everything? 'Gordon, if you don't take out the garbage now, it will overflow.'"

She started to mimic herself. I'd never seen anything quite like it. In a whining, nagging voice, she said, "'Gordon, if you don't mow the lawn today, the homeowner's association will send us a nasty note.' 'Gordon, you look absurd with duct tape all over your coat. Buy a new one.'"

She slammed the filter holder of the coffeemaker shut and whirled on me, her eyes blazing with anger. I took a step back. "Why can't I just ask him to take out the garbage, mow the lawn, or buy a new jacket? Why do I have to explain it to him? Why does he need to know that old lady Kauffman is trying to pick up my daughters' dates, so we need to feed her dessert and get her the hell out of here? Why can't he just take the goddamn dessert to the goddamn table?"

"Mama, he did take the goddamn desserts to the goddamn table."

"Fine, Emily, take his side. You always have. You've always been a Daddy's girl."

Normally, since quiet rebellion against my mother has been my hobby since I turned twelve, I would take being a "Daddy's girl" as a compliment. Under the present circumstances, it didn't seem like such a good thing.

"I'm not taking his side, Mama. I'm just making an observation."

She thrust some dessert plates and coffee mugs at me and didn't say another word.

We got through dessert without Ilse propositioning anyone else. At least I think she didn't. She had Milt alone for a few minutes while I got coffee, but nobody said anything when I came back. Then my father got Ilse and her daughter back into the Buick and took them home.

After a very intensely whispered conversation in the living room that left Leah looking tight-lipped and flustered, Joe left, too.

Jake helped clear the dessert dishes, then said he should probably go, as well.

"I'll walk you out," I said. The second we stepped out the door, the damp chill cut into me like a knife. I wrapped my arms around myself and shivered.

"Take my coat."

Before I could protest, Jake had draped his jacket around my shoulders. It smelled good. Like soap and peppermint and maybe a little bit of smoke. I wondered where he'd been, that his coat would smell smoky. I pulled it tight around me as we walked down the sidewalk.

"Sorry," I said.

"About what?"

"The little old lady in the wheelchair?"

"Oh, Mrs. Kauffman senior." He shrugged and I detected that grin playing at the corners of his mouth. He smoothed his mustache to hide it. "Don't worry about it. It's nice to know that someone still finds me desirable."

We stopped by his old tan four-runner. I gave it a playful kick with the toe of my boot. I remembered him buying it after he and Vince had graduated from college. I had still had two years left to go. "Are you ever going to replace this thing?"

He grinned, which made his eyes crinkle up. He knew I was joking; I felt like Abby did about his truck. We loved to be taken for rides in it. If we were dogs, we'd stick our heads out the windows and loll our tongues out while the wind blew our ears back when we rode in that truck.

"Why would I do a thing like that?"

"Because you could get a nice, shiny new one if you wanted. Maybe even one of those big SUVs with leather interiors and sound systems that aren't held in place with bungee cords." I peeked inside the truck. It was very Jake. Not spotless, but not trashed, either. A few paper coffee cups on the floor and CDs strewn across the passenger seat, but no actual food stuck to anything.

"Like I said, why would I want that? Those trucks have no substance. The four-runner has been around. She knows what's important, and if she's acquired a few dings in the course of her education, well, to me, those dings are beautiful."

I had a feeling we weren't talking about trucks, any more than we'd been talking about chairs last week. I knew what he meant, though.

"Thanks for coming. It made it a lot easier for me."

He smiled. "Thanks for inviting me."

"You want your coat back?"

"Not right now. I'll pick it up Saturday." He pulled the collar up around my neck.

When his thumbs brushed against my collarbone, my nipples responded with an intensity that they hadn't attempted in a long time. I fought back a wince—was it possible to sprain a boob? I really, really needed to get out more.

"Go back in now," Jake told me. "It's cold outside and I

think if your mother and sisters press up against that front window any harder, they'll go right through it."

He brushed a kiss across my cheek. As I whirled around, I managed to catch a glimpse of the three of them hightailing it back into the living room.

CHAPTER EIGHT

There's Nothing in Life that Can't Be Made Better by Having a Little Too Much Laundry to Fold

I'm sure they did something to their hair, but how the hell should I know how it turned out?

What's with the dark glasses?" I asked Leah when she walked in with her hair swept back in a clip and sunglasses on at five o'clock on a winter afternoon. We barely get enough sun in Seattle in the summer to warrant them.

"I didn't get much sleep last night." She took off the glasses. She looked like hell. If the circles under her eyes got any darker, someone was going to think she had been abused.

"Hot date with Joe?" Claudia asked, unpacking the bag.

She shook her head. "Joe's history."

"Really? Why?"

Leah shrugged. "After Thanksgiving he told me that my family made his eye twitch."

"So, why the dark circles?" I prodded.

"I haven't been sleeping much lately." She collapsed down into a chair.

Claudia tossed her an extra-large T-shirt with an exceptionally sickly sweet picture of a kitten on the front. Before Leah started wearing it for root night, it had just been icky. Now with smears of Titian Red and Apricot Glaze, it had a vaguely macabre look to it that we all liked much better.

"And I saw him again," Leah said quietly.

"You did what?" Claudia said at the same time that I said, "Saw who?"

The crostini with sun-dried tomatoes and goat cheese was halfway to my mouth when I felt their eyes on me. Oops. Imbecilic baby sister time again. I blinked a few times and then it came to me. "You mean Chase?"

Leah nodded.

"That's great!" I said.

Claudia glared. "No, it's not!"

I crammed the crostini into my mouth, washed it down with a sip of Chianti (it was Italian night), wiped my hands on my jeans, and decided to forgo the judgment call. It didn't matter whether Claudia and I thought it was great or thought it was a disaster, and arguing about it didn't make much sense to me at the moment. "How'd it happen?"

Leah sighed and rearranged herself in the chair. "Boredom, I guess."

I blinked a few times more. "I get bored all the time and it never leads to sex with hot club musicians. In fact, I was bored last night, too, and didn't get to have sex with anybody at all." I stopped to remember what I had done the night before. "I folded laundry."

I'd had a bonanza of five magnets drop out. I'd gotten "imagine," "funny," "squirrel," "apple," and "tree." I still didn't know what they meant. It could be that sometimes the universe isn't sending me messages through my laundry, but I didn't want to take the chance of missing anything important, either.

Claudia looked over at me. "Me, too. You should have called. We could have done it together. We could have rented a movie or something."

"Only if you'd been willing to come to my place," I said. "Abby needed to get to bed on time and I had piles and piles to fold."

"You don't know piles of laundry until you have two boys both involved in sports at the same time," Claudia scoffed.

Leah sighed even more deeply. Then one more time. Soon she'd heave a lung out onto the floor.

"Oh, right," I said. "How exactly did boredom lead you to have fantastic sex with a really cute guy again? I think this might be highly useful information for me to have."

"How do you know it was fantastic?" Claudia asked, pulling on the yellow polo shirt that used to belong to Mark that she wears on root night. "Maybe that was just a first-time thing."

"Because it was also fantastic the next time, when she tried to break up with him, and she wouldn't have those dark circles under her eyes if it had been lousy."

More sighs from Leah.

"Fine. Tell us about it," I said, "before you hurt yourself."

"I got back from my run. I took a shower. I had a bite to eat. It was only eight o'clock. Saturday night stretched out in front of me like a yawning maw of boredom that was going to eat me alive." She draped herself over the chair in a totally Greta Garbo move.

I blinked some more. Yawning maw? Being eaten alive? This didn't even sound like Leah. Leah was brisk and efficient, logical and dependable. Claudia is sweet and supportive. I'm the family flake. I say things like "yawning maw of boredom." I drape myself on doorways and say I want to be alone. Leah was totally encroaching on my territory. Interestingly, I did not feel threatened.

"You need more laundry to fold," I observed.

"Really?" Leah asked. "I thought I needed a little more intelligence and a whole lot more self-control."

"Failing that, more laundry will actually do the trick," I said. "If your day will be ruined because someone in your household does not have her favorite Powerpuff Girl underpants to wear the next day, laundry becomes a much higher priority." I wondered if it could be a higher priority than fantastic sex with a cute guy, but with the way things were going, I wouldn't ever get to find out.

"You called him," Claudia said accusingly.

Leah shook her head. Her hair slipped out of its clip. She was messy. Leah's never messy. Who was this person? Were there pods in the basement of her condo? Had she been taken over by the body snatchers?

"No. I just decided to go out."

"And you ran into him somewhere. Leah, this isn't a coincidence, this is fate," I said excitedly. "This is fate with a capital F. It's destiny. It's kismet."

"Emily, it doesn't take karma to look up where his band is

playing and show up there on a Saturday night," Claudia said, sarcasm practically jumping off her words.

I stared at her. Claudia isn't sarcastic. Leah is sarcastic. Had everyone exchanged bodies or personalities while I wasn't looking? I watch a lot of Disney movies with Abby and I was suspecting a little switcheroo. The Simon girls do *Freaky Friday.*

"I didn't actually look up where he was playing, Claudia," Leah said wearily.

"Oh?" Claudia arched her brows in disbelief. "You just happened upon him and his band someplace in all the places you could have gone in the entire city of Seattle?"

Leah waved her hand at her dismissively. "He may have mentioned he had a semiregular gig at this place on Saturdays."

"Oh, he just may have." More sarcasm, so deep and sharp and biting I was surprised we weren't bleeding.

"Claudia, does it matter how I happened to get there?" Leah ran her hand over her face. She looked exhausted.

"Yes, Leah. It does matter. Because you know this man is all wrong for you and yet you keep seeking him out. Letting him into your condo. Going to hear his band. Don't you see what you're doing?"

I felt steam starting to build up behind my eyeballs. I wasn't even sure where it was coming from; I just knew that I was starting to see red.

I stared at Claudia from on the couch, barely seeing her through the haze. "It's nice that you know what Leah is supposed to do, Claudia. Do you know what *you* need to do?"

"What, Emily?" She stood there with her hands on her hips, steam practically coming out of her ears.

I stood up and faced her. "You need to butt out. And so do I. Leah should decide what she wants and then act on it. It's not your decision or mine. It's hers. Neither of us has any business passing judgment on it. We're making her miserable."

Then I retrieved Abby from the other room and picked up our coats. "And you can get your own damn snacks tonight," I threw over my shoulder as I marched us out the door.

My sisters and I never fight. We bicker occasionally. We tease incessantly. We disagree about nearly everything. But we don't fight.

I don't know why. Blame it on my mother.

Her sister was her best friend and so she raised us to be one another's best friends. I don't know how else to explain it.

We are just as competitive, just as insecure, and just as contentious as any other set of siblings I know, but somehow it just doesn't express itself in the backbiting, petty rivalry into which I see so many other sets of siblings slide.

The problem with not fighting, however, is that we don't know what to do on the rare occasions that we do fight.

By the time I got home, I was heartsick. Why on earth had I been mean to my sister? I thought of the times that Claudia had rescued me. I thought about Joey Malone, whose eye she'd blacked when I was in kindergarten and he deliberately broke the shell I'd brought back from vacation and taken to school for show-and-tell. I thought of my first real date with Vince, when she lent me her best sweater and didn't even get mad when I spilled Coke on it. I thought of the times when Vince was sick that she took Abby out to the park or for ice cream, or sent me away to have a little time to myself. I thought of all those months after Vince died that she did my housework and took care of my kid and made sure I ate.

I was scum. I ticked off days on my fingers and realized I couldn't even blame it on my period. *The good news, ma'am, is that you don't have PMS. The bad news is that you're just a bitch.*

Abby didn't help. "But I don't understand why you were yelling at Aunt Claudia, Mommy," she said plaintively as I helped her out of the backseat when we got home.

"I'm not sure I do, either, sweetheart," I told her.

"You never yell at her. She never yells at you. You were both yelling." Her lower lip slithered out into a pout. "I don't like it when you yell. It's too loud. It hurts my ears."

I opened our front door and flicked on the lights. "Well, it hurts my whole head."

"Then turn this car around right now, young lady, and go back to Auntie Claudia and apologize this instant." She stood in the middle of our tiny foyer with her little fists on her little hips, looking just like my sisters and me and our mother and our aunt.

I wanted to obey her (or me or Mama or Aunt Nancy, I'm not sure which one of us Abby was channeling). I wanted to go back and apologize and cry and be hugged, but I couldn't. First of all, I didn't have the nerve to face Claudia so soon. Secondly, I suspected that I had been right.

It *wasn't* our business. I mean, our sister's happiness is certainly a concern of ours, but how she achieves it should be up to her. The more I thought about it, the more I felt that all of Leah's objections to Chase had to do with how other people might feel about him, Claudia's anti-Chase tirades being right up there in the front of that pack. None of Leah's objections had anything to do with how Leah felt about Chase. Or how Chase felt about Leah.

Granted, I'd married my high school sweetheart and would still be married to him if he hadn't had the most extraordinary bad luck to develop an extremely malignant brain tumor, so maybe I didn't know as much about relationships as people who had been out there dating. But I was still pretty damn sure that the most important thing was how you felt about each other, not how *other* people felt about how you felt about each other.

I also thought turning into a human volcano just because a guy looked at you sounded like an awful lot of fun. I vaguely remembered the sensation, but since I'd reached a point where I was having erotic thoughts about my electric toothbrush, I wasn't sure I could completely trust my memory.

"I'll call Aunt Claudia tomorrow," I promised. "It'll be okay."

Abby narrowed her eyes. "Do I have to go to bed?"

I laughed. "No. How about I make a bowl of popcorn and we watch *Aladdin?*"

Abby loves *Aladdin*. I think mainly she likes to dress up like Jasmine in those slightly slutty little harem outfits, but the story's fun and every time I watch it, I hear something else that the Genie says that I'd missed before.

The hands came off her hips and her little blonde brows went up. "Just you and me?"

"Just you and me."

Abby has the ability to fold herself up into the smallest of all possible human packages. She's tall for her age, but you'd never know it when she snuggles up against you, folded around herself. We wrapped ourselves in quilts and cuddled up on the couch.

When she was a baby, I was terrified of the soft spot on Abby's head. You know, that fontanel thing where the plates of babies' skulls haven't fused yet? The one all the baby books warn you to be so careful about?

I was so careful of Abby's soft spot that she developed cradle cap, because I was afraid to wash it too hard. Finally Vince took over the washing of her hair. To me, that soft spot summed up everything that was scary about parenthood: how vulnerable and dependent babies are and how completely dependent they are on us. I mean, not only do we have to feed them and keep them warm, clean, and dry, we also have to keep things from poking their vulnerable little heads. Menacing things are suddenly everywhere once you have a baby. Low-hanging branches, corners on coffee tables, lawn darts all become terrifying objects out there to harm your perfect little angel.

Now Abby climbed into my lap and I settled my chin on just where that spot had been, connecting back to the baby she used to be. I tried to make myself big and strong, so she could have that feeling of having a parent who was the biggest and strongest person on earth and who would never let anything bad happen to her, while she dreamed about sailing through the sky with Jasmine and Aladdin on their magic carpet. We watched Aladdin and Jasmine and Iago and the Genie until she fell asleep.

First I heard her breathing slow and then I felt that subtle release that comes as she relinquished total consciousness. Her little body curved into mine, echoing my own arcs in and out as completely and sweetly as it had when I still breastfed her. I inhaled deeply and could still in the back of my throat taste a little bit of the milky sweetness of those times. These moments would be as fleeting in retrospect, I suppose.

I wish sleep came to me as easily.

Right after Vince died, I used to have these incredibly vivid dreams where I'd meet him on this beach somewhere. It wasn't any place I recognized. More an amalgamation of a whole lot of different places. Vince is there, pretty much how he was when he died, the back of his head messed up from too many pointless surgeries and way too thin, wearing a pair of gym shorts and a tank top with the back slit open. We used to do that, Leah and me—slit the back of his shirts—to keep him from developing bedsores. But in the dream, he's walking like he did when he was well.

In the dream, we sit there together on this big piece of driftwood and watch waves pound against the rocks. You know that companionable silence that you develop with really good friends? Where you can sit there together and not talk and watch the world and not be alone? In my dream, it's like that. Like he's well again. Then he squeezes my hand and walks away.

I found those dreams immensely comforting.

You can interpret this dream any number of ways. Trust me, my sisters and I spent hours going over the possibilities.

Grief and bereavement experts will tell you that dreams in which the recently deceased appear to the bereaved with messages from beyond are extremely common. The most widely accepted explanation is that your loss is so new and so fresh that your subconscious helps you make the transition by conjuring up these little visits.

I think—Claudia agrees and so does Leah, even if she

doesn't always like to admit it—that it's equally possible that the person who died hasn't completely made the journey they're on yet, that until they're completely to wherever they're going, some essential part of them can still connect with the people they loved when they were alive.

The dreams become more infrequent as the person is further—psychically or spiritually—away. That's what happened to me. First days, then weeks, then finally more than a month would pass between dreams.

They stopped altogether about a year after Vince died. That's pretty much the same time I fell apart.

I hadn't dreamed that particular dream again, until that night.

I carried Abby to her bed and tucked her in, hoping I'd remembered to have her pee before we started watching the movie, but deciding that I'd rather wash sheets the next day than take the chance of waking her now. I was exhausted. I felt like Leah looked, and fell into bed and into deep, black sleep about two seconds after my head hit the pillow.

I was on that beach wherever, and up saunters Vince. The sunlight glinted off his blond hair and the corners of his eyes crinkled when he smiled at me.

"Been a while, Em," he said.

I stared at him.

"I've been busy," he apologized.

I felt a huge rush of anger surge through my body. "You've been busy," I repeated.

He shrugged. "It's a lot to adjust to."

He had a lot of nerve, even if he was dead. Really, *he* was busy? *He* had made a lot of adjustments?

For God's sake, I was the one who'd been widowed at thirty with a small child to raise on my own. I was the one who had to take care of everything by herself. I had to work and raise Abby and take care of the house and the lawn and pay the bills and take out the garbage and pack the lunches and do the laundry and help with homework and play catch and make all the meals and clean up after them and know which Pokemon were which and figure out which health insurance to get and how to save for college and . . . well, just everything else.

He gave me that smile of his. The one he used to give me when he got home late and dinner was ruined, or when he'd forgotten to take out the trash, even though I'd asked him a dozen times and the bag had leaked and left a brown sticky mess on the floor, or when he hadn't paid the credit card bill even though there was plenty of money in the account and I couldn't use it anymore. It had the same effect on me in the dream that it used to have in real life. He still annoyed me; I just loved him more than I was annoyed by him.

I sighed and took his hand. "I can't believe you have the nerve to say that to me. You do realize that I'm raising our daughter by myself now, don't you?"

He nodded. "I watch a lot. You're doing a great job."

"I'm still really sad, Vince. I miss you." I didn't look at him.

He patted my hand. "I know. I miss you, too. It's okay to start being happy again, though. I won't be mad."

I felt a rush of annoyance again. "Why is it always about you? Maybe I don't want to be happy again."

He laughed and slipped his hand away from mine. "You're gonna be fine, Em." He kissed my cheek and then I was sitting on the big driftwood log all by myself, dangling my feet in the sand.

When I woke up, I was sitting on the edge of my bed with my feet kicking at the carpet.

I did talk to Claudia the next day. Both of us fell all over each other apologizing, but I suspected that neither of us was actually sorry. She didn't feel any differently about Chase and I didn't feel any differently about it being none of our business. We just couldn't stand being mad at each other.

Besides, we are way too far into one another's lives to function alone. Claudia's boys come in and out of my house and Abby goes in and out of her Auntie Claudia's house like they were their own. Who would pick Abby up from the bus stop on the days I couldn't leave early? Who would supervise Randy's homework on the nights Claudia worked? Who would check either boy's homework for spelling errors? Claudia can't spell her way out of a paper bag.

So it was strange, having something that I couldn't talk to Claudia about. I've always talked to her about everything. Without reservations. Without fears. Without hesitation. Even though this business with Leah and Chase was just one little item, I felt like someone had pulled the life raft a little bit out of my reach and I was going to have to swim extra hard to get to shore now.

Part of me felt a little sense of loss, but another part of me—a new part of me that I hadn't realized even existed—felt great about it. This new part of me felt like it was about time I tried to swim to shore on my own. This new part of me thought I was strong enough, smart enough, and tough enough to do it, too.

This new part of me also felt it was time to do some more shopping, because my clothes still simply didn't reflect the bold, sassy woman hiding inside me.

I'm sure that's why I found it particularly gratifying when Jake walked through the door on Saturday, handed me a latte, and said, "Zowie!"

"Thank you." I smiled. I had on a gauzy peasant blouse and a pair of low-cut jeans with an ever-so-slight bell to the bottoms. Not a full Britney, mind you. No butt cleavage or belly button showing, but still I felt kind of zowie in it. I don't know when the last time I got someone to feel zowie-ish about me was. I certainly hadn't felt internally zowie in ages. I liked it.

"You look great," he said, not moving from the door.

"Thanks," I said again. He stared at me. I started to feel a little uncomfortable. "Do I have something hanging from my nose?"

He shook himself and came the rest of the way in so I could shut the door. "No. You're fine. You're better than fine even. You just . . . I don't know . . . look different."

I held my arms out and spun around. "New outfit."

"I noticed." He shook his head. "More than that, though."

"Lost weight? Gained weight?" I pressed. Had I bought new jeans that were going to make my butt look fat?

"No. Not an outside thing. You just look different. Like inside different."

I smiled again. I guess internal zowie can show just as much as external zowie.

*   *   *

One of the big advantages to my job is flexibility. Since it basically entails laying out the same brochure, proposal, and report for essentially the same small office buildings over and over again, it isn't exactly exciting, so the flexibility is a pretty big deal. It does also provide a modest income, decent health insurance, and the feeling—erroneous or otherwise—that I have some identity outside of my family life, even if I don't do it particularly well.

I try hard not to use people's pity. It bothers me to be "poor Emily" all the time, so I feel like it's dishonest to reap too many rewards from it. Sometimes I can't help it, though. After I came back to work the second time (after my little breakdown), Darrell Anderson (the big boss) called me into his office. He explained why Karen would be my supervisor in the kindest terms possible. He made it clear that the office would also do anything they could to help me get back on my feet again.

Most places would have probably canned me.

Anyway, in the spirit of helping poor Emily get back on her feet, they let me take work home and finish it there most afternoons, which allows me to come home at the same time Abby gets off the school bus. On the rare afternoon that a deadline or a meeting keeps me in the office past three o'clock, I can usually call my mother to meet Abby's bus. Or Claudia, if she isn't working.

When Claudia is working or has something else going on, my flexible schedule also gives my nephews someplace with adult supervision to hang out in the afternoons. Because she usually works a twelve-hour shift, they also get fed. Why it seems more like a dinner when I make chicken nuggets than when they make them for themselves, I'm not sure, but at least we eat them in something like a family atmosphere. That means at the kitchen counter, usually with a TV blaring, but with as much barbecue sauce as they can eat.

It also keeps me connected at some level with my nephews, which I don't think would be possible otherwise. They are adolescent males and as such are an alien species. Even little boys and grown men regard them that way, so I feel almost no guilt in admitting that I think of them that way.

My nephews happen to be good boys. Even though their habits, tastes, and speech are completely inexplicable to me, I regard them in a sort of good-natured anthropological way and am happy that they tolerate me.

So Randy and Todd were at my house on a Wednesday afternoon while Claudia went to a doctor's appointment. Mark, Claudia's ex, came to pick up the boys from my place to take them out to dinner. He's been in one of his "good daddy" phases for a month or so now, meaning he's actually showing up and taking the boys out to dinner or a movie or to shoot some hoops on a fairly regular schedule.

Good daddy phases tend to come and go with Mark. Leah and Claudia and I have decided that regardless of how we feel about Mark at this point, it should be our role to support good daddy phases as long as they last, and protect Todd and Randy as soon as they start to wane back into bad daddy phases. As hard as marriage to a drug addict was for Claudia, being a drug addict's kid is even harder for Todd and Randy.

When good daddy Mark showed up at my door, I tried to be pleasant.

"Hey, Mark, how are you doing?" I asked, letting him in. I used to make him wait for the boys outside the house. I felt he was an unsafe person to have in the house, but I could see how much it embarrassed Todd and Randy, and started letting him in. It's been okay so far.

"Not bad, Emily. How are things with you?"

Clean-cut and dressed like an ad for Yuppies "R" Us, you'd never believe Mark was a heroin addict to look at him. I honestly believe that "hitting bottom" for Mark might mean losing the tassels off his loafers.

"Todd, Randy, your dad's here. Gather up your stuff and get your shoes on."

A muffled chorus of "okay, Aunt Emily" emanated from the family room.

"Mind if I use the bathroom while I wait?" Mark asked.

I hesitated. Mark has been known to be careless with the stuff he uses to fix, and the last thing I wanted near the kids or me was the used needle from a drug user. Even one with tassels on his loafers. On the other hand, he was quite clearly in good daddy mode. I decided to compromise.

"Why don't you use mine," I suggested. "It's probably cleaner."

This offered the dual charms of being true (I love my nephews, but bathroom cleanliness is not one of their virtues) and isolating where Mark could hide any nasty stuff.

Todd and Randy came out, gathered their homework up from the dining room table, and put it in their backpacks, put on their incredibly gigantic shoes (I still have trouble reconciling that anyone whose diaper I changed could have feet that size) and waited. And waited some more.

The boys and I had started shifting uncomfortably from foot to foot. Abby climbed around on Todd as if he were a jungle gym rather than a person, an activity that he seems to encourage more than discourage. I told you he's a nice boy. We were all getting a little uncomfortable when Abby finally said, "Boy, it sure takes your dad a long time to go potty."

Both boys snorted.

"I'll go see what's taking him," I said with one of those big, bright, no-problem, stupid smiles that kids see right through but adults can't stop themselves from giving.

I walked down the hall to my bedroom with my heart in my throat. Visions of what I might find behind the door were making my stomach churn: Mark slumped over in a corner with a needle jutting from his arm, or writhing on the floor with froth spilling from his lips.

Nothing my imagination could conjure up, however, prepared me for what I saw when I walked into my room.

Mark stood in front of the mirror, stripped to the waist. He was turning from one side to another. "Do you think I'm starting to grow . . . breasts?"

CHAPTER NINE

To Soothe the Savage Breast

Leah

One part Harvest Wheat (#42), one part Golden Copper (#40), one part developer. Forty-five minutes. Maybe if we keep making her blonder, she'll get stupider and stop showing us up.

Claudia

One part Light Ash Brown (#32), one part Apricot Glaze (#38), one part developer. Thirty minutes. Still great, but a few sighs now that it had become old hat. Maybe trash the Light Ash Brown next time and go even redder?

I couldn't wait to relate the story of Mark's breasts to my sisters. I expected them to howl with laughter. When I finished telling them, I waited for the squeals and giggles.

Claudia choked.

Leah pounded her on the back. "Are you all right?"

"No," she said, turning very pale. "I think I might have done something very, very bad."

Leah stopped combing Claudia's hair. I stopped slicing cheese. It looked as if Claudia had stopped breathing.

"What did you do?" I whispered.

"Remember when I told you about Mark stealing Randy's medications?"

Leah and I both nodded.

"Remember when I made that comment about little white pills in the bottle and how would he know what he was taking?"

We both nodded again. I felt like a jack-in-the-box.

"Remember when my doctor put me on those progesterone pills to see if they would help with my PMS? Those little white progesterone pills?"

I gasped. Leah snorted.

"You didn't," Leah demanded.

"I did," Claudia wailed.

"That is *so* excellent," I breathed.

"I didn't think it would actually make him grow breasts!"

"Then why did you do it? You must have thought it would change something," Leah said.

"Well, I kind of hoped it would do something like that, but I didn't really think it would. It's a really low dosage."

Claudia had gotten even paler than usual. She has gorgeous skin. She has the perfect complexion for someone living in Seattle. Her skin is so white that it's practically translucent, with the faintest blush of rose on each of her cheekbones. She looks like a Renaissance painting of the Madonna. For color to actually drain from her face, she has to turn a color that's even whiter than white. Sort of like a gelatinous jellyfish.

"Well, if it's the pills, they're only growing little ones on him." I spoke with the authority of the only one who had seen

Mark's mammaries. I bit into a crab puff. As I chewed, another thought crossed my mind. "I wonder, though . . ."

"What?" Claudia asked. "What else?"

"Just . . . if it's making something grow, could it also be making something else shrink?"

We all looked at each other wide-eyed.

The only part I like about the holidays is decorating. I was raised Jewish; Vince was raised Protestant. We celebrated everything. I have dreidel lights and one of those Santas that dances and sings when you walk by it. I have a little candelabra with angels suspended over the top, so that the heat from the candles makes them spin around. I have a silver-and-blue Happy Hanukkah banner and several big garbage bags full of fake mistletoe and holly.

I'd celebrate Kwanzaa if they would start selling some decent decorations for it at Bed Bath & Beyond.

Abby loves decorating for the holidays, too. We still get our tree from the same little tree farm we used to go to when Vince was fine. I'm not sure Abby really remembers going there with him, but the first Christmas after he died she insisted on going there, and we've stayed with the ritual.

It's a darling little place with a sleigh ride and a little booth that sells hot cider and popcorn. Just make sure not to say yes when the friendly old man offers to take you on a sleigh ride. We made that mistake last year, but luckily his sons caught us before we actually left the property. It's nice they want him to live at home, even though his Alzheimer's is getting pretty advanced.

You might be wondering by now where Vince's parents are.

You may have even decided that they're cold and heinous people who would desert their daughter-in-law and granddaughter after their son died.

You'd be wrong.

Wayne and Brandi Kinney are genuinely the salt of the earth. They were wonderful to me from the second Vince and I started dating in high school and still are. They did, however, decide to retire to Florida after Vince died. Would they still have done that if Vince was alive? I have no way of knowing.

I know only a fraction of the pain that Brandi has had to live with since the day Vince died. From before that, really, as the tumor took more and more of him away from us.

Having a husband die when you've just turned thirty is devastating, horrible, and heartbreaking.

There are no good words to describe the pain of having your child die before you. Ever.

I felt as though Vince had taken a piece of my heart with him when he died. Brandi felt like he'd taken the whole thing. Wayne couldn't even say his name.

Staying here, where every corner and every street and every restaurant seems to have some connection to some memory of Vince, is hard for me sometimes. For Brandi, it was like walking around on a bed of nails day after day. You may eventually become tough enough to tolerate it, but you pay a price for the calluses.

They love Abby. They visit. They send presents. When she's older, she might even go to visit them by herself.

In the spirit of the season and knowing my taste, Brandi had sent us a fake stuffed fish wearing a Santa hat mounted on a plaque. The fish sings Christmas carols. How many people have a mother-in-law who would get them that? Especially since Brandi's taste runs more toward understated, lovely, tasteful decor.

"I think it should go over the buffet in the dining room, Mommy," Abby said. She picked up the package and scampered into the other room with it and held it up at the wall where she thought it should go. Of course, since she's only a little over four feet tall, she held it a lot lower than it would hang.

"You think so? But we hardly ever eat in here." We eat probably ninety percent of our meals at the kitchen counter. If we eat in the dining room, it probably means my mother is here.

"But we sit in here to play games and do puzzles," Abby pointed out.

"Quite true. We could enjoy him then."

I extricated Billy Bass from his box and tacked him to the wall, while Abby did little pirouettes around me. Sometimes being her mother is like having one's own little fairy princess.

We stood back and surveyed our handiwork.

"He looks kind of lonely," Abby said, her lower lip starting to extend.

The wall hadn't seemed quite so big and bare before I'd tacked Billy up there. A lonely singing fish in a sea of beige. Depressing. Not the effect we'd wanted at all.

I chewed my thumbnail and thought fast. I didn't like the look of Abby's pout, and I wasn't in the mood to paint the dining room. "We could put lights around him," I suggested.

Abby pondered for a moment. "Which ones?"

"Chili peppers?"

She shook her head.

"Dancing dreidels?"

She shook her head again.

"Santa cows?"

She clapped her hands. "Absolutely!"

We dug through the strings of lights until we found the set of cows with Santa hats. Abby was right: they were the perfect complement to a carol-singing fish.

We were discussing the addition of some gold ribbon and perhaps a little fake holly when the doorbell rang.

"I bet it's Uncle Jake." Abby danced over to the door.

"Why?" I hadn't heard his truck pull up, but I hadn't been listening for it, either.

"Because he comes every Saturday, you big silly. Haven't you noticed?" She cracked the door open. "It *is* Uncle Jake," she announced.

I hadn't noticed. Every Saturday? I thought back through the past few weeks. Abby was right. Every Saturday morning.

"Are you going to let Uncle Jake in?" a voice said from the other side of the door.

She considered for a moment and looked over at me.

"What's in it for us?" I yelled.

"I have a grande nonfat latte with a caramel shot," Jake shouted through the crack.

"For God's sake, Abby. Don't just stand there. Let the man in. He has coffee."

Abby didn't move. "I don't drink coffee."

"And a blueberry muffin." He rustled what sounded like a waxed paper bag in an inviting fashion.

Abby let him in. She took the bag from him and skipped

off to the kitchen without even saying hello. I took the coffee.

"You two are getting to be high maintenance," he observed.

I smiled. I'd never been high maintenance before. "Hey, you're the one who started these little Saturday-morning stopovers. Not that I'm complaining, mind you."

We went into the living room. I moved the bag of fake holly from the couch to the floor and put the boxes with the light-up menorah and the dancing Santa there, too, and we sat down.

"Do you ever talk to him still?"

For a bad moment, I thought he meant the dancing Santa. It's not out of the question. I talk to our cat, Shadow, all the time, but he isn't inanimate. I've been known to cajole and swear at appliances, but not to really chat with them.

I finally realized that Jake wasn't looking at me anymore; his gaze had traveled up to the shelf where Vince resided.

I know some people (all right, most people) think it's ghoulish, but I have Vince's ashes. I hated the idea of sticking them in some weird mausoleum and I kept coming up blank on a place to scatter them. He'd told me he wanted to be cremated, but we hadn't taken it further than that. In the end, I decided the place Vince had been the happiest was with Abby and me, so that's where I had him. On a shelf in the living room, with some of our favorite pictures of him.

"Sure. Sometimes," I said. "So does Abby."

Jake sighed and rubbed his eyes. "I miss telling him stuff."

"Me, too." I pulled one of the throw pillows onto my lap and hugged it.

He smiled one of those smiles that people make when they

don't think something is funny. "I imagine you do," he said dryly. "I mean, more like problems. He had that way of asking questions. You know what I mean?"

"Yeah." I gripped the pillow tighter. I knew exactly what he meant. Vince had had this way of never telling you what to do, but making you realize what you wanted or needed to do. I'd be bubbling over with frustration or confusion or just plain craziness about anything, from how to deal with someone at work to trying to plan a menu for a dinner party, and he'd ask me a couple of questions and suddenly I'd see exactly the right course to take.

It was an amazing skill. One I never mastered. I figured I should try anyway. "Can I help?"

Jake smiled at me and shook his head. "I don't think so," he said, his voice thick with irony. "I wish you could."

"Is it Sandy?"

He shot me a quick sideways glance and grimace. "No. That's pretty final."

"That didn't take long." I took another sip of coffee.

"No, it didn't. In fact, it occurred to me the other day that the incredible ease with which we divided everything up was one more sign that Sandy and I weren't ever meant to be together."

"Really?"

"Yeah. We didn't even argue over the CDs. What was important to her wasn't important to me and vice versa. Like I said before, we just didn't want the same things."

"So, if it's not Sandy, is it work?"

"Nah. Work's fine. Better than fine, even." He squeezed my knee and got up and put on his coat. "Don't worry, peaches.

I'll suss it out. I just wish he was here to ask me one of those weird questions that would turn everything on its head and make it make sense. Although this one might be beyond him, anyway. I know I sure can't figure it out."

Jake looked up at the shelf with the strangest look on his face, part wistful and part something that looked an awful lot like anger. My tummy flip-flopped. Darn those butterflies. They were there again, and I wasn't entirely sure why.

"If there's anything I can do . . ." I stood up to walk him to the door.

"You'll be the first to know."

I was still pondering what Jake's problem was and why thinking about it too hard made the air in my lungs go all hot and thick, when my mother called to announce that they were selling their house and moving to a condo because of my father's "condition."

"What condition, Mama?" I asked. I knew it wasn't going to fly. I'd tried it at Thanksgiving, and still had to choke down a plate of those god-awful mashed potatoes.

She sighed one of those long-suffering sighs. "His heart condition, Emily. Remember going to the hospital to see him in the middle of the night?"

"Of course I remember, Mama, but I thought the doctors said Daddy's heart was okay. That those palpitations were a fluke. Like when George Bush Sr. threw up on the Japanese prime minister's shoes."

She sniffed. "It was a warning. If it's not a condition now, it will be soon enough."

It's hard to argue with logic like that.

"Besides," she continued. "I'm tired. I'm tired of keeping a house this big, and with your father's condition, I'm going to have to do the yard, too."

I didn't want to have the "what condition" conversation again. It occurred to me that if we kept having it, Mama might eventually tire of it and stop playing whatever little game she was into this way, but it wasn't likely. Once she gets hold of something like that, she's like a woman with a Prada handbag at Nordstrom's semi-annual sale. Try to get it away from her and you could lose an arm.

"You could get a service," I suggested. "A cleaning service for the house and a landscaping service for the yard."

My mother made her noise. Mama's noise is a little hard to describe. It's a cross between saying *accchhh* and loosening a big loogy from the back of your throat. It's the noise she makes when she's disgusted by something or with someone.

I've heard that noise a lot in my thirty-two years.

"I should pay someone a king's ransom to do half as good a job as I could do myself, while I stand and watch them from the kitchen window?"

"You wouldn't have to stand and watch them," I said. "You could go do something else."

"What else should I do?" she asked.

"I don't know, Mama. Read, shop, relax, go to a museum, meet a friend for lunch. Do something that doesn't make you tired."

"No wonder you have no savings!"

I decided to ignore the crack about my financial standings. I'm doing fine. I used most of Vince's insurance money to start a college fund for Abby. Social Security supplements help with the mortgage. I run a little hand to mouth during some parts of the year, but I get by. "So, have you picked a place yet?"

"Not yet. I'm looking around, though. I'm supposed to have lunch with Hannah and Ilse Kauffman over at their place next week."

"That's nice." I waited. This didn't feel like a I-just-called-to-let-you-know-my-plans phone call. She had something else she wanted.

"Before I do anything," Mama said. "I need to clean out the basement. I want you girls to come and help. We'll do it next Sunday and you can have dinner here afterward."

I thought about telling her that I would have been happy to come help clean out the basement without the histrionics over Daddy's heart and threats to sell the house I grew up in, but who am I to rain on my mother's parade?

That's Leah's job.

"Nice job with the Brennerton proposal, Emily," Karen said. "I liked the redesign of the medical office building brochure you did, too."

"Thanks," I said. Then I waited.

But she just said, "You're welcome." And then she left.

"What's with all the assisted-living condo brochures?" I whispered to Claudia.

She glanced over her shoulder and whispered back, "I'm not entirely sure. She's up to something, though."

"Who's up to something?" Leah asked. Her voice sounded like a bullhorn. She held a collection of mismatched wineglasses in her hands.

"*Sssshh,*" Claudia hissed. "We're talking about Mama."

"What about her?" Leah whispered this time, too, as she put the glasses into the box Claudia and I hovered over.

I squinted at her to gauge her reaction. "The brochures about those apartments."

"What about 'em?" Leah's voice returned to normal. "Mama's just being practical. They're not getting any younger. If they want to be the ones to make those choices, they need to check out their options now, while they're still healthy and able to make their own decisions."

Leah had a point. Our father was a scientist. While he could be completely dispassionate and objective about laser beams and subatomic particles, those skills didn't translate into his personal life. He's just a big softie and vacillates back and forth about important decisions like a giant weathervane on a windy day.

Our mother, on the other hand, cries at long-distance commercials and Christmas specials even though we're Jewish, and can be sent into a complete panic if she doesn't have enough matching silverware for a dinner party, but she can make life-changing emotional decisions with the surgical calm of a brain surgeon and the military precision of Colin Powell.

"I disagree." Claudia shook her curls as she plunked an assortment of unattractive napkin rings in with the glasses. "She's making a point or she's manipulating. Either she's trying to get Daddy to snap out of his funk by forcing him into fighting over this move, or she's trying to get us to convince her that she's not that old."

"Daddy's in a funk?" I asked. "He's seemed so cheerful lately."

"You don't think this scrapbooking thing is part of a funk?" Claudia asked.

"No. I thought it was a hobby," I said.

"I think it, along with this hiking obsession, is a very thinly disguised attempt to reconnect with his youth."

Claudia reads a lot of self-help books.

"Honestly," Leah snorted in disgust. "Not everything everyone does is aimed at something else, Claudia. Maybe Daddy just likes doing scrapbooks. Maybe Mama would just like to move to someplace where somebody else did some of the work. Even Freud said that sometimes a cigar is just a cigar."

"And sometimes a cigar is just a big fat smoking penis, Leah. That's why Freud had to say that in the first place." Claudia stuffed a wad of unevenly yellowed doilies in around the glassware.

"Leah might be right," I murmured.

They both swung around on me.

"What did you say?" Claudia demanded. For thirty-some years, I'd pretty much followed Claudia's lead if she argued with Leah. Most of the time it took two of us to combat her. I guess I surprised Claudia when I didn't automatically side with her. I surprised me, too.

I shrugged. "I know that a whole bunch of their friends have moved into those places over the past year or so, and most of them seem pretty happy about it. Hannah Kauffman even has a boyfriend."

Claudia stared at me, openmouthed. "Hannah Kauffman has a boyfriend?"

I nodded. "He used to be in some purchasing department for the state government. I guess he's got a fabulous pension and a lot of benefits and all his teeth, too. Mama said Hannah was quite smitten."

"Hannah Kauffman, a seventy-eight-year-old, half-senile, half-blind diabetic with a sex-addicted mother, can get a boyfriend and I can't?" Claudia's lower lip trembled.

"Do you really want to date a retired purchaser for the state in his early eighties, whose best physical attribute is that he has all his teeth?" Leah looked Claudia up and down. "Maybe you should hang out at the assisted-living condos. I bet there are a lot of guys with good pensions that would be willing to give you a whirl."

Claudia blew her nose on one of the tissues we were using to wrap the glasses. "No. That's not the point."

We waited for her to go on, and when she didn't, I prompted her. "What is?"

She sighed. "Every day in the ER I see these women come in. Horrible women. Disgusting women. Filthy women. Women in polyester stretch pants with gigantic rear ends and missing teeth. Women who smell like urine. They all have boyfriends. All of them." She looked at us, wild-eyed. "And I don't. What am I supposed to think about that? What am I supposed to do?"

"Knock out a few teeth and wet your pants more often?"

"That's not funny, Emily," Leah snapped.

Actually, I disagreed. It was a funny comment, just not a funny situation. I decided not to argue, however, since Claudia looked close to tears.

"I don't know what I'm doing wrong," Claudia moaned. "What's wrong with me?"

"Nothing," Leah and I said in unison. Then we both

whipped our heads around to stare at each other. This was getting creepy. If we broke into a synchronized dance routine, I was going to move to another city.

I shivered and hefted the box onto my hip. "There's nothing wrong with you, Claudia. You'll meet someone when the time is right. I'm taking this up now."

Up in the kitchen, Mama had created three huge piles of stuff. The pile by the refrigerator was destined for Goodwill. The pile by the stove was intended for the storage space she'd rented. The pile by the table, the dejected-looking pile that had slumped in on itself like a rejected suitor, was meant for the dustbin.

I gave Abby a kiss on top of the head. She'd pulled an old cracked tea set from the Goodwill pile and was having a tea party with a one-eyed, half-bald baby doll whose name when I had played with her had been Maria, and a very disreputable-looking stuffed monkey that Claudia had called Jack-O. Personally, I thought Maria was lowering herself. She could do better than Jack-O. He wasn't in her league in either the looks or the brains department. But I was happy that Abby was so busy with the tea party that she seemed to be oblivious to the screaming match going on between my parents.

"It's a perfectly good coat," my father yelled. He picked his down jacket up from the sad, dejected pile and headed toward the hall coat closet with it.

My mother breathed noisily in and out through her nose while she watched him hang it up perfectly straight on its wooden hanger and then shut the closet door. She then marched purposefully over, took the coat off the hanger, shut the closet door, and flung the coat back on the trash pile. "It's being held together with duct tape and even that's coming apart. You need a new coat."

"I don't need a new coat! I have a new coat. I'm saving it for good. What I need is some more duct tape!" he yelled, grabbing the coat back and clutching it to his chest.

"For God's sake, Gordon! What "good" are you saving the new coat for? Your funeral?"

Daddy's eyes narrowed. He kicked at the tall potty seat that my grandfather had needed after his hip surgery ten years ago, when he'd still lived with my parents, before he'd gone off to eat his borscht with heavenly sour cream. The potty seat sat in the storage pile. "This? This you're going to save, but my coat has to go into the trash?"

"That was expensive. Papa only used it for a few months. We're not getting any younger, Gordon; one of us could need it someday soon. It's not out of the question for one of us to break a hip."

The two of them both reflexively knocked on the table, oblivious to the "piece of the true cross" underpinnings of the superstition. We're equal opportunity loonies.

"All I'm saying is that if the potty seat is staying, then my coat is staying." My father's chin jutted out and he looked down his nose at my mother.

She shrugged and gave him a look that was all fake I-don't-care-what-you-do. "Fine. But then it goes to the storage shed like the potty seat."

His eyes darkened. "Then how will I get it when I need it?"

"You'll have a key. I'm just saying that if the coat stays here, then the potty seat stays here."

They glared at each other. Kind of a Jewish–Mexican standoff thing. My father blinked first. He tossed his coat on the storage pile.

"Where do you want these?" I interrupted. Maybe distracting them with glassware would get them to stop arguing. I don't know why I thought anything would ever get them to stop yelling, but I kept hoping I'd find something.

"Put it on the table, Emily. I'll sort it out in a minute."

"There's not much to sort, Mama. I don't think there's more than two or three from any given set in here."

"Ah, but I'm sure they're more worth saving than my favorite coat." My father stalked off to his study, mumbling something under his breath about needing to sort through files.

"Which sets?" Mama asked brightly as if my father hadn't just stomped out of the room in a major snit.

"The water glasses with the daisies on them and the little juice glasses with the ducks." There wasn't much left of the ducks. Most of the white had flaked off, so they were pretty much just beaks and feet.

"Oh, the duckies," Mama cooed. She crouched down next to Abby with one in her hand. "For two years at least, your mother wouldn't drink a drop of juice unless I served it in a duckie glass."

Abby took it in her hands and turned it round and round like an archaeologist holding up some ancient pot, wondering about the people who might have eaten or drunk from it. "Can I have it, Grandma?" she asked with eyes like saucers.

"Of course you can, dear," Mama said and gave her another kiss.

I had a bad feeling about this. Suddenly I had visions of

transferring all the contents of Mama's basement to my garage. Maybe I should take Daddy's coat now and be done with it. I walked down the hallway to the study. He was hunched over the filing cabinet, leafing through folders. A pile of papers strewn on the floor looked like they might be destined to go out with his coat.

"So, Daddy, how do you feel about this whole moving thing?"

He looked up at me with a confused, almost bewildered look on his face. "What moving thing?"

I hate it when he does that. It makes me think he's going senile. But he's been doing it since I was a little girl and if he wasn't senile at that point then he isn't now. He just has such exclusive focus that he can block out even the reason he's doing something while he's doing it. "This moving thing. The one that has you and Mama arguing over what to keep and what to get rid of, so you can sell this house and move into a condo near a shuffleboard court."

He smiled. I love it when I make my Daddy smile. It's a youngest child thing; I can't help it.

"I think it's great. I think this house is too big for a couple of old coots to rattle around in. I think it'll free us up."

"Free you up?"

"Sure." He closed the file drawer and opened the one below, and began leafing through those papers. "No more yard work. A lot less housework. We'll have lots more time."

"Time for what?" It hadn't occurred to me that my parents were feeling pressed for time.

"More time to get out. More time to do things. Maybe we'll finally get to travel a little."

I was stunned.

Let me explain. My father loves my mother's cooking. This sounds sweet, I know. But understand that it means that he loves *only* my mother's cooking. Anything that is cooked in a different way is not just different, it's wrong. Perhaps immoral, even. When I offered to do the Thanksgiving turkey a few years ago and said I was going to soak it in brine and then roast it breast side down, you would have thought that I'd suggested committing lewd and illegal acts with that bird that most people have to go to Thailand to see.

My mother cooks like the good 1950s housewife she was trained to be. They don't make pot roast like that in Paris. I'm pretty sure the Parisians don't even make *any* kind of pot roast.

I'm not sure he could handle foreign toilets, either. This is the man who came out of the bathroom at my house and complained that we'd hung the toilet paper improperly, because we had the paper coming over the top and it should hang down next to the wall. Once again, this wasn't just an observation about a different way of doing things. He was affronted.

Even if he might be able to find some food he could stand to choke down someplace, and a place to relieve himself of it later, he'd hate it. My father is miserable anywhere but home. My parents went to Arizona once for a little vacation. He found the endless sunshine unbearable. In Canada, he complains that they talk funny. He's the original bloom-where-you're-planted guy; transplanting him for even a short time makes his normally happy green leaves turn brown and spiteful.

"Exactly where do you want to travel, Daddy?" I asked, all innocence and blue eyes.

He threw up his hands. "Who knows? Some place exciting! Some place exotic! Maybe we'll go to the Caribbean or India or Norway. The point is, we'll be free to go without worries."

"I didn't know you wanted to go any of those places."

He leaned back in his chair and sighed. "I'm not sure I do, either, Emily. I think what your mother wants is simply to have the freedom to choose those things. She's worked hard all her life. I certainly wouldn't begrudge her that. Would you?"

The phone was ringing as I walked in my door. I raced through the dark dining room to the kitchen and grabbed it without even looking at Caller ID.

"Hello," I said. Nothing but breathing and a lot of background noise answered me. Was that a siren?

"Hello," I repeated. It would piss me off if this was one of those telemarketers with those obnoxious computer-calling devices that keeps them from saying hello until you're about ready to hang up, so that they waste even more of your time before you finally hang up on them.

"Emawee," a strangled voice said.

"What? Who is this?"

"Emawee," the voice creaked again, this time with more urgency. "Ith Cwaueea. Had acthident. Odd. Wandy. Hep."

I finally got into a position to look at the Caller ID. The call had originated from Claudia's cell phone. "Claudia? Claudia? Is that you?" I can't describe the adrenaline surge that went through my body. For a moment, there was no answer. I felt sick. My knees felt rubbery and I wasn't sure they'd hold me up anymore. I sat down.

A male voice came on the line.

"This is Detective Bob Parsons. Is this a friend or relative of Ms., uh, Claudia Simon?"

"I'm her sister. What's happened? Is she okay?"

"She'll be all right. Her car's pretty bad and she has a mild concussion. They have her strapped to a backboard mainly as a precaution. She seems very worried about her kids."

Relief flooded through me. Feeling came back to my face. I don't think I'd even noticed that it had gone numb in the previous seconds. An accident. But she was all right. Mild concussion. Nothing to it.

"Tell her I'll get Todd and Randy." They'd been spending the afternoon at a friend's house rather than take part in all the fun of cleaning out their grandparents' basement. I had the phone number. "Tell Claudia that I'll send Leah to the hospital for her. Where are they taking her?"

"Hold on. Let me check," the officer said.

I listened to muffled voices in the background. He came back on the line. "St. Elizabeth's seems the most likely bet."

"Eeew. She's not going to like that."

"She have a problem with St. E's?" the deep voice asked cautiously.

"She works there." Think about it. In the ER, they routinely slice all your clothes off when you come in. And if you think they don't talk about you later, well, then you've never hung out with someone who works in an emergency room. I've heard about more interesting tattoos and physical anomalies than I can possibly begin to share.

"Oh. I see."

Another pause. More muffled voices.

"I can't change where they take her, but I can stay with her until this, uh, Leah person comes."

"It's another sister. The Leah person, I mean."

He chuckled. It was a nice sound, all rumbly and deep. "I figured that out."

"So exactly what happened, anyway?"

"Well, we're not entirely sure yet. As near as we can tell, your sister was sitting at a stoplight behind another car when she got rear-ended. The kids in the car that hit her were going fast enough to smack her wagon into the car in front of her."

"Oh, my God. Was anyone else hurt?" A three-car pileup? That didn't sound like nothing to me.

"Mainly bumps and bruises. Actually, your sister would have probably been okay, except for . . . uh . . ." His voice trailed off, which isn't all that easy for a voice that sounds like a growl coming out of a very deep volcano.

"Except for what?"

"Well, she had a whole lot of stuff in the back of her car." There was a question in his voice even though the words weren't phrased that way.

"We were cleaning out our parents' basement. Claudia was supposed to be taking that load to a storage shed," I explained.

I heard a sigh of relief. "Oh, that explains it. We were trying to figure out why anyone would have that collection of stuff in their car. I mean, even if she'd been living out of her car, we couldn't think of any reason to have that many sets of silverware, and then there was the thing that hit her . . ."

There he went, trailing off again. Asking a question without actually asking it, and I was ready to hop right in there and tell all. This guy must be a great cop. I couldn't see his face and I was ready to confess everything.

"What thing? How did it hit her?"

He answered my second question, but not my first. "Well, our best guess is that when she was rear-ended, this thing flew out of the backseat and whacked her in the back of the head. We think it might have been sitting on an old down coat, which has a slick surface that wouldn't have given it any purchase during the impact. Anyway, when it hit her, that's when she must have bitten her tongue."

That would explain the way she was talking. Eeeew. "What thing hit her?" I asked again.

Another long pause. Getting information out of this man was not easy. "It looks like . . . well, it seems to be . . . actually, we think it's a . . . well, a giant potty seat."

I couldn't help it. I snorted. Then I laughed outright. "Claudia was concussed by Grandpa's potty seat? And it hit her because it was sitting on Daddy's down coat?"

"It appears so, ma'am."

I, for one, would make sure that our parents never, ever lived this one down.

CHAPTER TEN

A Knight in Faded Levi's

Leah

One part Harvest Wheat (#42), one part Golden Copper (#40), one part developer. Forty minutes. Making her blonder might be working. She seems really spacey these days. Or maybe just preoccupied . . .

Claudia

We're waiting for Claudia's stitches to heal.

I got to be the one to pick Claudia up from the hospital. Mama and Daddy were picking all the kids up from their various bus stops, and meeting us back at Claudia's house after I checked her out of the hospital that afternoon. Jake had offered to drive me, but I'd said no. I wanted to try and do it by myself.

We planned to eat popcorn and watch TV while Mama made spaghetti. Leah would stop by after work. It was a regular party.

I started having trouble breathing when I pulled the car into the parking garage. By instinct, I drove up to the fifth floor. No one wants to go that high up; everybody bails by the fourth floor, since they're already a floor past the covered pedestrian walkway to the main hospital.

From way too much experience with the ins and outs of St. E's, I knew the fifth floor had another, less-advertised walkway. Almost no one wanted to go that far up and walk back down, so I was nearly assured of parking close to the entrance. This had been very handy information when taking Vince to various chemo or radiation therapy appointments, especially when he was weak and having trouble walking, or that horrible week when he threw up every time he stood up and we had to carry a trash can with us so he could stop and barf every few feet.

By the time I'd gotten my Jeep wedged into a space striped too small for a Geo Metro, much less a good-size SUV, my breath bellowed in and out of my lungs as if I'd run the whole way up.

I walked down the hall of St. Elizabeth's with a horrible queasy sensation in the pit of my stomach. The dingy floor, the shabby walls, the icky disinfectant smell that didn't cover the body fluid odors it was meant to disguise were all having way more effect on me than the situation required.

I wasn't going to neurology or oncology. There would be no more waiting in the waiting room for good news that never comes. I was just picking up my sister after she spent a night being kindly ignored under the pretense of observation.

I focused on breathing in deeply through my nose and out through my mouth. It kept me from hyperventilating, but it wasn't making my stomach any less queasy.

Claudia was sitting up in her wheelchair, a bouquet of flowers in her lap, when I came into her room.

"Hey, sweetie," she said with a wave.

I rushed over to her. A big white bandage covered a good part of her forehead over her left eye. An Ace bandage was wrapped tightly around one ankle, and her foot was extended out from the wheelchair and propped on a pillow. Ironically, her cheeks had a rosy glow about them and her eyes were bright. Maybe she was running a fever.

"Oh, you poor thing!" I said, checking her forehead with my cheek for temperature.

Claudia made a dismissive gesture, pushing me away after giving me a kiss. "It's just a bump or two. I'll be fine." She hesitated and looked over my shoulder. "Emily, I'd like you to meet Bob."

I couldn't believe I'd missed him. A great big guy rose up out of the side chair by my sister's hospital bed to shake my hand. A *really* great big guy. Like Norman Schwarzkopf big. Big thick shoulders. Big wide chest. Giant hands that nearly eclipsed my man hands in his when he shook mine and said, "Bob Parsons. You must be the sister I spoke to on the phone last night, not the one who came to the hospital. Or you dyed your hair fast."

Without thinking, I said, "No. I'm the one who still has her real color."

I heard Claudia hiss behind me. "This is Emily. The youngest of us three, as I'm sure she'll let you know right away."

I blushed. It was hard to think straight with Bob in front of you like that. Bob took up a lot of space, and he did it well. He had on a plain blue dress shirt with the top few buttons undone and a white T-shirt peeking out of the V and the sleeves rolled up over his bulging forearms, and a pair of faded Levi's. A suit jacket hung over the back of his chair and he wore what looked like trail-running shoes from REI on his feet.

He wasn't a pretty boy. His eyes were a little too wary. His jaw was a little too square. The fact that apparently neither God nor genetics saw fit to grace him with a neck and decided to have his head settle directly on his wide shoulders ended any chance of him achieving pretty-boy status.

What Bob had in spades is presence. Bob had presence out the wazoo. Bob's wazoo might actually ooze presence when he wasn't looking.

I turned reluctantly back to Claudia. "Nice flowers. Did we send them?"

We all take turns doing things like sending flowers, baby presents, bar and bat mitzvah gifts, and other items. There's a floating twenty-five dollars between the three of us. Rarely do we ever stop to tot up who owes what to whom, because we know it'll all come out right in the end, so sometimes you've sent flowers or a thoughtful gift to someone without knowing it. That doesn't mean you don't get credit for it, though, and if I sent that nice bouquet to Claudia, I wanted to make sure she got to thank me.

"No. Bob brought them."

I turned back to Bob and looked at him again. I wasn't really up on the police procedure manual, but I was pretty sure that bringing bouquets for minor accident victims wasn't part of their responsibility. On the other hand, it could definitely boost their standing in public opinion polls.

As I looked him up and down again, he blushed. It was

darling. It started right at the neck of that T-shirt and crept right up his face to the bristly edges of his light brown crewcut hairline. Adorable!

I looked back at Claudia. She blushed, too! I'll be damned if she wasn't all shook up over this guy!

A tired-looking nurse bustled in with a clipboard. "Just a few items to take care of, and then we can let Ms. Simon go home." She gave Bob and me a bright, artificial smile.

"Why don't you two wait in the hallway," Claudia suggested. "Fiona will let you know when we're done."

Bob and I trooped obediently out into the hallway, where wc could hear every word about pain medications and when to check with her regular doctor anyway, but I suppose it at least gave Claudia the illusion of privacy.

I leaned back against the wall and started my deep-breathing exercises again. It's a little embarrassing, but I felt proud that my family thought I could handle picking Claudia up. I didn't want to blow it by hyperventilating in the hallway or barfing in the parking garage. Maybe I should have let Jake drive me. I always felt a little calmer when he was next to me, like I could handle things a little bit easier if he was there to back me up. It just seemed like I should be able to do this by myself. Really, it wasn't anything terrible; I just had a hard time walking into hospitals since Vince died.

Right now, however, I felt a little like I did when I was seven and Mama trusted me to set the table with the good china for the first time. To most people, it wouldn't look like an honor. But in my little seven-year-old heart, I knew better. There's no greater honor than trust. So I didn't want to drop my sister and shatter her on the floor on my way from the cabinet to the table, as it were, and I wanted to do it without assistance.

Deep breathing, however, is boring, and the frantic movements next to me soon distracted me.

Bob was twitching. When a guy that size twitches while leaning against a wall next to you, it's a little like a minor earthquake.

I'd been so busy with my own deep breathing, I hadn't considered how he might be feeling. Truly, I hadn't considered him at all. It occurred to me that if Leah were here, she'd already know his rank with the police department, his educational background, and certainly his marital status. I only knew that he'd brought my sister flowers and looked pretty nervous.

"You okay?" I asked.

He nodded and gulped. I bet if he'd had a neck, I would have been able to see his Adam's apple bobbing up and down.

"You sure?" I pressed. "I don't like hospitals, either. That's why I'm doing this breathing thing. Wanna try it?"

"It's not the hospital." He heaved his shoulders around again. "It's not that I like hospitals particularly, but they don't really bug me, either. It's, uh, well . . ."

"Yes?"

"It's your sister," he blurted out.

"Claudia?" Smart question, Emily.

"I don't quite know how to explain it. I mean, I've seen hundreds of accident victims. But when they strapped your sister to that gurney and her hair billowed out around her like a halo and she looked up at me with those big brown eyes, and that incredible skin, I just . . . I mean . . . I wanted . . ."

I waited while he gestured with those big blunt hands, as if he could grab the right word out of the air with them.

"She's single." I thought that might be helpful.

He put a hand to his forehead. "I figured that out. I was wondering more if you thought she'd mind if I asked her out. I mean, I know it's irregular. It feels funny, but on the other hand, it's not like she's part of an investigation or a witness or something."

"No," I agreed. "No, she's not." He didn't need me to talk, though. He was on his own roll.

"I was so relieved to find out she wasn't homeless, either. When I saw all the crap in the back of her car, I was afraid she was living in it and I thought, there you go again, Bob. Always falling for the broken ones."

"Nope. Just somebody whose mother can't bear to give up giant potty seats." I thought about what he'd said and something occurred to me. "Bob, do you have any siblings?"

"A younger brother and a younger sister," he rushed to tell me. "So I know exactly how you feel. I always want to shield my little brother and sister from anything bad, even though they're completely grown up now, with families of their own and everything. There's something about a brother or sister that brings that out in people. So believe me when I say that I know how you want to protect your sister. I don't drink a lot. I don't do drugs. I have a good job, even though my hours are a little weird sometimes, and I wouldn't purposefully hurt your sister for all the world."

I stared at him again. He was an oldest child. A protector. Not a spanker, not a seducer. Not an empty facade. Bob was a champion. A knight in faded Levi's.

I put my hand on his forearm. It was like grabbing a log. "I haven't talked to her, but my guess is that Claudia would like it if you asked her out."

At the Bereavement Party on Wednesday night, after the small group meeting but before the candle-lighting-and-singing thing, Joanie took me aside. She said she felt it was time for Abby and me to "close," to graduate from the group. To stop eating pizza, laughing, crying, lighting candles, and singing with them.

I was stunned speechless.

"It's time, Emily," she said kindly while I stared at her lips and wondered if I would ever have the courage to tell her that with her coloring she should go with lipstick that has a little more red in it. "There are times when one needs a group like this one to keep moving forward. Then there comes a time when a group like this can keep one from moving forward."

"We're not as together as we look," I pleaded, realizing how craven I sounded, but not being able to stop myself from begging. "We're still really, really sad."

"Emily," Joanie remonstrated. "Stop."

"But I don't want to leave," I wailed.

Joanie started to nibble on those coral lips a little. I think I was making her a little nervous. "Well, of course we wouldn't throw you out, but I think it's time. Think about it, Emily."

"A man touched my hand and I practically flung a table over. That doesn't sound like a well woman, does it?"

"But you went on the date, Emily. That was a big step."

I stood there with tears welling up in my eyes. "But I don't want to close," I repeated.

She put her arms around me and held me while I cried.

"I know you don't want to close, sweetheart," Joanie whispered. "When you've been feeling a certain way for a long time—even if that way is sad—it's comforting, because it's familiar. Learning to feel a new way—even if it's happy—is scary because it's new and unpredictable. You can do it, though. You can be that brave for Abby and for yourself."

"No." I shook my head vehemently. "No, I can't. I don't want to and I won't."

"Emily, you don't know how much you've changed since you started coming here. You walked in here eighteen months ago, acting like you were fine. You were going to work, washing your hair, taking care of your daughter and your house. You thought you were done with it all, but you were going through the motions of living as if you were in a trance.

"You're through that, now. I can see it on your face every time you turn around, with every word you say, every bite of pizza you eat. You're really here now. You're experiencing the world around you. You're awake and aware and noticing things you haven't probably noticed since Vince was diagnosed with his brain tumor.

"It's time to go out and do that in the real world all the time. To savor all the pizzas the world has to offer. Don't limit yourself to Papa John's Veggie Delite on the second Wednesday of every month."

The wonderful thing about finding a good support group isn't the stuff you actually say, it's all the stuff you don't have to say. These are people who have walked in your shoes.

So if they already know most of what you need to say anyway, why bother, right? The answer to that is, because you need to say it. You need to lay the terrible feelings and hurts and fears out on the table and look at them under the annoying flickering fluorescent light of a church basement, and you need to do it with people you know won't judge you. They won't judge you because they understand what you have to say.

The terrible thing about finding a good support group is that because they already know what you need to say, they also know when you're full of it.

So nobody believed me when I said I wasn't ready to close. They just hugged me and told me they'd miss me.

CHAPTER ELEVEN

Happy Freaking Holidays

Leah

One part Harvest Wheat (#42), one part Golden Copper (#40), one part developer. Forty-five minutes. We're going for an updo tonight. It's one I saw in *Cosmo*. I know, I know. I'm way too old for it, but I make up for it with my immaturity.

Claudia

One part Light Ash Brown (#32), one part Apricot Glaze (#38), one part developer. Thirty minutes. She had to tell Bob that she dyes her hair. He accepted the news graciously. What was she worrying about?

You know, the lighting in here is terrible," Leah said from behind Claudia.

Claudia didn't even bother to turn around. "You say that every time we do this here."

"I say it every time because it's true."

Claudia sighed, but didn't argue. Leah reached for the brush in the bowl of dye.

"Careful, Leah. You're dripping," Claudia warned.

"Do you want me to put down a towel?" I offered. I didn't

have much to do; we weren't having snacks. Leah and I were both going to our office Christmas parties afterward, and Claudia was going to order pizza for her, Bob, Todd and Randy, and Abby. I was going to put Leah's hair up for her as soon as she was done with Claudia.

"If you put a towel down, she wouldn't have anything to bitch about," Leah said in a sour voice.

This is not entirely true. Claudia complains nonstop about having her hair combed and routinely begs Leah to dye her roots without combing it through. So she'd always have that.

I got the pink towel with the ratty edges out of the bag anyway and put it down under Claudia's chair. Claudia looked down to see what I was doing.

"Hold still," Leah commanded.

"You're pulling my hair," Claudia cried.

"I am not," Leah snapped.

"You two need a time-out," I said.

That shut them up long enough for Leah to finish Claudia and then clean up.

We sent Claudia off to shower and I started on Leah's updo.

"You're going alone to your office Christmas party?" Leah searched my reflection's eyes in the mirror. We'd moved to Claudia's bedroom, and Leah was seated on a chair.

I was standing over her, pinning tendrils of hair into little ringlets. "Yeah. Why?"

She was not going to her office Christmas party alone. She was going with Joe's replacement, Max. As near as I could tell, they were entirely interchangeable. Nice looking. Well groomed. Responsible jobs. Great buns. We were not going to introduce Max to Ilse Kauffman.

"Emily, you don't go alone to your office Christmas party; it makes you look pathetic." Leah tried to turn to look at me directly, but I kept a good strong grip on the lock of hair I was twirling and she couldn't quite do it. Not if she didn't want a bald patch on the back of her skull.

"What does pathetic mean, Mommy?" Abby asked, handing me another bobby pin. She was acting as my assistant. To dress for the part, she had selected a pink leotard with a tutu and a headband that had bee antennae attached to it. I never throw out Halloween costumes; they can provide years of enjoyment.

"Like a loser," I told her.

Leah gasped. "That's not what I meant. Ouch!"

She'd tried to turn again. Fool.

"No, but it is what you implied," I said while I continued to twist tendrils with great calm. "Besides, it's too late to do anything about it now. I'm leaving for my party about ten minutes after you leave here."

The others had rented all three Indiana Jones movies to go with their take-out pizza. I would have rather stayed with them. I was pretty sure I could ditch the party in time to get back for the third movie. I never liked the second one anyway, and Claudia would no more show them out of order than she would sprout wings and fly.

"Besides," I continued, "it's a big step for me to even go to the stupid thing. I haven't been since Vince got sick."

Leah tried to shake her head and hissed a little as I wouldn't let her. "You have no idea how much damage you do to your career path by skipping things like that, Emily. It makes you look like you're not a team player."

"Yeah, well, I think being incompetent probably had more negative impact on my career path than skipping the Christmas party."

"What does incompetent mean, Mommy?" Abby asked.

I took the bobby pin from her. "It means being a loser."

"You shouldn't say things like that to her," Leah remonstrated, but she didn't try to turn her head again. I can win small battles if I try hard.

"What if she believed you?" Leah asked. "It's unfair to confuse a little girl like that."

I sighed. She was right. I let go of her head.

Leah swiveled around on her chair so she was eye to eye with Abby. "Your mommy is not a loser. Nor is she incompetent, which actually means that you're not capable of doing your job. She had a tough time going back to work after your daddy died, and she made some mistakes. She's been trying very hard to do better, and everybody understood why she made the mistakes and forgave her."

She swiveled back and I went back to pinning tendrils up on her head. "It's still too late to do anything about it," I pointed out.

"You could call Jake," Leah suggested.

"You should have asked him this morning, Mommy," Abby added helpfully.

Leah's and my gaze met in the mirror again. "You saw Jake this morning?" she asked.

"Sure. It's Saturday," Abby chirped.

"And that means . . . ?" Leah's eyebrows climbed her forehead a fraction or so.

"It doesn't mean anything," I said quickly.

Abby began to dance around us, pausing occasionally to admire herself in the full-length mirrors on the closet doors. "Saturday morning means . . ." Pose. Pause. Twirl again. ". . . that Uncle Jake stops by . . ." Pose. Pause. Twirl. ". . . with a yummy muffin for me and a big tall coffee for Mommy." Pose. Pause. No twirl, just a little bow.

Now the corners of Leah's lips threatened to climb up with her eyebrows. "Uncle Jake stops by every Saturday morning with coffee and baked goods? How nice of Uncle Jake! What does Uncle Jake get in return?"

Abby cocked her head to one side while she thought. Her brows drew down in concentration. "Get? He gets to spend time with us, I guess." She pirouetted away, bored with her assistant status.

"It's not like it sounds," I said. "Since he and Sandy broke up, I think weekends are a little lonely. That's all. He's just looking for a little . . ."

"Companionship?" Leah suggested, no longer fighting the big wide smile on her lips.

"Maybe."

"Just remember, dear," she said, clearly relishing every word. "There comes a time in a relationship when a man wants more than just companionship."

I had no comeback. After all, picking out produce was becoming an erotically charged experience for me lately.

Twenty minutes later, we stood side by side in front of Claudia's mirror.

Leah looked fantastic. She had on a bright red halter dress covered with sequins. Her hair (if I do say so myself) looked charming, half pinned up with ringlets spilling around.

I looked presentable. Okay, a little better than presentable, but not glittery and fantastic. I'd managed to find a long, midnight blue velvet dress with a wide scoop neck that fit like a glove down to my hips and then flared out wide. I hadn't wanted to fuss with my hair. I figured I wouldn't stay at the party long enough to make it worth my while, so I had it long and straight like it always is.

"This better be the best night of your whole year," I told Leah.

"Why?" she asked, examining herself in the mirror, turning this way and that. "I'm just going to the office Christmas party, Emily. It's not Cinderella going to the ball."

I caught her gaze in the mirror. "Because you've basically sacrificed the other three hundred and sixty-four nights for this one, babe. I just hope it ends up being worth it."

Abby danced back in. "Aunt Claudia's ordering pizza. She wants to know if you want any."

"No," Leah and I said in unison.

We turned to look at each other. The real each others, not the mirror ones.

"What is with you these days, Emily?" Leah demanded.

I shrugged. "I don't know what you're talking about." But I knew exactly what she meant. I'd been talking back, not taking suggestions. Being stubborn and smart-alecky. Basically, turning back into myself. Well, maybe not the same self I'd been. I'd seen too many things I hadn't wanted to look at and done too many things I didn't think I'd be capable of. The road back to the old Emily was permanently blocked by those obstacles. But I could, I thought, find my way back to some place closer to her than where I'd been residing.

"Well, Grandpa would have said you're full of P and V, my dear," Leah observed. Then she smiled, and as she swept past me she said, "It's kind of nice."

"What's P and V, Mommy?"

I smiled at Abby. "Piss and vinegar, my dear. Piss and vinegar."

I have the best big sister in the world.

Ah, New Year's Eve. That night of the year when you get to confront exactly how much of a loser you are.

I planned to spend New Year's Eve with my child and my parents at their place in Edmonds. Mama promised to make brownies. We were basically going for the chocolate.

Okay, I admit it. We were going for the company, too. I'd wanted to wear sweatpants and bring my slippers with me, but Abby begged me to wear the matching velvet overalls she'd somehow managed to wheedle me into buying on one of our recent shopping sprees. She looked precious in them. I suspected that I looked like a pregnant twelve-year-old in them.

My mother confirmed my suspicion by gushing over my outfit as soon as I took off my coat. She loves me in oufits that make me look like a pregnant twelve-year-old.

Loser girl. Loser outfit. It made perfect sense.

I went to the kitchen to have a brownie. It took only one bite to know that they were low-fat. Great—even loser brownies.

My nonloser sisters with their nonloser dates were planning on stopping by before they went off on their nonloser evenings.

Claudia and Bob got there first. Todd and Randy were both off at overnights at different friends' houses. At thirteen and eleven, they were old enough to be left alone for the evening, but I don't think Claudia would have done it on New Year's. She's pretty watchful. But for the happy accident of invitations to houses with trustworthy parents, she'd be having a loser fest with me at Mama and Daddy's, instead of making a cameo appearance.

They were going for dinner and dancing. Bob apparently danced divinely, being quite light on his feet for a big guy. Claudia had on a black suede skirt that went from her narrow little waist all the way down to her ankles, and a glittery sequiny top. She'd pinned her hair up in one of those loose buns that look so sexy when your hair is curly and starts to come down.

I'd pulled my long straight hair back into a barrette.

"Nice outfit, Emily," Bob said. "It makes you look so, uh, young."

"Thanks, Bob," I said. I went to the kitchen and got another brownie. I heard Leah and Max arrive. I looked in the freezer. Nonfat frozen yogurt: cappuccino vanilla swirl. Loser ice cream for the top of my loser brownie.

Maybe I'd stick my head in the microwave.

"Emily, come out of the kitchen. Your sister is here," my mother yelled.

I sighed and went out. Leah looked almost as good as Claudia. She had on tight black pants and a plunging halter top, also glittery and covered with sequins.

Leah would have looked as good as Claudia if she hadn't had a funny, tight-lipped expression on her face. Every time

Bob touched Claudia's hand, she glowed. Leah didn't let Max touch her hand. At least not in front of us.

Leah kissed my cheek. "You look so sweet and pretty, honey."

I rolled my eyes.

She laughed.

I stuck my tongue out at her as soon as her back was turned, and grinned when I heard Max whisper to her, "Exactly how much younger than you is Emily?"

Claudia put her arm around me and whispered in my ear, "Relax. In five years, Abby will not only not want to wear matching outfits with you, she won't even want to be seen with you. And certainly not on New Year's Eve."

My father poured champagne for everyone except Abby. He had a bottle of sparkling cider for her. "Might as well start with the good stuff while we can still taste it." He meant while we were still awake.

It didn't totally suck, which was a relief. To my dad, the "good stuff" is anything that costs more than nine bucks at the grocery store. Still, it had bubbles and I like that a lot in a wine.

While we sipped, my mother sidled over to me. "Do you think your sister is wearing a bra?" she whispered in my ear.

"Which one?"

"Leah."

I looked at Leah's halter top. She'd lost more weight recently and the top hung loosely on her. She looked like a fashion model. Another reason she's a difficult sister: always working to keep that weight on. "I don't think so," I whispered back to Mama, hoping it would end there. The last thing I wanted to do was sit and contemplate the fact that my older sister was the one with the fantastic figure who was going out without a bra on New Year's Eve.

But my mother has strong opinions about foundation garments. "Don't you think she should?" Her whisper wasn't exactly that whispery anymore.

"Not with that top," I observed. I couldn't imagine a bra that you could wear under that top. I don't think you could even get away with Band-Aids over your nipples with that top.

"Which top?" Daddy asked.

My mother blushed. She hadn't realized how nonwhispery she'd gotten.

I said, "Leah's top."

"That's a top?" he asked. "It looks more like a handkerchief with glitter stuck to it."

"It's a top, Daddy," Leah said, lips tight.

Max blushed. "I think she looks very nice."

"Gordon, don't embarrass Leah in front of her friend," Mama said in a warning voice.

"You have children, Matt?" my father asked, completely ignoring my mother.

"Max. His name is Max," Leah hissed.

Max said no to the children question.

"Well, someday you might have a daughter." My father propped himself up against the mantelpiece, one elbow up, and gestured at the three of us with his champagne. "Then you'll know that what Leah has on is not a top. And personally, I doubt if she's wearing a bra."

Did I mention that our family doesn't hold its liquor well? The good news is that my father's decision to start waxing eloquent on the trials and tribulations of raising three daughters prompted the happy couples to immediately start off on their respective evenings. At least I didn't have to sit and watch my sisters being nonloser-esque any longer.

We turned the television on to watch the MTV countdown. Abby and I started a game of Monopoly. My parents went to sleep on the couch. I tried to remember how I'd spent last New Year's Eve. I'm pretty sure it was an identical scenario. Daddy might have fallen asleep in the armchair instead of on the couch, but otherwise it was the same.

By 10:30, Abby and I had finished the pan of brownies and she owned Park Place, Boardwalk, Marvin Gardens, North Carolina, Pacific Avenue, Ventnor Avenue, Atlantic Avenue, Illinois, Indiana, Kentucky, New York, and the Reading Railroad. I had the other three railroads, both utilities, and the light blue properties. They're my favorite because they match my eyes. Abby's favorites are the ones that get her lots of money. She's a good little capitalist and way better at staying focused on the game than I am.

We decided to go ahead and eat the nonfat cappuccino vanilla swirl. We also decided not to use bowls. My mother snored gently on the couch, mouth slightly agape. She'd never know.

The doorbell rang.

I shoved the ice cream under the coffee table just as my mother gave a big startle and jumped up, saying, "What is it? Who's there? Where are we?"

My father opened one eye. "Who's where?"

"I'll get it," I said, heading toward the door. "Were you expecting anyone?"

They certainly hadn't been expecting Jake. I hadn't been expecting Jake. I'm not sure Jake had been expecting Jake.

"What are you doing here?" I asked as I took his coat.

He sighed. "I was over at Tom and Carolyn's party."

I nodded. They'd invited me, but I knew they didn't expect me to show up. It wasn't a kid-friendly thing. It occurred to me now that I probably could have left Abby with my parents and gone to the party, at least for a little while, but I hadn't even considered it.

"Not a good party?"

He shook his head, looking a little confused. "It was a great party. Everybody laughing, eating, drinking, dancing. I just had to leave."

"Oooh," I said, wondering what it might be like to go to a great party again, or to even go to any party that my parents weren't also attending. "I know what you mean. I hate those parties with laughing, eating, drinking, and dancing. That's why I come here, too."

He laughed, then his brows creased again. "It didn't feel right. I couldn't quite get in the groove. I knew you'd be here, so I thought I'd stop by to wish you and Abby and your folks a happy new year. I hope it's okay."

"You know it is."

He smiled at me.

My knees felt wobbly and I wondered why. I'd had only one glass of champagne and that had been hours ago.

"Nice outfit, by the way." He ran a finger down the strap of my overalls. It made me shiver. "Can I take you out for ice cream later?"

"You can try," I said, turning to head back into the living room, in part to hide the shiver and also because I wasn't exactly sure where it had come from. "But it's under the coffee table and I don't think we'll both fit."

"I'm not going to even try to figure that out," he said as he followed me in.

By the time we made it into the living room, my parents had gone back to sleep. They actually looked pretty cute that way, side by side, little snores and grunts emitting from their open mouths from time to time. At least they weren't fighting.

We pulled the ice cream out from under the coffee table, and I sent Abby to the kitchen for another spoon (I am not a complete heathen, after all). Jake, after assessing the situation, decided to team up with me for the rest of the Monopoly game. There wasn't much he could do, though. The damage from my thoughtless and profligate spending had already been done.

"I hope you're doing better with your real money than you are with this game," he said. Brows creased, he lay on his side on the floor, propped up on one elbow, trying to add up in his head whether or not mortgaging Mediterranean, Baltic, St. Charles, and Tennessee would net us enough to stay in the game. We'd already sold all my houses back to the bank.

"I don't handle it that much," I admitted. "I pretty much handed it all over to Derek Zaretsky."

His head came up and he shot me a look of sheer surprise.

I threw my hands up in the air in a gesture of defeat. "I know. He's a complete nudge, but he's a wizard with money."

Jake laughed. "I'm surprised he hasn't proposed yet."

"I think he's waiting for my portfolio to become more stable." I'd been sitting tailor-style on the floor. I brought my knees up higher and wrapped my arms around them.

"The ice cream's all gone, Mommy," Abby said sadly.

She looked like an advertisement warning kids against sugar. Her ponytail was askew. She'd taken off both shoes and one sock. She had chocolate smeared across her face and ice cream splatters down the front of her overalls, which now had one strap undone. She burped.

"What did Mommy teach you about empty ice cream containers?" I asked in the most sickly sweet tone I could pull up.

Abby looked thoughtful for a moment and then brightened. "To throw them out before Grandma sees them, but to be sure not to throw out the spoons!"

"Good girl!"

She trotted off to the kitchen, bouncing the empty container against her leg. I hoped she'd remember about the spoons when she got to the sink.

Jake shook his head. "And the Mother of the Year Award slips through your grasp once again."

"It wouldn't, if that damn Russian judge would vote fairly. People should get their priorities in line."

Jake looked at me, his face suddenly serious. "Do you think you have your priorities in line, Emily?"

I searched his face for clues of where he was going. Sudden bouts of New Year's introspection weren't a Jake thing, under normal circumstances. "Yes, I do. I've had to get them in line. What about you?"

"That's one of the things I'm trying to figure out." Still sitting on the floor, propped on one hand, he leaned toward me.

"What things aren't in line?" I asked.

He grimaced. "Where certain lines are, for instance. Which ones you can cross and which ones you can't. Which ones you might be able to cross but then regret it, if you couldn't get back to the other side."

I leaned toward him. Dick Clark started counting down the seconds to midnight. Jake's face was so close I could smell his pepperminty soapy smell, almost feel the rasp of his beard against my face. My breath caught in my throat.

"It's midnight! It's midnight! Grandma! Grandpa! Wake up! It's midnight!"

Abby charged from the kitchen door and launched herself onto Jake's back. *Whump!* Leaning forward and not anticipating a full-body attack, his balance wasn't quite what it usually was, and he landed facedown in my crotch just as my parents jumped up to wish us all a happy new year.

I'm not sure, but from the look on his face, Jake had just gotten pushed across one of those lines before he was quite ready to leap.

CHAPTER TWELVE

Too Many Ironies in the Fire

Leah

One part Harvest Wheat (#42), one part Golden Copper (#40), one part developer. Forty-five minutes. Being a blonde is good. Being a blonde who kicks ass is even better, even if the ass-kicking is hypothetical.

Claudia

One part Light Ash Brown (#32), one part Apricot Glaze (#38), one part developer. Thirty minutes. Her hair almost matches the glow on her face. She's never been prettier.

This isn't as much fun without Claudia." I slit open a soybean pod with my thumbnail and popped some soybeans in my mouth. Leah's idea of an appropriate post-root-dyeing, movie-watching snack was edamame. You know, those soybeans they serve you at sushi bars? Low fat, high protein, healthy, healthy, healthy. *Blecchhh.*

"Thanks, Em. It's great to hang out with you, too."

I kicked her. It wasn't a hard stretch, since she was on the other end of the couch. I actually had to work *not* to kick her. "I didn't mean it like that."

"I know." She sighed. "Everything's sparklier when she's here."

"And now she's sparkling for Bob and leaving us here to be unsparkly all by ourselves."

Leah gave me a sharp look. "You don't think we can be sparkly? I could sparkle if I felt like it. I just don't feel like it right now."

She is sooooo competitive. I'm glad I'm the baby and not the oldest.

"Me, neither."

We settled back on our respective cushions.

"Don't you think it's interesting that she got those feng shui books, rearranged her house, and then like instantly met Bob?" I asked.

"It's a coincidence, Emily." Leah searched through the afghan covering her for the remote control.

"What if there aren't any coincidences? What if it was fate?" I shifted and felt the remote with my hip, and pulled it out from under me. Leah grabbed it from me. "Let's fast-forward to the part where she sings that song while she's sitting on the rock in the snow, and watch it with the sound turned off," I suggested.

I'd done Leah's roots for her tonight for the first time. Since Claudia wasn't there to do, we had some extra time and we were watching *The Bodyguard,* whose main amusement value to me is counting how many of Whitney Houston's molars you can see when she sings. I'm not sure I've ever seen such a skinny woman open her mouth that wide.

"Nah. I want to see the part where the sister confesses that she's so jealous that she hired a hit man to kill Whitney." Leah pulled the afghan up over her shoulders and kept a death grip on the remote control. Why did it bother me, and yet not surprise me, that that was her favorite scene?

"Okay. We can do that if we get to watch her sing the song twice, once with sound and once without."

Leah's eyes narrowed for a moment while she thought. She looked like Abby trying to decide between chocolate cookie dough ice cream and rocky road. "Deal," she said finally.

The phone rang. Leah looked over at the Caller ID box.

I paused the movie. "Who is it?"

"I don't know. It says 'unavailable.'"

"Well, if they're unavailable to us, then let's be unavailable to them," I said with great superiority.

Leah gave me a withering look. "What if it's Mama or Daddy calling from a hospital payphone? What if it's Ed McMahon telling me I'm a millionaire? What if it's George Clooney asking me out on a date?"

I shrugged. "You wanna answer it, go right ahead. I didn't want to watch the movie with the sound on anyway." I grabbed the remote back and hit the mute button with a flourish.

She picked up the phone. "Hello."

She sat up straight. "Claudia? Why did you come up as unavailable on my Caller ID?"

She put her head in her hands. I nudged her with my toe. "What'd she say?"

Leah covered the mouthpiece with her hand. "She said it's because she isn't available anymore. She's taken."

I mimed sticking my fingers down my throat and gagging.

"You're coming now?" Leah said back into the phone. "Fine. See you in a few." She hung up.

"I thought she was with Bob," I said.

Leah shrugged. "He got paged and had to go. She's on her way over."

Within a half an hour Claudia had arrived, so we decided to go ahead and do her roots.

My sisters donned their sacred vestments and I scoured Leah's refrigerator for something to eat that had a high-fat or processed sugar content.

"Does Bob getting called away like that bug you, Claudia?" I asked.

"That's his job," she said. "It's part of who he is."

"Oh. So it's okay that he has irregular hours? That he's in and out at all times of the day and night?"

"Emily, he's a cop. He goes when he has to. What are you getting at?" Claudia sounded annoyed. I didn't blame her; I was trying to be annoying.

"Oh, nothing really. I just thought you felt strongly about a family needing a schedule," I said airily.

Claudia didn't seem to want to comment on that one.

"How are things going with Max?" I asked Leah.

She shook her head. "No more Max."

"No more Max?" I looked over at Claudia to see if she'd known about this. She looked as surprised as I did.

"He seemed nice at New Year's," I said. I knew it was an inane thing to say, but nobody else was saying anything.

"Yep. He did." Leah agreed. Then she kept on combing.

I was a little frustrated at the lack of forthcoming details. Claudia seemed bizarrely content to sit and be combed out, which was annoying because she can get details on anything from anyone about the most personal and embarrassing subjects just by looking at them. She wasn't interested in helping this time, I guess.

"So that means he wasn't actually nice," I said.

"Nope," she said with what seemed strangely like satisfaction. "He was a prick."

"Oh."

The comb snagged in Claudia's curls and she yelped.

"This would be a lot easier if you'd let me add in the conditioner," Leah pointed out.

"You know the color doesn't take as well with conditioner," Claudia said.

"How did you find out he was a prick?" I asked.

"I passed out."

This finally got Claudia's attention. She turned in her chair to look up at Leah. "You did what?"

"It's not a big deal. I got a little dehydrated. I went for a long run and didn't drink enough. It's not that weird or uncommon. It's happened to me before."

Claudia's eyes narrowed. "You haven't been eating enough, either. You're losing weight. You're not taking care of yourself. What's going on? How many times has it happened before?"

"Nothing's going on. I just forgot to take a water bottle with me and then I was out longer than I'd expected, and I didn't stoke back up enough before I met Max for dinner." She shoved Claudia's head back around a little more roughly than I thought strictly necessary.

"So you passed out. How does that make Max a prick?" Claudia asked.

Sometimes it's best not to delve too far into motivations. At least not if you want to find out what actually happened first. Although Leah did look a little on the thin side. And now that I was looking, she seemed a little pinched, too.

"Didn't he catch you before you fell?"

"He caught me. And took me home. Which was stupid, because I didn't need to go home. I needed about a liter of water."

"So he's a prick because he took you home?"

"No. He's stupid because he took me home."

Claudia yelped again. "Do we have to comb it through?"

"Stop whining," Leah commanded. "You know we have to comb it through or there'll be big chunks that get nothing on them. It's the price you pay for curly hair."

"So why's he a prick?" I asked.

She sighed and stopped combing. I got the impression she was a lot angrier than she wanted to let on and maybe a little embarrassed, too. "We got back here. We sat down. He asked what was wrong. I told him I thought I was dehydrated. He asked if I might be pregnant."

Claudia turned around. Leah didn't shove her back this time. "What did you say?"

"What could I say? I told him that I wasn't!"

"You aren't, are you?" Claudia asked.

I can't believe the stuff she gets away with asking. If I asked Leah if she was pregnant, she'd smack me for sure. She gave Claudia an exasperated look and said, "Of course I'm not pregnant. I told you; I was dehydrated."

Both Claudia and I let out breaths that I sure didn't know I was holding. Then I realized we still didn't understand the Max story yet. "So he's a prick for asking if you might be pregnant?"

"No!" she yelled. "He's a prick because about an hour later, I asked him what he would have done if I'd said that I was pregnant, and he said he'd want to know if the baby was really his!"

It's rare that a room holding my sisters and me is actually silent. This was one of those occasions.

I couldn't believe my ears. From Claudia's slack-jawed face, my guess was she couldn't believe hers, either. Finally, I broke the silence. "He said that? He said that to you? He's not just a prick. He's a prick . . . a prick . . ." I cast through my mind for a word bad enough.

"A prick mongrel," Claudia suggested. "A prick-and-a-half. A giant hippo prick. A purple and green giant hippo prick."

I felt our point had been made. "What she said."

"More to the point," Claudia said. "What did you say?"

Leah blushed a little. "I kind of went off at him."

This was going to be good. I just knew it. "What did you do?"

"I told him that it most certainly *would* have been his baby, and that I didn't appreciate the implication that it might not be."

"And what did he do then?"

"He got all flustered, and asked why I was getting so mad about a hypothetical situation."

"You're kidding," Claudia said. "He didn't understand what he'd said wrong?"

"Oh, I'm pretty sure he knew what he'd said was wrong. He just wasn't ready to admit it was wrong."

"Are they ever?" Claudia sighed.

"He said any man would have had the same thought, especially since the situation was, as he had already said, hypothetical. So I explained to him that he was most certainly the hypothetical father of this hypothetical baby, and that if he didn't want even hypothetical responsibility for it, I would go out and get a hypothetical lawyer and sue his hypothetical ass off."

"And then what?"

"I showed him the hypothetical door."

So, Abby and I attended our final Bereavement Party. Abby seemed fine. It's hard to tell with her sometimes; she is her father's daughter and has a great poker face. I can usually tell when she's stressed, though, just like I knew when Vince was uptight about something. Of course, with Vince it didn't generally take the form of wetting his bed at night.

Me? Well, I kept it together pretty well until the very last part. That singing-and-candle-lighting thing always sends me. Everyone stands in a circle holding hands, with a candle in the center of the circle. We all sing this song about how it's better to light one little candle than to be alone in the dark.

Usually I sniffle a little. It doesn't matter how many times I've heard the song, it makes me cry. I also cry at "The Star Spangled Banner" and Abby's elementary school's song, especially the part where they sing that a school is not just a building. I can't even tell you the words to any of them right now without embarrassing myself with a sniffle, so you can imagine what the candle-lighting song does to me.

To make matters worse, the kids had been asked to bring

mementos of the person that had died. All around me were little children clutching worn cowboy boots and tattered pictures and well-washed T-shirts and watches to their skinny little chests. It was just an assortment of old stuff like you'd see at a garage sale or out on the curb for the Salvation Army to pick up, but to these kids these were treasures. I looked at Abby sitting with one of Vince's Mariners caps in her lap, the one she was wearing in one of her favorite pictures of her and her dad at a baseball game, and I felt my heart break all over again.

I started to cry for real. Christine threw her arms around me and started to cry, too. In a matter of minutes, we were all on the floor in a heap, sobbing our hearts out. Kind of a group catharsis.

But you know, I walked out of there feeling like I'd done what I'd come in there to do.

CHAPTER THIRTEEN

We Are Reminded of How Little Hair Color Actually Matters

Emily, I have breast cancer."

"What?" I could have sworn that Claudia had just told me that she had breast cancer. Since that simply could not be the case, maybe I needed to have my ears checked.

"I have breast cancer, Emily," Claudia repeated.

Okay. So I'd heard wrong twice in a row. Maybe someone she knew had breast cancer. "Who has breast cancer?" I asked.

"*I* do." To be honest, she sounded like she was getting a little miffed at me.

"No." That was the only response I could think of. "That is not okay with me."

Claudia sighed. "No one asked for my approval, either. Trust me, I wouldn't have given it."

"But . . . but, how did you find out? Did you find a lump? You didn't say anything!"

She started to cry. "When I went in for my annual exam, my doctor wanted to get a baseline mammogram on me. They saw a lump. They did a fine needle aspiration right there in the office. No big deal, they said. Probably nothing, they said. They just gave me the results yesterday. I'm going to have surgery next week. They'll try to do a lumpectomy if they can get a clean margin around the tumor, but they might have to do a mastectomy."

"No," I said again. "No. No. No. No."

"Emily, that's not going to change anything."

I knew that. I maybe knew it better than she did. I couldn't help letting the universe know exactly how I felt about it, though. And what I felt was *no*. Not acceptable. Not tolerable.

"No," I said. Then I hung up the phone and cried.

After half a box of Kleenex or so, I picked up the phone to call the one person who would know exactly what I was feeling, the one other person I knew who would feel as angry and upset as I did.

If Leah said hello when she answered, I couldn't make it out through the sobs.

"She talked to you?" I sniveled.

"Uh-huh," was the muffled response.

I knew instantly that Claudia had called her first. Not just because Leah was already in full hysterical sob mode, either. Claudia always calls Leah first. Mama always calls Leah first, too; then she calls Claudia. I'm always the last to know anything.

I suddenly remembered that this wasn't about me. "What are we going to do, Leah? What can we do?"

I might as well have thrown cold water in her face. The sobs stopped almost instantly. "We're going to do what we always do. We're going to love one another and take care of one another the best we know how. What else is there, anyway?"

What else indeed? Before I could formulate a response, my call waiting beeped at me. "Just a second, Leah. Let me see who it is." I changed lines.

"Stop talking about me behind my back," Claudia said. "It's one of the things I hated most about telling everybody. I knew you'd all immediately call each other and start talking about me. I bet Ma is talking to Aunt Nancy right now. Her line is busy."

I froze. "What makes you think I'm talking about you?"

"Leah's line is busy and you can't lie worth a damn."

"Hold on a second." I clicked back to the first line. "Leah, it's Claudia on the other line. She wants us to stop talking about her."

"Tell her to stop being paranoid."

I clicked back over. "Claudia, Leah says to stop being paranoid."

"Tell her it's not being paranoid if I'm right."

I switched lines again. "Claudia says she has good reason to be paranoid, and if you want to tell her anything else get off your ass and come over here. I'm going to tell her the same thing."

"Okay." Leah snuffled.

"And Leah," I said.

"Yes?"

"Bring cinnamon rolls. Lots of them."

I told Claudia to grab the boys and get in the car, and I even called Mama and Daddy. I practically hung up the phone on my mother as she argued that her house was the better place to meet. When will she understand that until our children are older, the best place to get together is the place that has video games? The doorbell rang.

I stared at it for a second. Leah's fast, but she's not that fast. Then Jake's face peeked around the side window. His brows creased and he rang the doorbell again. I let him in.

"Are you experimenting with telekinesis?" he asked, handing me my latte.

"Huh?"

"Well, most people don't just stare at the door when the doorbell's ringing. They actually answer it. I thought maybe you were trying to open it with your prodigious mental powers."

I laughed, just a little. I couldn't quite summon up a real laugh. It sounded weird and echoey to my own ears. I could tell Jake noticed. His brows furrowed again.

"Emily, what's wrong?"

I stared at him. I couldn't say the words out loud. I wouldn't say them. Maybe if I didn't say them, it wouldn't be real. It wouldn't be happening. Maybe I also couldn't say them because my chin was trembling so much.

"Is it Abby? Is Abby okay?"

Oh, sweet Jake. The first thing he thought of was Abby. I shook my head yes.

"Then what? What is it?"

I said it then, right out loud. "Claudia has cancer."

And then I was crying. He tried to hold me, but I couldn't

let him. I felt too stiff, too brittle, like if he held me I might break into a thousand little pieces that I could never put back together again. So he led me to the couch, found a box of tissues for me, and sat next to me, patting my back until Leah got there with the cinnamon rolls.

CHAPTER FOURTEEN

When the Going Gets Tough, the Tough Go Shopping

Leah

One part Apricot Glaze (#38), one part Golden Copper (#40), one part developer. Forty-five minutes. Added conditioner, too. She seemed a little brittle. Her hair did, too.

Claudia

One part Light Ash Brown (#32), one part Apricot Glaze (#38), one part developer. Thirty minutes. We asked her if she wanted to skip it, but she said she couldn't stand the thought of those snooty surgical techs talking about her gray roots when she was under anesthesia. She's not allowed to wear toenail polish, but we gave her a nice manicure, too.

I picked my parents up to go shopping. My mother was dressed for a full-out suburban commando raid on the mall—tasteful pantssuit, sensible shoes (by Rockport, of course), and pearls.

My father, on the other hand, was dressed for a back country assault on a big climb. His nylon canvas pants had pockets everywhere. There were slant pockets in front with special little change pockets with zippers. The back pockets had Velcro closures. The side pockets had little plastic clips hanging from the zipper tabs. The legs zipped off in case he got too warm later. The ankles had zippers, too, and more little hooks at the end. He wore a nylon shell jacket with cape vents and a storm flap. A compass dangled from one pocket. I refuse to discuss his shoes.

We were going to Victoria's Secret to buy some loungewear for Claudia to recuperate in. I suggested Daddy might want to take some bottled water or a purifying kit. After all, the store was on the second floor of the mall. My mother gave me a dirty look and marched out the door with her pocketbook tucked into the crook of her arm.

I love going to Victoria's Secret. It always smells so nice in there. I love all the pretty little lacy things, even if they are displayed on headless, armless, legless mannequins with ridiculously perfect proportions and no cellulite.

January was almost over. February was right around the corner. Valentine's Day is to Victoria's Secret what Christmas is to our little Christmas tree farm. It's bonanza time, and Victoria wasn't keeping it any secret. I have never seen that much red in one place. Or that many hearts. Or that much lace. Or that many uncomfortable-looking men holding up little pieces of heart-covered red lace and trying to figure out what to buy for their sweeties that wouldn't get them in trouble.

Mama zeroed in on a rack of pretty little sets almost immediately. Say what you will, the woman knows how to shop. Do not even attempt to distract her from her mission. Mannequins in red lace teddies an obstacle? *Pah!* Child's play to Jessica Simon. Embarrassed computer geeks imagining their girlfriends in tap pants and push-up bras littering her path? They don't even slow her down.

My father, on the other hand, kept staring at the mannequins and then at his shoes, then back at the mannequins again. "Maybe I should wait outside," he suggested.

"Don't be ridiculous, Gordon," Mama snapped. "It's just underwear. You've seen women's underwear before."

"Not underwear like this," he whispered to her, a deep flush building up his face. "Not for my daughter."

"We're not buying that kind of underwear for Claudia. For God's sake, Gordon. This will only take a minute."

A whole bunch of the pajamas buttoned up the front, so Claudia wouldn't have to lift her arms to put them on. Mama leafed through the rack and then selected one with lace trim.

"What do you think of this?" She held it out at arm's length. "I think it's practical enough to wear and it's not too bridey, but I do want her to still feel pretty afterward."

We looked at each other. I could see the horror that was mounting inside of me mirrored perfectly in my mother's eyes. My mind flashed past all those pictures of one-breasted women that the plastic surgeon had showed us when we went with Claudia for a consult. The puckered scars. The empty space. The idea that Claudia might have a reason not to feel pretty after her surgery completely undid me. Apparently it undid Mama, too.

We fell into a weeping fest among the thongs and garter belts.

My father backed slowly away from us as if we might suddenly turn against him and become violent, which, given the way Mama was talking to him these days, was not completely out of the question.

"I can't stand it," Mama gasped, clutching the pajamas to her chest. "My baby. So beautiful. So sweet."

"It's not fair," I sobbed onto her shoulder. I was aware of movement from the corner of my eye. Daddy continued to back away from us until his way was blocked by a round table of thongs in every color of the rainbow. "Totally unfair. Why her?"

"When is it ever fair?" My mother pushed me away and held me at arm's length, her eyes searching mine for answers we both knew didn't exist. "Why her? Why Vince? You know better than anyone that there's no rhyme or reason to it."

I touched her cheek. "I thought I was the only one who'd given up on trying to get it to make sense."

She bowed her head. "How could you think that? You think I could watch my baby girl's heart break and see her withering on the vine in what should be the most glorious years of her life, and think there was any plan that could justify this? I tell you, Emily, if there is a plan, it's a lousy one."

Daddy could back up no farther, but that didn't stop him from trying. The table began to tip. What little control I had left dissolved, and I gave myself over to the tears that were going to come, whether I wanted them or not.

Mother held me.

She stood there in the middle of Victoria's Secret, surrounded by garter belts and thongs and push-up bras and computer geeks and my father and unnaturally pale, slender salespeople, and held me while I cried.

I felt a little tug on my jacket. I looked down. Abby gazed up at me, all big blue eyes and golden curls. "Mommy," she asked. "Why are Aunt Claudia's new jammies making you and Grandma cry?"

Mama looked at me and I looked at her, and then we started to laugh. Then we both knelt down and hugged Abby and started to cry again.

After a few minutes, we got ourselves back under control and headed for the cash register with the pajamas.

My father followed, head bowed and trying to pretend he didn't know us. As we left the store, alarms began to go off. Three slender, pale salespeople came whooping after us, yelling, "Sir! Sir! Stop, sir!"

We looked around. The only sir standing right outside Victoria's Secret was Daddy. He turned around to see what the salesladies wanted, and I froze.

Hanging down the back of my father's cargo pants, suspended from the many Velcro tabs that covered his many pockets and loops, was a long, lacy, pastel tail of thong panties.

Apparently they had attached themselves to him when he had backed away from us.

"Grandpa's got a panty tail!" Abby shrieked.

The salesladies ushered him back in to quiet the electronic alarms, and quickly detached their merchandise from my father's ass.

I fell apart laughing, unable to do more than gasp and point. Abby did wild pirouettes around everyone. Mama berated my father, then announced we'd have to skip lunch and go back to the car if I didn't stop cackling like a harpy.

I wish I could learn to titter.

Claudia's phone rang.

"Let the machine get it," she instructed.

It was the night before her surgery. All the kids were spending the night at Leah's. I was spending the night at Claudia's. As the one most familiar with the registration and check-in procedure at St. E's—Claudia only sees things from the nurse's side, not from the patient's side—I was designated to drive her to the hospital in the morning.

"You sure?" I asked. "I don't mind."

She shrugged and licked ice cream off the serving spoon, savoring it, because she wasn't to be allowed another thing to eat after seven o'clock. "If it's important I'll pick it up."

We listened as her voice told whoever was calling that she couldn't come to the phone right now, but if they'd leave their name and number she'd get right back to whoever it was.

The machine clicked and whirred and then Bob's voice came on.

I waited for her to rush over and pick it up. It stunned me when she didn't, but not as much as what Bob said next.

Bob's voice said, "Claudia, please, whatever I did to make you angry, at least give me a chance to apologize for it."

"What did he do?" I mouthed at her silently as if he could hear me.

Claudia shook her head and nibbled on her lower lip. Her eyes looked wet.

"Please, Claudia," Bob continued. "Please, give me another chance. I miss you."

The click of his phone hanging up was the only noise for a little bit.

"You're not actually angry with him, are you?" I asked finally.

Claudia shook her head.

"You didn't tell him what was going on, did you?"

She shook her head again.

"Why not?" I probed.

She shrugged.

"I know you've only been seeing him a little while, but I thought you really, really liked him." I liked Bob, too, as a kind of brother-guy to have around. He was funny, smart, and good at fixing things. Not quite as good as Jake, but close enough for when Jake was tied up or decided that he'd done enough baby-sitting of me and Abby—which, come to think of it, didn't seem to ever happen. Anyway, Todd and Randy had liked him easily as much as I had, and trust me, gaining that accolade from teenage boys is not easy. Speaking of not easy, Mama and Daddy liked him, too, and even Leah was starting to warm up to him.

"I did really, really like him, which would have made being rejected by him really, really painful," Claudia finally responded.

Once again, she had stunned me. My mouth fell open. "Rejected? Why on earth would he reject you?"

"Because, Emily, tomorrow morning they're going to hack out a chunk of my left breast—they can't tell me how big a chunk, and they might end up having to chop off the whole thing—and then they're going to burn it with radiation. After that, they might possibly shoot my body full of hazardous chemicals that will make my hair fall out. If that doesn't make me into damaged goods, I don't know what does."

"Damaged goods? You can't be serious."

Claudia sank down in her chair. "Oh, I'm completely serious."

I looked at my beautiful sister with her brunette curls and her little cupid's bow mouth. One side of her bodacious set of ta-tas would be compromised, but I honestly thought Bob would be able to handle that. I thought he could handle it if her hair all fell out, too. It blew me away that she wouldn't even give him a chance to be the kind of guy I thought he was. "Claudia, I know what you're feeling, but I think Bob is bigger than that."

"What did you say?"

I should have been paying more attention. If I had, I would have probably noticed the way she was pulling her shoulders up. Our mother does the exact same thing when she's pissed. Her eyes don't spark quite the way that Claudia's do, but once again I rose to the occasion.

"I said, I thought Bob could handle this."

"Before that. What did you say before that?"

I stared at her, drawing a complete blank. "I don't know."

"You said you know what I'm feeling." Her eyes had narrowed down to slits.

I knew I was in trouble. I just wasn't sure what I was in trouble for, although I knew it was too late to get out of it. "Yeah. So?"

"So, Emily," Claudia snapped. "Let me make this perfectly

clear: you do not know how I feel. No one is going to cut into your body. You aren't walking around knowing that malignant cells are rapidly multiplying inside your body and possibly spreading, as we speak, through your bloodstream to other parts of your body that you might want to hang onto, and you are not wondering if you'll live to see your children graduate from high school. So, basically, you don't have a clue as to how I feel."

She stomped off down the hall and slid over the part of her dresser that protruded into the doorway (have I mentioned that Claudia's stubborn?) and into her bedroom.

I waited a few minutes and then followed her down the hall, over the dresser, and into her bedroom. I lay down next to her on her bed. We stayed that way for a few minutes without talking, just watching the ceiling fan go around in circles.

Finally, I said, "I'm really sorry."

She took my hand. "I know."

Then we propped ourselves up on the bed pillows and watched *Austin Powers*—the first one, the one that was actually funny; not the second one, which was basically gross except for the whole Mini Me thing—and I didn't bring up Bob again.

I have no idea why hospitals are always so cold. I understand why the operating rooms are like that, but I'm sure they have separate controls. The waiting room was freezing and without Leah and Mama and Daddy flanking me on the couch, my extremities began to lose sensation.

I drew my knees up to my chest and pulled the big shaker sweater I was wearing over my legs. I banded my arms around my shins and rested my cheek against my knees. I rubbed my jaw against the pattern of the sweater, trying to focus on the raspy feeling instead of how scared I felt. I hoped concentrating on details like that might help me stay in the moment, and keep me from drifting back into unpleasant parts of the past or into unknown parts of the future.

"You look about twelve years old. Again," a deep voice said.

I jumped up from the sofa. "Jake!" He looked so reassuringly himself. A little shaggy, a bit rumpled. Just seeing his face made the knot in the pit of my stomach ease up a tiny bit. "Well, you look like you've been living out of the back of your van."

He snorted and gave me a hug.

"You didn't have to come," I said into his fleece jacket. "I'm glad you did, though."

"It's good to be appreciated." He released me and grinned down at me. Then, plopping down on the hard sofa, he yanked me down with him. He pulled me close, wrapped his arm around me, and tucked me into the space next to him. My body stiffened for a second. I hadn't sat this way with a man to whom I wasn't related since . . .

Well, probably since Vince could sit up, which had been quite a while. It managed to feel both comforting and a little scary all at once. I shivered.

He pulled me closer and landed a kiss on top of my head. "Where is everybody?" he inquired.

"Down in the cafeteria getting a cup of coffee."

He pulled back from me in mock shock. "You gave up an opportunity to caffeine load?" He shook his head. "And I thought that news report I heard about snowballs in hell was a fluke."

I gave him a dirty look. "I don't think the stuff they serve down there has enough caffeine in it to matter; it tastes like brown water. Besides, I thought somebody should wait here just in case." I glanced at the clock. "She's only been in a little while, but you never know."

He nodded. "I'll walk you down to the espresso stand after they come back. I still remember where it is."

"Me, too, but it's a whole different crew now. They don't remember me from when Vince was here."

Jake gave me a funny look. "It's been more than a year, Emily. You can't expect them to remember you."

I sighed. "It's weird, how it can seem so long ago and so much like just yesterday at the same time."

Jake pulled me close again. That's one of the nice things about Jake. He often knows exactly when not to say anything. We sat quiet for a while.

The problem with making conversation in hospital waiting rooms is that nothing ever seems quite appropriate. If you chitchat with whoever is waiting with you, it's easy to feel callous and uncaring. You're talking about trivial things like the video you rented the other night or local politics or your mother or the new sweater you want, while someone you love is having a body part sliced open, their heartbeat and respiration slowed, their consciousness taken away.

If you take the other tack, however, it's easy to ride the hysterical swell of fear and horror that's rising up, and weep the whole time. This is exhausting for you and horrifying for the people with whom you're sharing the waiting room, even the complete strangers who are waiting for someone else.

I've tried both ways. Neither works for me. I've tried reading, drawing, even embroidery. No matter what I bring with me, I mainly end up staring into space a lot.

Jake and I stared together for a little bit, then I felt him get restless. He crossed his left leg over the right one. Then he uncrossed them and stretched his leg out straight. Then he put the right one over the left. I stopped trying to count how many times the little seascape appeared in the wallpaper border and turned to look at him.

"You holding up okay?" he asked.

I considered the question for a minute before I answered. "Not really."

We were quiet a while longer.

"Anything I can do?" he asked.

"You're doing it."

More silence.

A surgeon came in to talk to the people whose couch was back to back with ours. Another thing about waiting rooms is that unless you're deaf, it's impossible not to eavesdrop.

The doctor's words drifted over to us in bits and pieces. " . . . couldn't get a clean margin . . . metastasis through the chest wall . . . possible involvement of bone and liver . . . palliative care . . . will do everything we can for her pain . . . so terribly sorry."

Someone (her daughter? her sister? her friend? I don't know; I couldn't look) let out a single sob.

The perfect pitch of grief. It's the wrenching single note of sorrow that sears through your soul, leaving a path of destruction like Sherman marching through the South. You may think you don't know it, but the second you hear it, you'll recognize it. It's universal. And universally devastating.

The room that had been so cold a little while before suddenly became very hot. There didn't seem to be much oxygen in the air, either. I gasped in a breath, but it didn't seem to fill my lungs. I gasped in another. My stomach rolled. The back of my throat burned with bile. I clasped my hands over my mouth and prayed I wouldn't throw up.

Jake stared at me.

Probably everybody else stared, too, but I couldn't see them. They were a blur. I couldn't focus on anything farther away than I could reach.

Jake's mouth moved. I heard his voice as if it were coming from a long way away, plus it was hard to hear over the pounding of my heart and the sound of me gasping in air like a fish on the beach.

"Are you okay?" I thought he said.

I shook my head no.

"I'm getting you out of here," he said in slow motion.

I nodded my head yes.

Jake half dragged, half carried me down the hall. He kept trying doorknobs on unmarked rooms until one opened. He shoved me inside and crammed himself in next to me, pulling the door behind him.

We were inside a linen closet. Between the shelves of threadbare sheets and scratchy blankets, there was barely enough room for us to stand. Something in the air tickled my nose. I felt a giggle start to rise in my throat. The absurdity of ending up in a linen closet with Jake while Claudia went under the knife started to overtake the panic attack.

"Emily, look at me," Jake commanded.

I focused in on his eyes.

"Are you all right?" he asked again.

"No. No, I don't think I am," I said and gasped. I was still hyperventilating; my heart was still racing. Ordinarily I'm not claustrophobic, but I don't think the towers of linens were helping me breathe easy. They had that funny, fuzzy smell that too much industrial laundering can create. "I don't think I can do it again, Jake."

"Do what?" he asked, his voice wary.

"You heard what that doctor said. 'Metastasis.' 'Palliative care.' You know what those words mean. You were there when they said some of them to me."

"But they weren't saying them to you this time. That doctor wasn't talking about Claudia. He was talking about somebody else."

"Somebody else's sister. Somebody else's mother. Somebody else's friend. Does that make it any better?" Suddenly I was cold again. Really cold. So cold my fingertips lost sensation. I started to shake.

He held me by my shoulders. "It doesn't make it any better, Emily. It just makes it not your problem."

"Yet. It's not my problem yet." My voice started to rise. It was the oddest sensation. I felt like I was floating above us, around the ceiling fan vent, watching myself become hysterical. If this is what out-of-body experiences were like, I didn't think they were all they were cracked up to be.

"I can't do it again, Jake. I'm sorry. I know it's selfish, but I can't. I can't take it again. I can't take the smells and the sheets and the bed pans and the IVs and the medications and the horrible vacant look in their eyes as their insides get eaten up, and they try to make the world still make sense."

The words tumbled out of my mouth so quickly I almost couldn't understand them myself. My teeth chattered with cold.

"You want to know why I can't do it?" I didn't wait for an answer. I knew he didn't want to know; *I* didn't want to know. But I'd been carrying it around for so long, it had started to feel like a tumor inside of me. "Because I hated every second of it, Jake. I could barely stand it. The tumor ate away so much of who and what he was. The hours of doing nothing and then the frantic racing, trying to do too many things at once, trying to stop something that couldn't be stopped, no matter what I did or didn't do. I prayed for it to stop. I prayed for him to die, Jake. I prayed for my wonderful Vince, the father of my child, to die, because I was tired. And heartsick. And selfish. So unbearably selfish."

"Emily, you have to stop this." His fingers dug into my shoulders. He looked like he wanted to give me a good shake. "Vince's last months were horrible. It was a nightmare, and you have to stop dragging yourself through it over and over."

"How am I supposed to do that?" I asked through clenched teeth. It didn't help; they still chattered. I still shook. "How am I supposed to forget it when I see his eyes every time I look at Abby's face, when I come to a hospital and hear someone else get a death sentence and know what they're in for? How am I supposed to get over it when he keeps showing up in my dreams?"

Jake's face seemed to melt. All the edges went soft. "Oh, Em." He folded me into his arms. This time, I let him.

I cried. Not a pretty little movie cry, a real cry. I sobbed great big boo-hoos that felt like they ripped their way up from the bottom of my gut. Jake kept on holding me.

He didn't tell me to stop. He didn't tell me it would be okay. He didn't recoil with disgust when I kept blowing my nose on a towel I grabbed from the shelf behind me. He just held me.

Finally, I stopped crying.

He still kept holding me.

And it felt good.

In fact, it felt better than good. It felt great. It felt wonderful.

His arms were warm and strong, and there was a little hollow where his shoulder met his chest that my head rested in as if it were custom-made for me. The closet didn't seem so cold anymore. In fact, I was warming right up.

A little *ping* went off in the back of my head. What if Leah and Claudia were wrong? What if Jake didn't have a thing for me? What if I had a thing for Jake?

But what if it didn't matter? What if the only thing that mattered was how good it felt to have my body pressed up against his? I couldn't believe that in all the times I'd hugged Jake, I'd never noticed how perfectly our bodies fit together. I couldn't believe how good it felt to press my lips to his.

I couldn't believe . . .

. . . that I was doing this in a hospital linen closet while my sister had her breast hacked open.

I pushed him away. "Jake, I can't . . ." My voice trailed off while I struggled to come up with words to express all the thoughts that were racing through my head, and the feelings that were racing through my other body parts. Then I looked at his face.

He looked horrified. I don't know how else to describe his expression, except complete and total horror. I couldn't tell what precisely was horrifying him; the possibilities were endless: my swollen red eyes, my streaming nose, the thought that I might think he was interested in me as anything more than his best friend's widow.

What he said as he released me was, "Emily, I'm sorry."

"No." I gasped. "No. It's my fault." Then I bolted from the closet back to the waiting room.

He didn't follow.

What was I thinking, I wondered, as I scurried down the linoleum-covered, dingy hallways. Just because my sisters think I'm smart and pretty and tell me that any man would be lucky to have me doesn't mean it's true. Hadn't I learned that when they'd assured me that my rendition of "Tomorrow" was practically Broadway material, to be nearly laughed out of the auditions for our high school production of *Grease* my junior year?

I wanted so much to be Olivia Newton-John, and was sure I could be. I'd even had my hair permed like Olivia's at the end of the movie. I'd longed to wear that slutty little outfit with the leather pants and bustier. I knew there was a chance I wouldn't get the part. I mean, I'd never even enrolled in the chorus class, so Mr. Brott, the chorus teacher who was directing the play, didn't know me. I hadn't had singing lessons of any kind either, but was sure I could at least have the part of Rizzo.

The truth is that I can't carry a tune in a bucket, but when you can't carry a tune, you don't know that because you can't hear it.

I did get a part in the chorus, but throughout the long agonizing weeks of watching Kim Camp rehearse the part I thought I was destined for, and enduring everyone humming off-key bars of "Tomorrow" every time I walked through a room or backstage, I'd never been so humiliated.

Until now.

When I got back to the waiting room, my family had returned from the cafeteria. They looked at me accusingly.

"I thought you were going to wait here," my father said.

"I had to go to the bathroom."

In my family, going to the bathroom is an inalienable right. None of us would ever have been able to pull off the little Dutch boy's heroic feat, because feeling all that water on the other side of the dike would have made each one of us have to pee too bad. As the countryside flooded, the rest of the family would have shrugged and said, "Well, she had to go. What do you expect?"

"You've been in the bathroom for fifteen minutes?" Daddy asked.

I mumbled something about losing my way in the labyrinth of hospital hallways, but I saw my mother take in my puffy, swollen face and elbow Daddy hard in the ribs. Everyone scooted over and I sat down.

CHAPTER FIFTEEN

Qué Será, Será!

Leah

One part Apricot Glaze (#38), one part Golden Copper (#40), one part developer. Forty-five minutes. We're considering going back to the Titian Red. This vacation from reality has been a little strange.

Claudia

One part Light Ash Brown (#32), one part Apricot Glaze (#38), one part developer. Thirty minutes. Never drop your standards.

Claudia belongs to the you-never-know school of makeup and clothing. That means she wouldn't dream of going to the grocery store for a gallon of milk without properly applied mascara and an outfit that matches.

Why?

Because you never know.

You never know who you might run into, who might be shopping at the same time, what might happen, or where you might end up. Claudia blames it on wearing scrubs to work. She says that if people didn't have free will over what they wore to work each day, they'd pay more attention when they did get to choose. She's convinced that if more people went to work in scrubs, you'd see fewer plaid pants on the street and no horizontal stripes ever.

I, on the other hand, know. I know that if I go to the grocery store without showering, brushing my hair, or putting on makeup that I will run into everyone I've ever met in my entire life. I know that borrowing a pair of white pants from one of my sisters is a guaranteed way of getting my period to start. I know that if I wear a pair of leggings with no underpants that a large hole will develop along the butt seam.

We both make Leah crazy, but that's a given and an added perk.

So the day after her lumpectomy, as soon as she was given the go-ahead to shower, Claudia washed her hair. I dried it for her since it hurt to lift her arm up and would for a while.

"So, now that you know that it's not so bad, are you going to call Bob?" I asked, leaning my chin on my fist as I watched her smooth on the first coat of eye shadow in the hospital bathroom. I love watching Claudia put on makeup. I've never gotten the knack. I always smudge the mascara or get the eyeliner crooked.

The news from Claudia's pathology report had been about as good as it could get. None of the lymph nodes they'd harvested had shown even microscopic signs of cancer. They'd gotten a clean margin from the lump in her breast, and it had been very small—less than one centimeter. They wanted her to take a drug called tamoxifen, but didn't want to do any of those terrible chemotherapies that make people so sick, or even hit her with radiation.

She'd have a nasty scar. She might even want to consider plastic surgery later, but it really wasn't that bad. Who gets to be our age without a few scars to show for it, anyway?

"I don't know." She started the second coat of eyeshadow. "I haven't had time to think about it."

"Oh." I held my breath while she made her mouth into a perfect little O and started to apply mascara. I wish I knew why we all do that. I can't put mascara on without making that face, either. "When do you suppose you might have time to think about it?"

Claudia put the mascara wand back in the tube and set it down with excruciating gentleness on the Formica countertop. "Drop it, Emily."

Our eyes locked.

"Okay," I finally said. "But only because you didn't put mascara on your other eye yet and it's making you look like that psycho guy from *A Clockwork Orange,* and it's scaring me."

Claudia's face went blank for a second. She turned and looked back in the mirror. Suddenly she slapped the counter and guffawed.

We laughed until we cried. The freshly applied mascara ran down to her chin. Then Claudia had to take all the makeup off and start all over again.

It might have been the first moment that I let myself truly believe that Claudia was going to be okay.

I helped her into the boxer pajama set that Mama and I had bought her at Victoria's Secret, and helped her back into the bed.

Leah showed up with Mama and Daddy not too long

after Claudia and I got started on the crossword puzzle. We shmoozed. Claudia started to yawn. We turned on the news. Claudia dozed off, looking way more like Show White in the glass box than I was completely comfortable with. We decided to go have lunch in the cafeteria while Claudia napped. They were serving tuna surprise today, and Daddy loves tuna surprise.

"Are you going to eat that or play with it?" Leah demanded.

Just the smell of hospital tuna surprise or the very dubious-looking chicken cordon bleu in the cafeteria line was enough to make my stomach roll. I'd opted for the salad bar, but it wasn't much more appetizing. For a couple of months, I'd eaten nearly all my meals at the hospital. I'd lost about ten pounds, so it did have its good points. Those good points, however, didn't include actually eating the food. We started calling it the Despair Diet.

Now I shot Leah a look across the table and then gave my canned peach half a very deliberate spin. "Mama, tell Leah to stop bossing me." I stuck my tongue out at Leah for good measure.

"Emily!" Leah yelped.

"Leah!" I mimicked back.

"Girls," Mama said. The weariness in her voice made me immediately wish I hadn't been such a brat. She set her hand on mine.

I hadn't realized how papery her skin had become. Everything blurred a little and I blinked to clear my vision.

"Eat something, Emily," my mother said, her voice gentle.

"I will," I assured her. "Just not right now. I want to go check on Claudia. We've been gone a while."

I saw Leah open her mouth to argue, then close it without challenging me—a sure sign that I looked as awful as I felt.

By the time I'd gotten past the gift shop, the chapel, through the dingy orange-carpeted lobby, and up to Claudia's floor, my stomach had settled a little. My mother had already damped my spirits. Kindness can be amazingly cruel. When Vince was dying, kindness was the thing that could knock me to my knees. Give me an arrogant resident over a hug from a friend any day. So we had a little rule about not being too nice. At Vince's memorial service, some of my closest friends whispered their condolences to me along with some of the nastiest things you can call a woman. Now, that's true kindness.

Claudia's door was within sight when I heard Bob's voice.

He is one of those big men with a big voice to match. It bounced and echoed off all the tile and right down the hall to me. I slowed my steps.

I heard the murmur of Claudia's voice, but couldn't make out the words.

Then Bob said, "I'm a detective, Claudia. It's my job to find things out, and finding out you were here wasn't exactly solving the Jimmy Hoffa case."

Claudia's voice murmured again.

Bob answered. "I called your mother. She still likes me, at least."

I took a few more steps. Claudia's voice got clearer. "I just didn't want you to . . . I mean, I didn't want you to feel . . ."

I didn't have to see her. I knew what her face was doing. The lower lip of her little cupid's bow mouth would be trembling, her chin would be wobbling slightly, and her big brown eyes would have filled with tears. No one cries prettier than Claudia. No giant rivers of snot for her, no sirree.

By this time I was at the door to Claudia's room, pressed up against the wall for maximum eavesdropping.

I heard Bob sigh. "Oh, Claudia. Don't cry." I grinned with satisfaction. Did I know my sister or what?

"I'm trying not to," she said softly. "That's the whole point. I didn't want you to feel manipulated."

"I don't feel manipulated," he assured her. "I feel . . . I just want . . ."

There was a long pause. I took a deep breath, held it, and peeked around the corner.

Bob sat at Claudia's bedside. He clasped the hand that didn't have tubes running into it tightly between his two hands. I couldn't see anything but the back of his head and his big beefy neck. I wanted to see his face.

Claudia was propped up in the bed. Her dark curls splayed across the white pillowcase and two spots of color shone high on her cheeks. She looked like an angel from a painting by Rossetti.

"I feel better when I'm with you," Bob finally blurted out.

"Better about what?" Claudia's brows creased in confusion.

"About everything! About life! About me!"

Claudia's big brown eyes got even bigger. "Oh, Bob. That might be the nicest thing anyone has ever said to me." She breathed in deeply and sat up in the bed.

He kissed her.

I ducked back around the corner and headed back to the cafeteria, feeling much lighter. Maybe the Jell-O would be edible.

*   *   *

There is something completely heartrending about the sight of a woman sobbing in an empty hospital waiting room.

So, even though I knew Claudia was okay, I nearly panicked when I found Leah doubled over and gasping for breath between big, wrenching boo-hoos in the fourth-floor lounge.

For once, I kept my mouth shut and just held her while she cried.

Leah almost never loses the iron grip she keeps on herself. When she does lose it, it tends to be spectacular.

The last time she fell apart was right before Vince died. She'd spent weeks trying to manage things at her office during the day before rushing over to spend her nights with me and Abby and Vince, learning how to give IV medications, doing the endless loads of laundry, waiting for something to happen, and dreading that something would.

I'm not sure if she'd slept more than a few hours at a time for weeks. Of course, I hadn't either. Even if we did get a stretch where we could stay in bed, no one could sleep. So I wasn't in any shape to judge what kind of shape she was in.

Anyway, she just fell apart. Overnight she went from being completely in charge, to not remembering where we kept the medications or how to turn Vince in the hospital bed.

I sent her home, one more thing I'll always wonder about. Did I make the right choice? Should I have kept her with me?

Vince died the next morning. Without her there.

Leah, of course, had predicted that he'd die then. She was the one who'd explained to the hospice nurses about how I'd always teased him about forgetting our anniversary, about how

I'd programmed all our security codes and PIN numbers to be our anniversary date. She said that he was waiting until then so I'd know that he never would have forgotten, no matter what. That this was his last message to me.

She knew him so well. Adored him.

He'd adored her, too. Not in an icky, can-I-dance-with-your-sister way. Vince had appreciated Leah's intelligence and drive, and he'd known and understood her soft side, too.

I think that was another reason he chose to go when he did (and I do believe it was a choice). I think he wanted to spare Leah watching that last bit of him slip away.

I also think he wanted me to be there. So I would know it was real. So I would know it had been peaceful.

The night before he died was the last time I'd seen her cry like this, with her body wracked by sobs, out of control. I hadn't been able to comfort her then. There was no way to feel better. The best you could hope for was numbness.

I hoped I was doing a better job of helping Leah now while she sobbed uncontrollably. We didn't have to go numb this time. This time, things were going to be okay.

"She's all right, Leah," I whispered. "Claudia will be okay."

"But she might not have been," came the muffled reply. "We could have lost her."

"But we didn't."

"It doesn't make sense," she wailed.

"Of course it doesn't. It never has."

She pushed herself away from me. "Then how are we supposed to do this?"

I stared at Leah blankly. "Do what?"

"This!" she yelled, gesturing first at herself and then waving her arms around. "Life! How are we supposed to do this if it doesn't make any sense?"

"The same as we always have, I guess." I shrugged. "How else?"

She whirled on me. "Fine. Let's say that's a logical and reasonable answer for the moment. The next question would be why?"

I felt my entire gut condense and freeze into a tiny, hard rock. "Because the other options are untenable."

"Emily, I've based my whole life on the idea that if I worked hard and did my best, good things would come my way."

"And they have. You have a great job, a beautiful condo, a nice car. All kinds of good things."

She pounced on that. "But what does any of that mean? When I look around the world, nothing important makes sense. Why did Vince die? Why did Claudia get cancer? Why are babies starving all over the world? Why am I alone?"

"Because shit happens, Leah, and there's nothing any of us can do about it."

"Aha!" she shouted.

"Aha what?" Maybe the stress of Claudia's illness had pushed Leah over the edge. Never, ever had I seen her act like this.

"Why *can't* we do anything about it?"

I sighed. "Because we don't control everything, Leah. There's a huge portion of the universe that simply doesn't respond to being bossed. That applies to malignant cells, droughts, and getting a boyfriend."

"I know." She twirled a strand of hair around her finger

and tugged hard on it, something I hadn't seen her do since she thought she was going to fail organic chemistry during her sophomore year of college. "It suddenly occurred to me that Alan might have been right."

"Excuse me?" Alan was Leah's last truly serious boyfriend, the one before the endless succession of Joes and Maxes. The one who was serious enough to share cookware with, if not vows.

"When he left, he said something to me that made no sense at the time. He said that if I wanted someone's involvement in my life, I might have to accept that they might not want to do everything my way."

"And that relates to Claudia's getting sick in what way?"

"The powers that move the universe are involved, whether I want them to be or not, and they clearly are not doing things my way."

I hate to laugh at other people's epiphanies. I mean, it's not like mine are incredible all the time. So I sat and waited.

"You have no idea how frustrating it is," she continued. "Every day, I see people making the stupidest decisions and the worst choices. I can see what they need to do, but even if I tell them, they don't do it. Everyone's so bullheaded. I have no authority over them, and I can't make them see reason."

Suddenly, it looked like a sunburst crossed Leah's face. "That means that I don't control everything! Everything is not my responsibility! Everything is not my fault!"

I stared at her. "You thought Claudia's getting sick was your fault? That Vince's dying was your fault?"

"No, no. Not really. I just finally understand that no matter how perfect I try to be, or end up being, it won't change anything. It won't bring Vince back to you or keep Claudia from getting sick or save Mama and Daddy from getting old. It will only twist me up into a bitter old woman who missed a million opportunities."

I put my head in my hands. "I'm so confused."

"I knew it wasn't my fault that bad things happened." She put her hand on my shoulder and turned her tear-streaked face to me. "But I've realized that it's not my responsibility to make them well, either."

I blinked hard. "You just realized that you don't have to cure cancer? Just now?"

Leah rolled her eyes. "No, Emily. I just realized that I don't control what everyone does or does not do. Or what happens to people and what doesn't happen."

My mind reeled. For a moment, I was even a little angry. Talk about being egocentric! How could Leah have felt she was that important in the universe, to have that kind of control? "Leah, it's just life. You can't control it; you can't direct it. Life just happens, and we have to ride the course as best as we can. You just have to hope you can look at yourself in the mirror every morning without disgust."

The truth of what I was saying hit me like a tidal wave. Maybe, just maybe, I was as guilty of egocentricity and hubris as Leah. All those times I'd wondered if I'd made the right decisions—wondered if something I had done had made his death come faster, or if something I hadn't done could have stopped it from happening—they were just attempts at self-aggrandizement. Or maybe we'd rather be wrong than helpless.

Leah was still talking. "So, then that means I'm free."

"Free to do what?"

"To lead my life."

I was still confused. "You weren't before?"

She blew her nose. "That's the sad thing, Em. I probably was and never even knew it. I've wasted a lot of time." She stood up.

I sat, feeling like the little boy at the end of *Shane,* watching his hero ride off without him. "What are you going to do?"

She smiled, then took my face between both her hands and kissed me on the forehead. "First, I'm going to call Chase. It doesn't have to be what I thought a relationship should be, or what Claudia thinks a relationship should be. He doesn't have to be what I thought the man I would fall in love with would be, or what Mama or Daddy think a man should be. I can enjoy the relationship and him and be happy, because I don't control the universe, and what will be, will be."

It was the most Doris Day moment my sister has ever had. For a brief moment, I expected daisies to spring up under her feet.

Jake has had a key to the house since Vince carried me over the threshold. It's handy. He's let us in when I've locked myself out. He brings in mail and feeds the cat and goldfish when we're on vacation. Lately, he's taken to dropping off little treats for Abby and me, like bags of the spiced tea from the Pike Street Market that I like, and Powerpuff Girls barrettes for Abby. So it didn't surprise me to find an envelope addressed to me in his handwriting sitting on my kitchen counter.

I was, however, unprepared for its contents. It didn't help that the whole thing appeared to be in some elusive guy code.

Dear Emily,

I wanted to let you and Abby know that I'm not going to be around for a while. A lot has been happening lately and I need some space and time to sort it out. I'm sorry I'm so confused, but I don't know how to work it all out. I've been trying, but I'm not sure which way to turn. Vince was always my compass and I'm not sure how to figure this out without him. I'll be in touch when I get my head together.

Love,
Jake

I took this to mean that he was going away for an indefinite period of time. And I was pretty sure that the clinch in the linen closet at the hospital had a lot to do with it.

CHAPTER SIXTEEN

Phantom Pains

Leah

One part Apricot Glaze (#38), one part Golden Copper (#40), one part developer. Forty-five minutes. She's fabulous. Great color. Great body. Great bounce. Her hair looks good, too.

Claudia

Claudia's not doing hers this time. Bob says he thinks touches of gray are sophisticated and elegant.

Why didn't you tell us?" Claudia stroked my hair as I wept on her shoulder.

"We had other things to worry about." I sniffed. "We were still waiting for your pathology reports."

"You should have told us anyway." Leah shoved the box of Kleenex closer to me. "It could have provided some welcome distraction."

I cried harder. I could feel Claudia gesturing at Leah, probably to shut up. Not that Leah would if she didn't feel like it.

"I can't believe I got dumped before we even started going out," I wailed.

"Technically, I don't think that it counts as being dumped, then," Leah mused. "I think you actually have to have some kind of love relationship before you're dumped. This case is more like plain old . . ."

" . . . rejection," I finished for her.

Claudia sighed. "Leah, do you really feel that's helpful?"

"No," she admitted while she patted my hand. "But it is honest."

"She's right, Claudia. I have to face it. You should have seen the look on his face. Who could blame him? Here he thinks he's comforting his best friend's wife, and I turn it into a pass."

"You're not his best friend's wife anymore," Claudia said softly. "You're his best friend's widow."

I sat up. "I'm not sure that's completely true for him. Or for me."

"Semantics aside," Leah said. She filed harder than necessary at the nail on her pinky finger and studiously kept her head down. "What are you going to do about it?"

I picked at the damp, shredded-up Kleenex in my hands. If I crumpled it just right, it looked a little like Australia. I pondered the fact that Australia is the only landmass that is both a country and an entire continent. My mind was clearly working on shuffle—completely random.

"Nothing," I finally said.

"Nothing," Leah repeated.

"Why nothing?" Claudia probed.

I sighed. "Nothing. If I do nothing, the situation is still salvageable."

"Explain," Leah commanded.

"Right now, if I don't say or do anything when—and if—

Jake comes back, it's almost like nothing happened. I mean, really, nothing did. I figured out that I loved him, and five seconds later he rejected me. It's got to be the shortest love affair on record."

Claudia put her hand over mine. I wondered if she could feel the icky Kleenex and didn't mind because she was so used to other people's body fluids.

"Is that true?" she asked. "Do you love him?"

"I think so, but how am I supposed to know?" I sniffed and put my head back down on her shoulder. "I've known Jake since grade school. All of a sudden, in the middle of a panic attack in a hospital linen closet, I noticed that my buddy of almost twenty-five years happens to be a great-looking guy that I adore spending time with, and we both happen to be single and our bodies fit together like two puzzle pieces. How do you expect me to untangle that?"

"We don't," she assured me as she stroked my hair. "But if you mean what you said, if you love Jake, you owe it to both of you to try."

"Don't listen to her," Leah said. "She's just flying high on this whole Bob thing."

The Bob thing was indeed going very well. Nightly phone calls, pet names, the works.

"Like the whole Chase thing doesn't have you all giggly and giddy?" Claudia asked.

Leah smiled. "I know. I see all the endless possibilities of what can go wrong, and I still can't convince myself to walk away."

As well she shouldn't. The Chase thing was going as well as the Bob thing. Maybe even better, since it seemed to involve lots of steamy sex all over Leah's condo and Chase's apartment, and apparently their cars and a few bar bathrooms, too. Really, you wanted to look very closely at the furniture at her place before you sat down on it. Either that or you had to keep your imagination under very tight rein on the topic of any stain you might see.

Amazingly, our parents even seemed to like Chase. He's hard not to like. Sweet and gentle, and finally there's someone younger than me to boss around! Once we all scraped our jaws off the floor (he really is tremendously sexy) and started to get to know him, we had to wonder why Leah had been wasting her time with all those Joes and Maxes. After a few beggars-can't-be-choosers remarks, even Mama relented and admitted that he was sweet and awfully cute. She even giggled as she said it.

I leaned my chin on my hands and wondered if the situation was at all salvageable, or if I was fooling myself.

"Emily," Claudia's voice broke into my reverie. "Don't you think it's worth a chance?"

I blew my nose. "It's too scary. I know how completely hellish it is to have my heart broken. You know how when someone loses a leg or an arm, they say that afterward they have these phantom pains? The leg that isn't there will hurt or itch or something?"

They both nodded.

"Maybe what I'm feeling for Jake is like a phantom pain from a part of my heart that isn't there anymore, the part that Vince took with him when he died."

Both my sisters became extremely still. Leah put her hand over mine. "You also know how wonderful it is to be in love, too. Don't forget that. You know better than most people. Is there anything better than to love someone and be loved in return?"

I thought about it, turning over the possibilities. My answer came out as a strangled whisper. "But what if that person can't give me what Vince gave me? What if I can't ever find that again? Should I settle for second best?"

Leah took a deep breath and let it out slowly. "Sweetie, Vince was one of a kind. There aren't many guys like him around. Trust me, I've looked longer than you. If you spend the rest of your life waiting around for another Vince, you'll die a lonely old lady."

"Maybe that's the way it has to be then," I said.

"Maybe you're too scared to try again," Leah said.

Sometimes I hate it when she's right. I didn't have a comeback, but as it turned out, I didn't need one.

Claudia's hand stopped stroking my hair, and she emitted a noise that was somewhere between a gasp and a squeak.

"Leah, come look at this," she said urgently.

"What is it?" I tried to sit up, but Claudia had my head tucked firmly against her chest and any struggling on my part could lead to untimely suffocation.

"Oh, my God," Leah said in a hushed voice.

"What is it?" I asked again, trying unsuccessfully to twist free. Oh, God, did I have lice?

"It was bound to happen sooner or later," Claudia observed thoughtfully.

"I suppose," Leah mused, her fingers dancing over the spot that Claudia had been stroking. "Still, it's shocking to see it."

"*What's in my hair?*" I squealed, stamping my feet.

Claudia released my head.

I sprang up.

Leah took my face between both her hands and said, "It's not in your hair, sweetie. It *is* your hair. You're starting to go gray."

Shit. Well, I supposed I'd earned it.

A little more than two weeks later, I woke up in a good mood. Not just a good mood, really. A mood so good that even an incipient yeast infection couldn't have ruined it.

It doesn't seem to matter how often this happens to me, these moments of clarity that bring on something like elation. I accept these days with open arms like they are the sun breaking through the clouds, not as the warning of impending doom or at least big trouble that I should know they are by now.

Magnets that said "bubble" and "dream" had fallen out of one of my socks that morning, and even that hadn't been enough of a warning.

Because I refuse to stop being that stupid little ant with the high hopes (and why on earth did he want to move that rubber tree plant anyway?), I was unprepared for the phone call from my mother summoning me to the emergency room again. Good God, could our family never catch a break?

I dropped Abby with a suitcase full of Pretty Ponies and her toothbrush, just in case, at her friend Kathryn's house to play for the afternoon. Kathryn's mom was very understanding and said not to worry if I needed Abby to spend the night.

I must have been moving faster than I realized, because even with getting Abby packed and settled, I beat Claudia to the hospital. Leah was already there, holding Daddy's hand and looking tense.

Even with all the machines they'd hooked up to him, it was hard to tell what his heart rate was. The numbers jumped up and down like a stock ticker on Black Tuesday. The EKG showed a rhythm that, at best, could be called syncopated.

As I walked in, one of the machines started beeping loudly. "That doesn't sound good," I said to Leah.

"Hello, Emily," Mama said.

I shook my head. When had she started using greetings again? And when had I stopped?

"It keeps doing that," said Leah with a nod to the beeping machine, ever focused on the matters of true import.

A second machine joined in. "Really, really not good?" I asked.

Leah shrugged, eyes huge in her unnaturally pale face.

A nurse in pink scrubs and what looked like giant electric-blue duck clogs bustled in. She flicked a couple of buttons and all the beeping stopped. She turned to my mother. "Has his heart rate ever gone this high before?"

We all looked at the machine to which she pointed. My father's heart rate hovered for a few seconds at about 212 beats per minute before dropping down to 140, and then pinged back up to 180. My mother shook her head.

Pink Scrubs said, "We've paged Dr. Shakira. He's on rounds and should be here any minute." She bustled back out.

Within seconds, the first machine began to beep again.

I sat down next to my mother and took her hand. It lay limp in my hand, as if she were so far away she couldn't even tell anyone was next to her. Her eyes were glazed. I don't think she even blinked when Claudia came in and sat down and took her other hand.

"Where have you been?" Leah whispered.

Claudia blushed. "I was at Nordstrom's Rack when you called."

Leah glared.

"There was a rack of dresses marked down to six dollars," Claudia whispered.

My mother still didn't react. Very scary. News of a bargain of that magnitude would normally have her leaping out of her chair. She didn't even blink now.

"Six dollars?" I whispered back to Claudia. "Were they cute?"

"Darling," she said. "Completely darling."

"Stop it," Leah hissed. "You're upsetting Daddy."

My father waved his hand. "Let them talk, Leah. What harm will it do?"

I looked from his face to Leah and back to him again. He looked resigned. She looked pissed. I decided to risk it anyway. I mean, really. Six dollars? "What kind of material?"

"Sort of a fuzzy knit. I'll show you later," Claudia promised.

"You bought them?" Leah yelped. "I call you to tell you our father is in the hospital, and you stop to shop?"

"I didn't stop to shop. I was already shopping. When you called, I was in the dressing room already. I'd already tried on three of them. It only took a minute to try on two more and then buy them. I came straight here afterward."

"You tried on two *more?*"

"Leah, they were six dollars! How long do you think they're

going to last?" Claudia threw her hands up in the air. "Besides, there's nothing I can do here that you weren't already doing."

Leah pressed her lips together until they were white.

Just when I thought the constant beeping of the machine or the waiting would make me completely insane, Dr. Shakira strode in with what looked like about twelve teenagers in white coats.

"Mr. Simon," he said jovially. "Nice to see you again. You've brought your lovely daughters and your wife this time, as well. How nice. Mrs. Simon, how is your ear?"

"Fine," Mama whispered.

"No more bugs, then?"

Wordlessly, my mother shook her head no.

Dr. Shakira made a peremptory gesture at one of the teenagers, who scurried forward and pressed buttons on the machine to make it stop beeping. Dr. Shakira looked at the readouts on all the machines and clucked his tongue. He held out his right hand, and as if by magic another nurse, this one in flowered scrubs with giant yellow duck shoes, appeared and put a thick file in it.

Dr. Shakira clucked his tongue some more. "Mr. Simon, I'm sure you know this is not good."

My father nodded. The machine started to beep again. The other one joined in instantly.

"Not good at all," Dr. Shakira said, his lips pursed. He turned to Flowered Scrubs and said, "The rate is too high. We're going to have to shock him, but I don't want to do it here. You and Marian get him to ICU. We'll meet you there."

He flew out of the room, white lab coat flapping. The dozen teenagers fled with him, each with their coat flapping, but not quite so briskly as Dr. Shakira's. Maybe a starched coat is a privilege of completing your internship.

Pink Scrubs came in and started grabbing bags off poles and tossing them onto Daddy's gurney. Flowered Scrubs thrust a bag at us and said, "Here are his clothes. You can follow us as far as the ICU waiting room. We'll let you know as soon as you can come in."

They started running through the hallways, pushing my father along like a bobsled on which they were about to jump.

"We're gonna have to shave him," I heard Pink Scrubs say breathlessly as they left us.

"He's a hairy one, all right," Flowered Scrubs agreed.

Right before they banged through the double doors that we weren't allowed through, I heard my father yell, "If you're going to shave me, watch out for my moles, and for God's sake, don't take off a nipple!"

The waiting room was empty except for a TV blaring CNN headlines. I switched the TV off before it could give me a headache.

Mama began to pace. Back and forth. Back and forth. She wrung the twisted piece of tissue in her hands. "The damned fool," she muttered. "The damned old fool."

"What?" I said.

"His heart had been racing up and down for two hours before he said a word," Mama snapped.

"Can you blame him?" Leah asked. "The way you've been complaining about him, I'm surprised he isn't frightened to open his mouth. Maybe that's why he didn't tell you his heart was acting strangely." Leah's tone was sharp, mean, even. "I haven't heard you say anything nice about Daddy for months."

"Leah . . ." Claudia, the peacemaker like always, broke in.

"No, Claudia," Mama said. "If Leah has something to say, she might as well get it off her chest."

"That's it," Leah said. "I've already said it. It seems like since Daddy had his first heart episode, you've had it in for him. Nothing he does or has done in the past few months has pleased you. All you do is complain about how he never pays enough attention or never helps."

"And why shouldn't I? He's a wrinkled-up old fool, Leah. Nothing but a wrinkled-up old fool." She ground her teeth shut so tight I thought her jaw might break.

This wasn't like Mama. Bickering with Daddy? Sure. My parents bicker 24/7/365. My parents bicker so much that my sisters and I couldn't figure out what was funny about that comic strip *The Lockhorns*. We thought that was how married people talked to each other.

But this meanness? That's just not them. Theirs is a loving bickering.

Leah threw her hands in the air. "Thanks, Mama. You just made my point for me."

"What do you know about it, Leah? That's what I'd like to know." I'd never heard Mama talk this way. She wasn't strident; she wasn't shrill. She was damn mad and determined to make us understand. "What do you know about forty years of marriage? What do you know about raising three children? What do you know about two lives so intertwined that sometimes I don't know where one of us stops and the other starts?"

We all stared. Leah's mouth opened and closed a few times, like a fish. No sound came out, though.

Mama stared as if daring us to talk back. "Then one day,

that other person shows you that they could leave without you. They could just up and die and leave you all alone. Leave you to an old folks' home with no one but a bunch of crazy old ladies for company. Or worse yet, leave you to live alone in a cold, empty house with no one to watch the news with or share a meal with."

Claudia put her hand on Mama's arm. "Mama, you wouldn't be alone. You'd have us. We'd always be there. We love you."

"No, Claudia." Mama shook her head vehemently. "It's one of the things I congratulate myself on. You three have your own lives. You're independent. You don't need me. I did my job well. I was a good mother."

"And a good wife," I added. "You're a good wife."

"Oh, Emily." Mama looked at me, her pain so close to the surface that I felt like I could reach out and touch it.

I stared at her and swallowed hard. We all have murky, nasty corners down deep in our souls. We've all done things we're not proud of, things that shame us. Or worse, things that make us look at ourselves in the cold, harsh light of reality and see ourselves for what we are, even if we don't like it much.

"Do you remember Vince's last big surgery? You know, the one where they messed up the back of his head so bad?"

Everybody nodded. It was the beginning of the end. Vince never healed from that. The next six weeks of his life had been an unrelenting nightmare of leaking cerebrospinal fluid, shunts, MRIs, confusion, and nausea until he'd finally let go and allowed himself to sink completely into the coma he'd been fighting off with sheer willpower for so long.

"Well, two nights before, it was Abby's turn to bring the snack for her preschool group."

"You should have switched with someone, Emily. Or had one of us do it," Claudia said.

"You're assuming that I was thinking straight, Claudia." I laughed a little at how screwed-up my thinking had been. I'd still been hanging onto some strange hope that Vince would pull through. I still thought he was going to beat that tumor. Two recurrences in less than eleven months, and I was still expecting him to get up off the couch and be himself again. "So I was putting cream cheese on two dozen miniature bagels, and then cutting them in half and wrapping each one in pink Saran Wrap. I still needed to wash the grapes and cut them into little bunches and put them into Baggies, and make sure that I had enough Dixie Cups for the juice, and Vince kept wanting me to come into the family room to see this Elvis special they were playing on VH1."

"You love Elvis," Claudia said.

"You're right. I do." I nodded and tried to think of a way to explain it. "And I love that special; Vince knew I did. It's the one where he's on that little round stage in the center of everybody, and he's wearing black leather pants and a leather jacket. He's so cute and his voice is so great. But right then, it wouldn't have mattered if young, black leather Elvis had walked through the door and offered to give me oral pleasure on the spot."

My mother gave a little gasp. I barely stopped to take a breath, much less apologize. "I still had to get the preschool snack made. It had to be done, and it had to be done right. I was tired and stressed, and Vince wouldn't do anything but sit there and watch TV and expect me to drop everything and come running whenever he wanted to show me something, even though I was the only one keeping our little family going."

"So what happened?" Leah asked. "Did you watch the special?"

I could tell that they wanted me to say yes. Hell, *I* wanted to say yes. I wanted to say that I'd dropped everything and sat on the couch holding hands with my dying husband, who had just been trying to find some way to stay connected with me. I wanted to say that I'd had the perspective to know what was important and what wasn't. Instead, I told them the truth.

"No. I threw the cream cheese knife at him."

"You threw a knife at your husband right before he had his third brain surgery?" Even Claudia was apparently going to have problems forgiving me this one. Who could blame her? I still hadn't been able to forgive myself for it.

"Yes. I did. And I yelled at him. For ten minutes, about how inconsiderate he was."

"What did Vince do?" Mama asked.

"He tried to convince me that things were going to be okay. He started to list everybody who had it worse than him. He started talking about how burn victims had it worse, and refugees from Serbia had it worse, and people starving in Africa had it worse." I remember listening to his litany and realizing that he'd been thinking about it for some time, keeping a little list of people who had it worse than he did in the back of his head, to comfort himself.

"And what did you say?" Leah asked.

"I informed him in no uncertain terms that I didn't care how many people had it worse or how many people had it better. I told him that I refused to be happy about him needing more surgery, and that the least he could do after all the inconvenience he was causing was to let me make the fucking bagels for the fucking preschool class without interrupting me every ten fucking seconds."

I took my mother's hand. "So you see, I've done it, too. I was so scared about how much it would hurt to lose Vince that I shut myself off from him before he was gone. I think some part of me thought it would make it easier."

Tears started to leak out of my eyes. "It doesn't work, Mommy. It just makes it worse. Vince still left anyway. And I have to face the fact that I wasted some of the precious little time I had with him because of some stupid bagels and grapes."

Leah walked over and put her arms around me.

In the strangest way, it felt so good to say it all out loud. Maybe confession is good for the soul. Or maybe those moments in the linen closet with Jake started the blood flowing back into that part of my heart that I thought Vince had taken. Maybe it wasn't gone so much as just gone numb, like a foot or a hand that's gone to sleep.

And maybe I'd finally found something positive that came out of watching my husband die. I could help my mother not make the same mistakes I had made.

I finally didn't feel guilty, either. So many times, when I would remember that last fight, I'd feel so bad. He was just trying to soldier on in the best way he knew how. I was just being bitchy.

But it was okay now. I'd been doing the best I could do back then. There was a lot of pressure and I hadn't always borne it with grace. I'm only human. I didn't have to feel guilty about being human.

"I saw people at my support group do it, too," I said.

"They did?" Mama asked softly.

I nodded. "They'd say they couldn't understand why they missed somebody so much, when that person was such a lousy husband or wife anyway. It's like that Aesop's fable with the fox and the grapes. You know, the whole sour grapes thing?"

In case you don't remember, the fox couldn't reach the grapes and when he couldn't have them, he walked away saying they were probably sour anyway.

Pink Scrubs came into the waiting room. "You can go in now. He's in bed four."

My mother gathered herself up. She took a deep breath, squared her shoulders, straightened the waistband of her slacks, and marched out after Pink Scrubs.

She marched all the way to bed number four. She marched right up to my father. She said, "Listen here, Gordon Franklin Simon. I've got something to tell you and you'd better be listening."

Daddy's eyes got big above the oxygen mask. It's not like he could interrupt with the mask over his mouth, but I doubt he even tried.

"You're a wrinkled-up old fool," Mama told him. "But you're my wrinkled-up old fool."

He reached up a hand to grab hers. There were a lot of tubes in his wrist. I could see it made it hard for him to even find her hand, much less hold it, but he took it. He pressed it to his chest.

"I don't want a different wrinkled-up old fool. I'm used to you. I don't want to try to get used to anybody else. So you'd better stick around."

My father brought her hand to his cheek, and then back to his heart. He lifted the oxygen mask and said, "I love you, too, Jessica."

The ICU nurse didn't want all of us in there at once. She'd let us all stay only if we could stay quiet and not disturb anyone else, which lasted about fifteen minutes. After the third time she had to shush Claudia, she booted the three of us out into the waiting room. Mama would have the first turn sitting with Daddy, then Leah, then Claudia, then me.

Daddy looked like he was napping as I tiptoed in. I pulled a chair up next to the bed and took his hand.

He opened one eye. "Hello, Emily. Your turn finally?" He coughed a little. His voice was gravelly.

I nodded. "Age order, as always."

"I know how hard this is for you, and I'm so sorry to put you through this," he said.

"Don't be silly, Daddy. You're not putting me through anything." A little knife edge of guilt flashed through my gut even as I said it, though. I had had a little flash of the "why me's" on my way into the hospital.

He smiled. Actually, it was more of a grimace. "Please, Emily. I'm tired. We both know diffcrent."

I put my head down on his bed. He stroked my hair.

"You know," he said. "I was brought up to believe that men were supposed to hide their deepest emotions. But there comes a time when it doesn't seem fair or kind to not respond to those who are less inhibited."

I looked up at him. He cradled my chin in his hand and wiped the tears off my cheek with his thumb, like he had when I was a little girl.

"It is impossible to be a perfect parent, and exceedingly difficult to be a good one, Emily. Seeing how well you girls have done in life in spite of my deficiencies as a father gives me so much pride."

"Daddy, you didn't have deficiencies," I protested. Okay, so he waited until I was thirty-two years old to have "the talk" about what boys want on dates, but he had gotten to it eventually.

He shook his head. "You know better than that, Emily. You're a parent now, too. You know that nobody can be a perfect parent all the time. I hope you know that all my mistakes were made with as much love in my heart for you as all the things I did right."

"I know that, Daddy. So do Leah and Claudia." I smiled. "I'm not sure about Mama, though."

He chuckled. Then his face went serious again. "I want to tell you, too, what an inspiration you are to me."

"An inspiration? Me?"

"I can only guess at the blow you suffered when Vince died. I know your heart broke. All of our hearts broke. But you went on."

"Only with help," I said. "Lots and lots and lots of help. Besides, I didn't know what else to do."

He shook his head. "See? That's what makes you an inspiration. You didn't consider another course. And when I watch you now, and see how you take care of Abby and how you love your sisters and how you stay connected to your mother and to me, I see that you know, on a level that most people don't know even exists, what's important in life. And you live it. Not many people can say that, Emily."

"I love you, Daddy."

"I know that, honey. I know that because you show me every day." His hand dropped to his side. "Now go home. Go take care of Abby. Tell her that her grandpa loves her."

I didn't notice until I was leaving the hospital that I hadn't hyperventilated or gotten the least bit queasy the whole time we were there.

CHAPTER SEVENTEEN

Feelin' Good Is Good Enough for Me

Leah

One part Apricot Glaze (#38), one part Titian Red
(#74), one part developer. Forty minutes. Back to her
fiery self. It's nice to take a vacation, but it's heaven to
come home.

Emily

One part Espresso (#12), one part Cinnamon (#14),
one part developer. Thirty minutes. It's a start. It's pretty
close to my real color, and it was kind of fun to get to
be one of the big girls.

"Emily, could you come to my office?" Karen said over the phone.

Yes, Karen has an office. I have a cubicle. I don't even have a good cubicle. The only thing good about my cubicle is that it isn't very far from the ladies' room.

I looked at my watch: 2:30. I had half an hour before I had to leave to get home in time to meet Abby's bus. I just needed to be sure I could scoot out the instant Karen was done with me.

"Sure, Karen. Just give me a second to straighten my desk and I'll be right up."

"Actually, Emily, I'd appreciate it if you left your desk until later. I need you to come right now."

This so didn't sound good. I climbed the stairs with leaden feet, my stomach dropping with every step. While my feet dragged, my mind raced.

What had I done? What had I worked on recently where I could have screwed up badly enough to warrant this summons?

Of course, that was the problem with my particular brand of screw-up. I operated in too dense of a fog to apparently notice even where I might screw up.

Karen's door stood half open. I knocked, using as little knuckle as possible. Maybe she wouldn't hear me and I could sneak out. Tomorrow I could honestly tell her I'd come right up, but she must have stepped out.

Even admitting that I thought that embarrassed me.

I closed my eyes and took a deep breath and knocked with more knuckle. Rip the bandage off, hair and all, nurse.

"Come in, Emily." Karen waved happily from behind her desk. "We were just talking about you."

Tony sat across from her.

I shut my eyes and hoped the instant vertigo caused by seeing him sitting there would pass quickly. I must have really, really screwed up to have the VP of marketing be there, too, but for the life of me I couldn't think of anything I had let go without triple-checking it. Had I sunk so low that even with checking a third time, some egregious error would still remain?

"Sit here next to me." Tony indicated the nubbly, burnt orange side chair.

I walked stiff-legged to the chair and sat.

"Karen and I wanted to talk to you about your work lately," Tony began.

I dropped my head to my chest. "I have been trying, guys. I check everything three times. I read stuff backward. I read it out loud." I desperately wanted them to understand the effort I was making; maybe I'd at least get some credit for that.

"And it shows," Tony said. "It's hard to believe that you're the same person who made the Angle of Mercy sign."

I winced, but thanked him anyway.

"In fact," Tony went on. "Everyone has noticed the improvement in your work. We're all so proud of you, Emily. You've pulled through."

My wince became an inward cringe of nails-on-blackboard proportion. Somehow, having tragedy enter your life makes you public property. Everyone feels entitled to have an opinion on how you're handling things. People often tell me how proud they are of me—an emotion that I'd heretofore thought required more than mere acquaintance.

Still, it pleased me immensely that Tony felt my work had improved, and even more that I wasn't going to be called on the carpet or fired.

"We'd like to reward that improvement, Emily." He leaned forward and smiled his slightly oily grin. "Would you like that?"

I all but bounced in my chair and clapped my hands together like Abby does when I ask if she'd like to go out for ice cream.

"Karen will be leaving us in a couple of weeks," Tony went on.

My eyes went wide. Karen? Fired?

"I've accepted a position with an advertising firm downtown," Karen threw in quickly. "It's a big step up for me."

I hoped she hadn't read my mind. I particularly hoped she hadn't read that dark, murky little corner of it that had been shamefully thrilled at the idea of Karen getting canned.

"We're sad to lose Karen, but we're also very proud of her." Tony beamed.

I smiled and nodded. Be a team player, Leah always advises. If Tony and Karen are happy and proud, you be happy and proud, too.

"That leaves my position open, Emily," Karen explained. "That's why Tony and I wanted to talk to you. It would mean a little less flexibility in your schedule, although I'm sure you could still work from home a couple of afternoons each week."

But what did Karen's job being up for grabs have to do with my afternoons?

I stared at them both for a moment, my mouth somewhat agape, before it hit me. They were offering me Karen's job! They were asking me to take the position that I'd wanted way back before everything went wrong. Maybe I wasn't an incompetent boob anymore!

"Me? Your job?" I finally choked out.

Karen smiled. "Yes, you. My job. Do you want it?"

I managed to make it to the parking lot before I did a wild polka of joy.

As I drove down I-5, the weekend stretched ahead of me, full of all the stuff that fill most people's weekends: vacuuming, dusting, grocery shopping, laundry. Somehow, it seemed relentless today. And lonely.

I wanted to *celebrate* my promotion. I wanted someone to pick me up and whirl me around and tell me how terrific I was. I wanted someone to toast my new success with, besides my seven-year-old daughter.

My sisters would be happy to do it, but I knew they both had plans for the evening. They'd probably be willing to stop by, but I hated to make them change things around at the last minute. Besides, they had lives of their own.

Unfortunately, I didn't. At least not that kind of life.

I picked Abby up from the bus stop. Instead of going home, we went out for hot fudge sundaes. Today was a celebration. Maybe not the kind with champagne and flowers, but pretty sweet nonetheless.

I was okay. Abby was okay. Claudia, Leah, Mama and Daddy, everybody was okay. So my parents were selling my childhood home and moving into a condo. Big deal. So maybe Jake didn't love me, and the thought that I might be interested in him was so repellent that he actually had to leave the state. That was okay, too.

I'd done denial. I'd done despair. I'd even been angry now and then. Maybe I was getting through being numb, and finally getting to a place where I could start my life again. It hurts when the blood flows back into sleeping feet and hands. Maybe a little heartache is unavoidable when your heart starts to wake up, too.

The next morning, I put on my Walkman and told Abby to answer the phone, since I wouldn't hear it over the combination of the vacuum cleaner and Janis Joplin wailing about freedom. Abby knew not to answer the door. Which was why I was so shocked when I turned off the vacuum, heard her talking to someone, and heard that someone answer. What they were saying didn't even register, just that a man was in the house with Abby.

I raced to the living room, my heart pounding. Visions of child-molesting, cannibalistic serial killers posing as innocuous door-to-door salesmen banged around in my brain.

"Mommy stopped going on dates," Abby announced.

"Is that so?" Jake asked.

"Jake! It's you!" I stood in the doorway, gasping for breath, as if I'd run from miles away instead of from Abby's bedroom, where I'd been trying to vacuum around the piles of Beanie Babies.

He stood up.

My heart flip-flopped. How could I never have noticed how handsome he was? How appealing his untucked shirt and rumpled jeans were? How could I not have noticed how cute he was when he smiled?

Abby sat on the floor, looking back and forth like a spectator at a tennis game. "Are you guys going to say anything to each other, or are you just going to look at each other until your eyeballs fall out?"

We had apparently exhausted her seven-year-old's store of patience with our googly eyes. She's always been one of those kids who demands action.

"We're going to stare at each other until our eyeballs fall out," I answered. "Then it's going to be your job to pick up all the eyeballs, because Jake and I won't be able to see them."

"*Blecchh!*" She shook herself. "I'm going to the park."

"Wear shoes," I yelled after her. Something you might not think you need to tell children when it's only fifty degrees outside, but was indeed necessary when it came to my daughter. I took her place on the floor next to the couch, where Jake had sat back down.

"Welcome home, stranger," I said.

He smiled. I did my best to ignore the cuteness.

"Thanks."

"Where'd you go?"

"Scuba diving. Mexico."

"Sounds fun. Sounds warm." I wiggled my toes against the carpet. I'd painted my toenails blue. Abby had picked the color, and I thought it was fun. Claudia had taken one look and told me not to fall asleep on any park benches, that it made my feet look like I needed CPR. I had considered sage green until Abby pointed out that then my toenails would look like Grandpa's. I opted for oxygen-deprived over fungal. "How long did you stay?"

He rubbed his eyes. "Not as long as I'd intended."

"Why not?"

"I don't know, Emily. I had the weirdest dreams down there."

"What about?"

He hesitated. "They were about Vince. Or at least Vince was in them." He leaned his elbows on his knees. "I'm not sure how to describe them. We were some place weird. I'm not sure where, but there was an ocean, because we were sitting on a piece of driftwood, watching the waves come in."

The hairs on the back of my neck started to stand up. "Yeah?"

"Yeah. And he's wearing those gym shorts with one of those T-shirts you and Leah kept slitting up the back. You know, at the end. When he was really, really sick."

"Yeah," I said again. The hairs on my arms joined the ones on the back of my neck. "Then what?"

"That's the thing. There isn't anything else. He sat there with me. Then he patted me on the back, and then he wasn't there anymore." He shook his head, looking a little confused. "So, what have you been up to?"

I shrugged, not trusting myself to speak right away. Finally, I said, "Not much. The usual."

"No more dating?" He seemed to be studying the carpet by my toes, too. He certainly wasn't meeting my eyes when I finally did look up at him. "Abby told me."

"Do you remember your senior year, when we took that school trip to Funtasia?"

Jake nodded. It occurred to me that he'd always been tremendously patient when I'd start to answer what seemed to be a straightforward question with a long, rambling response. I used to think he did it to needle Vince, who used to get a little impatient every now and then (okay, more than every now and then) with my metaphorical answers to questions that he felt could be resolved with a simple number or a yes or a no, but since Vince wasn't around anymore, I guess that wasn't the reason Jake listened to my weird responses. Another little something to ponder late at night.

"You guys were in those bumper boats on that little pond. Remember that?" I asked.

Jake nodded again.

"It was a great day. Not too hot, but mainly sunny. I remember watching you guys out there, and thinking it was funny that there always seemed to be a shaft of sunlight on Vince. Everybody else ended up in shadows every now and again, but it seemed like Vince never did."

I'd been watching my toes pretty carefully through all this, but now I looked up at Jake. He sat perfectly still, waiting, and he looked right back into my eyes. I gulped, but took it as license to continue.

"Then I thought that it seemed like there was always a light shining on Vince. That he just existed in some kind of golden spotlight all the time. It didn't seem to matter what he tried, it always came out right.

"After Vince died, I realized that it wasn't a light shining on him. It was a light shining from him. Those months that I was so depressed are all a blur to me, but what I remember feeling more than anything else is cold. I was so cold without Vince's light shining on me that I thought I'd freeze to death."

He made a little sound like a groan, and I stopped. He motioned for me to continue.

I shrugged. "Those guys that Kim fixed me up with were nice. They were nice-looking, they had decent jobs, they were funny. But there wasn't any light or warmth coming from them. It finally occurred to me that for some other woman, maybe there would be. Just not for me. So I asked Kim to stop fixing me up for a while."

"You know one of the things I finally realized while I was on my trip?" Jake asked.

I shook my head.

"He's really gone. Vince is really dead and he's not coming back."

I stared at him. "Was there some part of the whole cremation-and-memorial-service thing that you missed?"

"No. Stop being a smart-ass." He nudged me with his foot. "I think it finally sank in. He's gone. Nothing I do is going to bring him back. Nothing I don't do is going to bring him back, either."

He leaned forward, resting his forearms on his knees, and looked me right in the eyes. Were those green edges to his hazel eyes new or was I just noticing them now? "Emily, about that day in the hospital—"

"Don't," I interrupted him. I covered my eyes with both hands so I wouldn't have to look at him. "I'm so sorry. I was out of line. You were trying to comfort a friend and I turned it into something else. You don't have to say anything more about it."

I felt his hand on my shoulder; my whole arm tingled with warmth.

"Okay. I won't say anything more about it now, but I can't promise to leave it that way."

He gave my arm a squeeze. I almost wished he would take his hand away, but I wanted him to keep it there even more.

"What I would like to do is take Abby to a movie or something. I've missed her, too. Almost as much as I missed you." He smiled.

I ducked my head and wished my stomach would stop doing flip-flops. Had those dancing butterflies come back again? And if so, why were they doing their joy dance in my stomach still? They originally took up residence in my underpants, after all. I was beginning to doubt the fortune-telling properties of my magnets lately. The last one that had fallen from my panties said "jump." Since committing suicide did not seem like an option to me at that moment, I'd decided to ignore it.

"Abby told me you'd refused to take her to see the latest Pokemon movie. There's a three-thirty showing. Could I take her?"

"Jake, have you ever seen a Pokemon movie?"

"No," he admitted.

I wasn't surprised. Pretty much the only adult in the world who would willingly volunteer to take a child to a Pokemon movie is one who had never seen one. It's impossible to explain to the uninitiated how incredibly torturous the experience could be. "I know she'd love to go, and I know I'd love to not have to see another one."

He laughed. "Emily, you exaggerate everything. It can't be that bad."

When they came back two hours later, I could tell from the dazed look in Jake's eyes that he now knew better about Pokemon movies. They *are* that bad. They're even bad if you sleep through them. They slide into your unconscious memory to infect you with their badness.

Abby, however, was supremely happy. She skipped in, ponytail flying, detailed exactly how much junk food Uncle Jake had purchased for her (Gummi Bears *and* M&Ms *and* popcorn *and* soda) and then began wildly bouncing off the sofa, chairs, and walls of the living room because Jake had apparently given her caffeinated Pepsi along with all the sugar. The only good news was that when the sugar buzz wore off, she would crash big time.

"Thank you so much for taking her. I got so much done. And I'm so grateful not to have to sit through another Pokemon movie," I said. I chased Abby out of the living room and kitchen, and came back to the study I'd set up in the former breakfast nook off my kitchen.

Jake laughed. "Yeah, well, you owe me for that. That was pretty much the worst movie I've ever seen." He looked confused for a moment. "I actually dozed off during a big chunk of it, but somehow knew it was bad even though I was asleep. I'm not sure how they did that."

He pulled over one of the kitchen stools to sit next to me by the computer. "Whatcha doin'?"

"I told Kim I'd scan a photo of her, to put in her profile at that online dating service that Claudia used before she met Bob. She thought an accountant with a riding crop sounded like fun." I showed him the two head shots that Kim had given me. "So, if you were scrolling through a dating site, which face would be most likely to make you stop?"

"Yours," he said.

Before I could scrape my jaw off the floor, he'd kissed me on top of the head and walked out the door.

CHAPTER EIGHTEEN

Do Me

"Call him."

"Don't call him."

It was just like in the cartoons, when they have a little angel on one shoulder and a little devil on the other, except I didn't know which was which. I sighed. We were having an emergency meeting in Claudia's kitchen. I'd called them both as soon as I could make intelligible sounds.

"He opened up and showed her his vulnerable side," Claudia cried. "She *has* to call him, so his inner child knows it's safe to show himself to her."

"His inner child? What self-help trip have you been reading this week?" Leah pulled her tea bag out of her cup and carefully placed it on her spoon, then wrapped the string around it to squeeze out the last drops. "Men want to be the pursuer, not the pursued. She shouldn't call."

"Now, the kiss was on top of your head?" Claudia asked me.

I nodded, then shrugged. "Kind of more like the forehead than the actual top of the head."

"And he held your face with both hands?" She tapped her spoon thoughtfully against her lower lip as I nodded.

"What does it mean?" I asked, anxious.

"It means he wanted you to hold your head still." Leah dropped the honey jar down in front of us with a *thump*.

When I left an hour later, they were no closer to breaking the standoff. I wasn't, either.

As luck would have it, I didn't have to decide whether to call or to play it cool. Jake was waiting on the front porch when Abby and I pulled into the driveway.

Jake rewired a broken lamp while I gave Abby a bath. Then he read her a bedtime story while I picked up the kitchen. When I came out from tucking her in, he was standing in the middle of the living room, hands jammed into his pockets, rocking back and forth on the balls of his feet.

I walked right up to him. I mean right up to him. You couldn't even measure the distance between us in inches. Nano-inches, maybe.

He kissed me.

Now, I don't mean to sound like Goldilocks here, but it wasn't too hard and it wasn't too soft. It wasn't too dry and it wasn't too wet. It wasn't too fast or too slow. It was just right. I felt all warm and tingly inside, like a big golden light was shining on us.

I put my hands on his chest. "Why did you leave? Really."

He bent his head so our foreheads touched. "I didn't know what else to do," he said softly. "I'd lost my best friend. Then it seemed like I had a new best friend. It was my old best friend's wife, but that was okay. Just friends, right? So problem solved, right?"

I stayed very still.

It took him a while, but he went on. "Then it seemed like I might be in love with my new best friend. Except she still was my best friend's wife, and that made her completely taboo. So as long as it was a secret and nobody else knew about it, it was okay. Problem solved again, right?"

I still didn't say anything.

"Then you kissed me. And I kissed you back, and I didn't ever want to stop kissing you and holding you. But you were my best friend. But you were also my best friend's wife. The whole thing was giving me a very bad headache."

I laughed a little and put my head on his shoulder.

He kept talking. "I felt guilty, but I wasn't sure what for. I mean, are we going behind Vince's back if he isn't here to sneak around behind? Would it be better to let you find somebody else? Would it be better to let you be with whatever bozo Kim fixed you up with? Or run through the dating gauntlet that Claudia ran? Or should I try to be with you myself, and treat you the way I know you should be treated? I wanted you so much. But I wasn't sure if I should even feel that way, much less act on it." He sighed. "So I had to go."

"And why did you come back? Really."

"Because I was in love with my best friend and that might be the best thing that could ever happen to anyone, and I wanted to kiss my best friend and keep kissing her forever." He pulled me tighter against him. "I don't know if I'll ever be able to forget that we wouldn't be together if something terrible hadn't happened to Vince. On the other hand, we got each other through something terrible, and that has to be worth something, too."

Then he was kissing me again, and it was so good my toes curled up. He stopped for a minute to smile at me.

"So, what do we do now?" he asked.

I smiled sweetly back at him and said, "Do me."

Up Close and Personal
With the Author

HOW AUTOBIOGRAPHICAL IS *DO ME, DO MY ROOTS?*

Anyone who knows me even slightly can tell you that quite a few of the general details of this book are autobiographical. For instance, I am the youngest of three sisters. Like Emily, my husband died of a brain tumor. That said, I used more extreme versions of us for the story and changed a lot of the details such as, my oldest sister is very successful and bossy like Leah is in the book. My real older sister, however, has been married to the same intelligent, successful, charming man for twenty years now and is only scary when she gets mad. I'm happy for her. It just doesn't make for good copy. Oh, the duct tape of my father's jacket is real.

WHICH FICTIONAL CHARACTER LEAST RESEMBLES HIS OR HER REAL-LIFE COUNTERPART?

That's easy. Emily's mother resembles my mother only in that she wears Rockports and has great hair and skin. Like my sister's happy marriage, my mother's basically sweet nature doesn't make great copy.

I also especially tried to leave the kids alone. The three children in the book definitely have qualities that my kids and my niece and my nephews all have, but it seemed unfair to them to model characters too specifically after them.

WHICH FICTIONAL CHARACTER MOST RESEMBLES HIS OR HER REAL-LIFE COUNTERPART?

Probably Claudia. The sister on which she's based is our family reader of self-help books and is probably the sweetest and most supportive of the three of us, just like Claudia is in the book.

WHY DID YOU CHOOSE TO WRITE A BOOK THAT HAD SO MANY ELEMENTS OF YOUR OWN LIFE IN IT?

It wasn't so much that I wanted to write something autobiographical as that I needed to write this book. It was as much a therapy thing as it was a creative thing. I'd finished my first book (*Petals on the Pillow*, Avid Press) not too long before my husband died. It was almost exactly two years later when I started to write again. I had started work on a romantic comedy when a friend died in a bicycle accident. Trying to find some way to help his widow and still deal with my own pain became the impetus for this story about a young widow starting over.

ARE YOU AND YOUR SISTERS REALLY THAT CLOSE?

Yes. We are. The age gap between us is a little greater than that of the sisters in the book, but otherwise the relationships are very similar. I honestly don't know why or how we've escaped the problems and issues with which other sets of siblings struggle. Sometimes I think it's because we're all happy where we are in the birth order scheme. Other times, I attribute it to my parents' nearly pathological efforts to be fair. Whatever it was (and I suspect it's actually a combination of those things plus some others that I haven't figured out yet), I'm grateful for it.

WHAT DO YOU SEE AS EMILY'S BIG STRUGGLE?

Emily was very content being numb for a while. She is, however, too vital and passionate a person to remain satisfied with a life that's only half lived. She's torn between the safety of not feeling anything and the fear of opening herself up to having to experience another heartbreak.

SURELY JAKE WOULDN'T BREAK EMILY'S HEART.

Never on purpose, but people change and situations change. Often without anyone giving permission. Emily is all too aware that sometimes one person can't help but hurt another. I think if there's any message in this book, it's that you have to take a pretty big gamble to have a relationship and be willing to be hurt to have something work. In a good relationship, the stakes are often just as high as the reward.

DO YOU SEE ALL RELATIONSHIPS AS DANGEROUS?

In a way, yes. Being in a relationship requires that you allow another person inside all your defenses. Loving someone makes you terribly vulnerable. I think that is the struggle at the heart of this book for all its characters. From Jessica's fear of Gordon's death to Leah's fear of how people will view her relationship with Chase to Claudia needing to trust Bob to Abby refusing to talk about her father. All of these women's need for love pulls them to the men around them. At the same time they push the men away because of their fear of being hurt. The lesson that Emily learns and that she tries to explain to her mother and sisters, is that pushing the other person away doesn't make it hurt any less when you lose them.

Then don't miss these other great books!

Bite
C.J. Tosh
0-7434-7764-2

Liner Notes
Emily Franklin
0-7434-6983-6

My Lurid Past
Lauren Henderson
0-7434-6468-0

**Dress You Up
in My Love**
Diane Stingley
0-7434-6491-5

He's Got to Go
Sheila O'Flanagan
0-7434-7042-7

Irish Girls About Town
Maeve Binchy, Marian Keyes,
Cathy Kelly, et al.
0-7434-5746-3

**The Man I Should
Have Married**
Pamela Redmond Satran
0-7434-6354-4

**Getting Over
Jack Wagner**
Elise Juska
0-7434-6467-2

The Song Reader
Lisa Tucker
0-7434-6445-1

The Heat Seekers
Zane
0-7434-4290-3

I Do (But I Don't)
Cara Lockwood
0-7434-5753-6

Why Girls Are Weird
Pamela Ribon
0-7434-6980-1

Larger Than Life
Adele Parks
0-7434-5760-9

Eliot's Banana
Heather Swain
0-7434-6487-7

How to Pee Standing Up
Anna Skinner
0-7434-7024-9

Look for them wherever books are sold or visit us online at www.downtownpress.com.

Great storytelling just got a new address.

PUBLISHED BY POCKET BOOKS

doWn
tOwn
press

09503